HIGH COUNTRY AMBUSH

Sergeant Hugh O'Reilly legged the dark bay into a trot until a hundred yards of open grass stood between him and the side of the mountain.

The next instant the mountainside erupted as three rifle shots fired in quick succession kicked up spurts of dust in front of the horse. Nostrils flaring, the dark bay reared up on its hind legs, its forelegs raking the air.

O'Reilly's flashing dark eyes glared up at a ledge above him. "God damn it, quit that firing! You're scaring hell out of my horse! I know you won't shoot a man wearing scarlet!"

A long, raspy laugh sounded from up on the ledge, then a figure in buckskin and moccasins stepped out from the pines. He held a Winchester into his shoulder, the barrel pointing squarely at O'Reilly's heart . . .

#4 SERGEANT O'REILLY

IAN ANDERSON

ZEBRA BOOKS
KENSINGTON PUBLISHING CORP.

ZEBRA BOOKS

are published by

Kensington Publishing Corp.
475 Park Avenue South
New York, NY 10016

First printing: January 1987

Printed in the United States of America

Chapter 1

The lone scarlet rider cantered his dark bay around the south side of the perfectly still, mirror-top lake separating him from the dark green pine forest that swept thickly up the side of Mount Queen Victoria. On the other side of that mountain was the Palliser River and Fort Determination. It would be good to be back. He had been gone a long time. Or so it seemed. Actually it was no more than a month.

The turquoise water of Surprise Lake reflected the forest and mountains surrounding it, like two worlds—the real world and an upside-down one. Above, or below when he looked into the lake, the sky was a warm, incredible blue, with only a skiff of cloud off to the southeast.

There was no trail through the tall green pines fringing the south side of Surprise Lake, so the scarlet-coated horseman rode along the coarse-sanded shore, the bay's hoofs occasionally splashing into the water, disturbing its tranquility where the pines came too close to the water's edge, or where a boulder reposed to break the soft, almost imperceptible lap of the spring-fed lake.

He would not reach Fort Determination by the sundown that was only five hours away. It would take him that long to get around Queen Victoria. It would be tomorrow's noon or later, depending upon whether he struck any diversions along the way.

Off to the distant west in front of him, the mountain ranges broke to a valley, lined by snow-crowned peaks sharp and irregular against the azure sky. Over there lay the Continental Divide and the border between the Province of British Columbia and the North-West Territories' District of Alberta. The Palliser flowed along that valley, swinging off to cut north of Mount Queen Victoria twenty miles beyond Surprise Lake.

He loved these mighty, majestic, snow-jeweled mountains and the cool of the thick pine forests and jade-colored lakes. After the heat and carnage, the blood and fire, the dust and flies of a year on the South African veldt, the splendor and solitude of Canada's Rockies were a soothing balm to his soul. He could stay amongst them forever.

His reverie was suddenly broken by something on the far side of the lake. A sudden flash! Like the glint of sunlight off a rifle barrel. Abruptly he reined his horse to a stop. An instant later something zapped past his head as he felt a sharp force twang the wide brim of his tan, pointed-crown Stetson. Then a crack-like explosion shattered the mountain stillness.

The scarlet rider's reaction was instantaneous! In a blur of movement he snaked his Winchester from its

6

saddle bucket behind his right leg, kicked his feet from the stirrups, and hurled his one hundred and ninety pounds from the dark bay's back. Before the gunshot's echo finished rumbling across the lake, he had stretched his six-foot-two-inch frame behind a large round boulder marking a long, fingerlike spit jabbing into the water's edge.

With a shrill, piercing whine a bullet struck the boulder inches from his shoulder, sending tiny fragments of rock flying. Instinctively he ducked. Another memory from South Africa flitted across his mind—khaki uniforms were less conspicuous than red, a lesson the British had learned the hard way. At that moment he wished he were wearing a brown duck stable jacket instead of his bright scarlet tunic, with its shiny brass badges and buttons and the three gold chevrons and embroidered crown on his sleeve. Even behind the boulder he was too good a target. He would have to move. Whoever that rifleman was, he could slink unseen among the trees on the far side of the lake and get into position to snipe him from another angle.

Glancing quickly around he saw with relief that his dark bay had trotted off into the pines. At least the rifleman wouldn't be able to kill it. Apart from the personal sorrow he would feel over the horse's loss, Fort Determination would be a long walk.

Behind him were a few scattered rocks, an expanse of sand, then the trees. The rocks were too small to offer enough cover. Especially not for a bright red coat. The only protection lay in the trees. There he'd be on roughly equal terms with the hidden rifleman. But to get to them he would have to cover forty yards of open sand first.

Before he could make his move, he had to pinpoint that rifleman's position. Or come close to it.

Cautiously he inched his head around the boulder. The hidden rifle erupted a third time, and again tiny fragments flew from the boulder, stinging his ruggedly handsome face.

His dark eyes flashed! "God damn it!" he breathed, pulling quickly back and flicking tiny rock particles from his wide, upbrushed black moustache. But he thought he knew where the shots came from, and that was about where he'd seen the sun's reflection off that rifle barrel.

Bringing up his Winchester, the Mountie suddenly threw himself on top of the boulder, quickly aimed at the other side of the lake, and opened fire. Four times in rapid succession! *Aim—fire—lever—aim—fire—lever* . . .

The instant he'd fired the fourth shot, he whirled around and sprinted away, past the scattered rocks and across the forty yards of sand. His long legs pounded like pistons. For the last fifteen yards he expected to feel the force of a bullet smash into his back and drive him to the ground.

But he made it! No more shots followed.

From the cover of the tall pines he peered across the still turquoise water. He couldn't see anything he hadn't seen before. Nothing unusual. No movement at all. But the silence! . . . Had one of his bullets found a mark? He had to find out.

Letting forth a few long, low whistles, he picked his way amongst the pines searching for his horse. It took only a couple of minutes until he found the dark bay, its head down, walking toward the sound of the whistling.

Before taking the reins, he pushed four fresh cartridges into the magazine of his Winchester, then swung himself back up into the saddle. Taking a last look around to get his bearings, he rode off through the thick forest to the far end of Surprise Lake.

The sun had arced well across the blue sky to the west by the time the Mountie sergeant worked his way around to the north side of the lake, with the treed slopes of Mount Queen Victoria towering behind him. Before reaching the spot where he reckoned the hidden rifleman had fired from, he dismounted and covered the last quarter of a mile on foot.

When he got to within a dozen yards of the lake's north shore, where he could see the water through the trees, and over on the south shore the long fingerlike spit and the boulder he'd taken cover behind, he brought up his Winchester, ready for action.

He paused and listened intently, looking around carefully, his eyes flitting from tree to tree, from brush clump to brush clump. Then he crept stealthily forward, a few feet at a time, his spurred boots moving slowly, noiselessly over the soft, needle-covered ground. Then he stopped again and listened further, his eyes sweeping the forest ahead, blood pounding in his ears, his heart beating like a triphammer.

9

Could the rifleman be lying dead somewhere ahead? Or wounded? But if he were lying wounded, there should be some noise, some groaning or thrashing around or something. But his experiences in South Africa told him that wasn't necessarily so.

Once more he crept warily forward, half-crouched, his body and pointed Winchester moving as one in a continuous, swinging motion. Now he knew he was almost directly onto where the rifleman had fired from. But the rifleman wasn't anywhere around. So if he was wounded, he'd managed to shift position. One thing beyond doubt—*he wasn't dead*! The Mountie's skin crawled. The danger still existed!

But suddenly he saw something—something on the ground immediately ahead. Something small and bright. And around it moccasin prints and the sign of a man kneeling, with rifle pointed across the lake. He stooped to pick it up.

"My God!" he exclaimed, his voice no more than a hushed whisper. "Mad Old Mike! But it can't be. He's dead!"

He examined the small round object. A brass button—on it a buffalo head surmounted by a crown. Bright and freshly polished. It hadn't been there long. Otherwise it would have been dull and tarnished.

The Mountie lifted his head, his dark eyes probing the thick green forest. But he saw nothing—heard nothing. It was eerie—like a voice from the past! *A voice from the dead!*

After several minutes of looking, he dropped his eyes to the ground and studied the sign. There were no bullet marks on the trees around where the rifleman had kneeled. So his own bullets hadn't come anywhere near him. It hadn't been his shooting that had driven the rifleman away.

He could see where the rifleman had turned around, shouldered a pack that he'd leaned beside one of the trees, and struck off deeper into the forest. After a dozen yards there were no more moccasin prints.

The sergeant breathed a sigh of relief. At least he hadn't shot him. None of his bullets had touched him. *If* it was him. But the button? It *had* to be him!

The tall, square-shouldered redcoat dropped the button into his pocket, trailed his Winchester, and strode back through the silent pines to his horse.

He had only another hour or so of daylight left. Not enough to get around Queen Victoria before sundown. But he was damned if he would camp anywhere near here tonight.

Constable George Bailey, shiny brass trumpet up to his pursed lips, stood at the foot of the flag pole sounding *retreat*, Corporal "Dusty" Rogers lowering the Union Jack beside him, when Sergeant Hugh O'Reilly rode into Fort Determination.

Sergeant O'Reilly grinned behind his fierce black moustache as he reined his horse to and sat at attention until they finished. They looked smart, he reflected, in their scarlet tunics, yellow-striped blue breeches, spurred Strathconas and Stetsons. They

11

must have known he'd be back tonight.

As a detachment post, it was not necessary at Fort Determination to sound *retreat* when lowering the flag at sundown, or to blow *reveille* when raising it in the morning. Regulations made that standard routine only at the Regina depot and the larger, divisional posts. For that matter, trumpeters weren't even on strength at other than divisional posts. But then, George Bailey wasn't a trumpeter. Not officially. Not since 1890, thirteen years ago. But, unbeknown to the depot quartermaster, he'd taken his trumpet with him when he was transferred out. O'Reilly always knew when George had been drinking, because he'd hear wafting over from the barracks the calls George had learned at Regina, from *reveille* to *lights out* . . . *assembly* . . . *stables* . . . *mess* . . . *guardmount* . . . *last post*—sometimes a *general* or *royal salute*—and when he'd had two or three too many, *boots and saddles* and the *charge* as well.

Besides knowing the trumpet calls, George also knew his sergeant. He knew O'Reilly had a soft spot for the ceremonial side of Mounted Police life, and that despite a generally easygoing manner, he was a stickler for things of a ceremonial or regimental nature. He was fussy about a smart turnout in uniform, shined badges and buttons, polished boots and leather, tidy barracks, and the ritualistic raising and lowering of the flag. In common with the other half-dozen men at the post, Bailey liked O'Reilly, and to please him sounded *retreat* at the lowering of the flag each evening. And he had done so every evening

12

during O'Reilly's absence.

The moment George whipped his trumpet down to his side and Corporal Rogers started folding the flag, Sergeant O'Reilly flicked his reins and legged his horse forward again. He met them in front of a rambling log building with a veranda running along the front. Above the veranda was a rustic sign onto which had been carved the name: *North-West Mounted Police*. A smaller sign, fixed at eye level beside the front door, bore the words: *Fort Determination Detachment*, which the men jokingly referred to as *Determined Detachment*.

Corporal Rogers smiled up at O'Reilly. "Howdy, Hugh. Welcome back. Good patrol?"

A slim, dark-haired man with a perpetual smile, Corporal Rogers was an American. He'd ridden with the Texas Rangers and the U.S. Cavalry before drifting up to Canada and joining the North-West Mounted Police at Regina eight years ago. Why he was nicknamed "Dusty," O'Reilly couldn't imagine. They should have dubbed him "Smiley."

"Hello, Dusty, George. You must've had a lookout watching for my return."

They both grinned up at him.

"Not a chance, Hugh. We've been doing *retreat* every night you've been gone. Just as though you were here. Regina all over again."

O'Reilly grinned back at them. "Drunk or sober, eh?"

Both vigorously shook their heads. "Not us, Sergeant. That only happens twice a year—Dominion

13

Day and the Fourth of July."

"And the three days between," O'Reilly kidded.

Corporal Rogers protested laughingly. "And definitely not when I've got the responsibility of the post on my hands."

O'Reilly reached behind him, pulled the Winchester out of the saddle bucket, and climbed down off his horse's back.

George Bailey handed Corporal Rogers his trumpet and stepped forward to take the bays' reins. "I'll look after him, Hugh."

George was thirty-three, the same age as O'Reilly, and he had four years more service, having joined the Force at eighteen as a trumpeter. When O'Reilly took charge of the detachment two years ago, a brand-new sergeant with only nine years service, freshly returned to Canada after a year with Lord Strathcona's Horse fighting the Boers in South Africa, he had anticipated resentment from the stubborn, independent-minded thirteen-year constable with a defaulter's sheet recording several orderly-room convictions for drunkenness, fighting, and insubordination. But he had been quite wrong, for George saw in the tall, black-moustached Nova Scotian a man's man, and never gave him a moment's trouble.

"Thanks, George," O'Reilly replied gratefully, unstrapping his bedroll and lifting his wallets from the saddle. Tucking them under his arm he stepped up onto the veranda and entered the building, Corporal Rogers behind him. From the hallway O'Reilly turned into the sergeant's office, and dropped his bedroll and

14

saddle wallets onto a chair while Corporal Rogers lit the coal-oil lamp.

"Anything of consequence happen during my absence?"

Corporal Rogers shook his head. "Not much."

"All quiet down at Black Town?"

Black Town was a rough coal-mining community a dozen miles down the Palliser. Its proper name was Coal City, but the police and other residents of Fort Determination called it Black Town because of the coal-dust-blackened color of its shantylike buildings.

"Lasher, the mining company manager, has been yapping about no police protection. I sent a couple of the boys down there the last two Friday and Saturday nights to keep order. The first time, there was a brawl in that honky-tonk dance hall. The second time, there was a fight between miners and the Indians. Now Lasher wants the Indian village moved way back into the mountains."

Levering eight .45-75 caliber shells from his Winchester, O'Reilly replied, "He's always bragging about the political pull he has in Ottawa. He should get the Indian Department to do his dirty work."

Corporal Rogers grunted. "For my part, I'd like to see them Indians clean the hell out of that scumbag bunch of miners."

O'Reilly thumbed the eight rifle shells into his bandolier and placed the Winchester on a rack behind his desk. Glancing out the window he could see down toward the steamboat landing the lights of the settlement winking on in the deepening twilight.

15

"Oh, yes . . . something else," Corporal Rogers added with a smile. "Jake Raff, that prospector over on No Strike Creek, was shot at a couple of weeks ago on the south side of Queen Victoria. I know it sounds a mite ridiculous, but he reckons it was Mad Old Mike shootin' at him."

O'Reilly took off his Stetson and sat down behind his desk. "We have a report on file from Indians that Mad Old Mike was killed in an avalanche last winter."

Corporal Rogers shrugged. "I know. Like I said, it sounds a mite ridiculous."

O'Reilly slipped his hand into his pocket. His fingers touched the brass button he had found by Surprise Lake. "What makes him think it was Mad Old Mike?"

"The shooting. The bullets came so close they damn near singed his beard. He reckons no one could come that close without hitting him. No one but Mad Old Mike."

Frowning at his desktop, O'Reilly ran a hand through his thick black hair. "Raff was probably drunk."

Smiling, Corporal Rogers shrugged again. "Could be, Hugh. But if we get any more complaints like that, I guess we'll have to look into it."

O'Reilly didn't answer immediately, but when he did his voice was little more than a whisper. "Yes, I suppose we will."

Picking up from the corner of O'Reilly's desk the folded flag and George Bailey's trumpet, where he'd put them when he lit the lamp, Corporal Rogers

16

moved toward the door. "Well, it's suppertime, Hugh. George and I'll be heading down to Mrs. Merrill's hotel. Care to join us?"

Almost absently, O'Reilly shook his head. "No, Dusty. Not right now. I had a late lunch on patrol. I want to get squared away first. I might be down a little later."

"Whatever you say." With that, Corporal Rogers left the sergeant's office, leaving O'Reilly alone.

Sergeant O'Reilly sat at his desk for the longest time, staring moodily at a bright brass button in his hand.

Chapter 2

Moving deftly among the dining-room tables, Catherine Merrill carried plates of bacon and eggs, or eggs and hotcakes, to the dozen patrons of the Northern Lights Hotel. Each time she passed a window she glanced out, looking up Fort Determination's only street toward the Mounted Police barracks a hundred yards beyond the settlement. Each time she felt a tingle of excitement. She knew Sergeant O'Reilly was back, for she had seen him ride to the barracks at sundown the previous evening. She had been disappointed when he hadn't come down for dinner with Corporal Rogers and Constable Bailey shortly afterward. However, she knew he would be down for breakfast this morning.

The dining room was busier than usual this morning because of the four overnight guests staying at the hotel, who had arrived yesterday on the river steamer from Edmonton. They sat together at a table in the far corner, although one of them was just in the process of leaving. They had described themselves in the hotel register as businessmen. Catherine Merrill had noticed Corporal Rogers looking over at them quite frequently during his breakfast. He was obviously curious about them. The Mounted Police always made a point of finding out about the activities of strangers, and she knew it was just a matter of time before one of them asked about the four men.

She hurried back into the kitchen to bring a pot of steaming black coffee to one of the tables. She had just finished pouring when Mr. Meecher, manager of the Northwest Transportation Company, left his table and made his way to the cash register. Putting down the coffeepot, Catherine Merrill moved quickly to attend to him.

"I trust you enjoyed your breakfast, Mr. Meecher," she said.

"Sure did, Mrs. Merrill," he answered. "I always enjoy your meals."

She laughed. "Come now, Mr. Meecher. You know I don't cook them myself."

Mr. Meecher winked. "Oh, I know you've got old Ling in the kitchen back there keeping the cooking fires burning, but I like to think it's you that does the real meal preparations, especially that roast beef and Yorkshire pudding you serve on weekends. No Chinaman could ever cook good old English roast beef like that."

The transportation company manager grinned, although it was more a leer than a grin, like a mechanical movement of the mouth, with no corresponding reaction from the eyes at all, nothing to give the mouth movement any life. "But it's a shame that good cooking has to be wasted in a place like this . . ." And he waved his arm around the dining room, noisy with the scrape of cutlery on crockery, the chink of coffee cups, and the sound of talking men who all knew one another—except for the three strangers over in the corner.

"And what, may I ask, is wrong with a place like this?" Catherine Merrill asked, almost defensively.

"Nothing, nothing at all," Meecher quickly replied. "It's just that . . . well, a fine-looking woman like you ought to be cooking for one man alone, not half a dozen or more."

Catherine Merrill colored just slightly when she realized what he meant. "Well, this is my life, Mr. Meecher. Since my husband passed away—"

Meecher didn't let her finish. "That doesn't stop you when it comes to Sergeant O'Reilly, though, does it?" he demanded. "Oh, I saw you looking up toward the barracks. Now that he's back, I guess I'm not good enough—"

"*Mr. Meecher!*" Catherine Merrill exclaimed. "Please contain yourself."

The room had suddenly gone quiet, and a red-faced transportation company manager looked sheepishly around, to see several pairs of eyes on him, on them both, including those of Corporal Rogers and Constable Bailey, and Tom Barr, the Hudson's Bay Company manager.

"Anything wrong, Mrs. Merrill?" Corporal Rogers asked, rising to his feet.

"No, nothing at all, thank you, Corporal," Catherine replied. "Mr. Meecher is just paying his bill."

After the transportation company manager left, Catherine Merrill returned to her tables, pouring more coffee for her breakfast patrons. She had just finished this when she again glanced out the window in the direction of the barracks. Her heart leaped, for she saw Sergeant O'Reilly coming, striding manfully down toward the settlement. He was a fine figure of a man, she thought as she watched him come closer. The uniform he wore so well seemed a part of him, his dark features and big black moustache providing just the right contrast against the bright red tunic, close-fitting so that it emphasized his lean waist, deep chest, and broad shoulders. The leg-o'-mutton peg of his yellow-striped blue breeches was cut high above the knee so that it showed his long legs, with the morning sun flashing off his polished brown boots and glinting spurs. His tan-colored Stetson he wore with the stiff brim at a fifteen-degree tilt over the right eyebrow, providing the suggestion of a devil-may-care attitude. As for his bearing, he carried himself ram-rod-straight, the very embodiment of the trained soldier that was a dominant characteristic of men of the Mounted Police.

A scraping of chairs behind her caught Catherine Merrill's attention. Turning, she saw that Corporal Rogers and Constable Bailey, always inseparable when one or the other wasn't away on patrol, had finished their breakfast and were about to leave. Two of the other constables, sitting at another table, were almost finished.

"Nice breakfast, Mrs. Merrill," Corporal Rogers said with his customary smile as he stepped over to the counter to sign his bill.

"Sure was, Mrs. Merrill," added George Bailey. "Sure beats cooking our own in the barracks mess."

Catherine Merrill smiled back at them. "I don't

know whether I should take that as a compliment or a complaint."

"A compliment, ma'am," Corporal Rogers assured her.

She laughed graciously. "Then, I'll take it as such."

The dining-room door opened, to be filled by a blaze of scarlet as Sergeant O'Reilly entered.

"Morning, Hugh," Corporal Rogers and George Bailey chorused. "You're almost too late for breakfast," the slim, smiling American added.

A serious expression clouded O'Reilly's face. "Yes . . . well," he answered almost apologetically. "I guess it was that patrol. Must've tired me a little. I slept in."

Dusty Rogers held up his hand. "You don't have to explain to us. You're the boss-man around here. See you back up at the barracks, Hugh."

"Good to have you back, Hughie," Tom Barr called out from his table, where he sat with Mr. Grant, manager of the Canadian Bank of Commerce. Tom Barr always called O'Reilly *Hughie*, never *Hugh* or *Sergeant*.

Outside, Dusty Rogers and George Bailey started walking up the street toward the barracks.

"Now I know why Hugh didn't come to dinner with us last night," Dusty laughed. "Sly dog. He came down late purposely this morning because he wants to be alone with Mrs. Merrill."

"Can't say I blame him," replied George. "They'd make a right handsome couple."

Sergeant O'Reilly sat down at a clean table Catherine Merrill had led him to, where she poured him a cup of coffee. "What would you like for breakfast, Sergeant?" She almost called him *Hugh*, but caught herself in the nick of time.

O'Reilly took the menu she handed him and opened it, more from nervousness than from a need to read what was inside. She noticed his nervousness and it pleased her. It was little things like this that she observed about him that gave lie to his devil-may-care appearance. Without them, she would have liked him less, for she knew he didn't have this nervousness amongst men.

For his part, O'Reilly inwardly cursed the ill-at-ease feeling that gripped him whenever he was in the presence of this woman. He was afraid he would fumble the menu or drop his coffee cup or do some other clumsy thing and make a damned fool of himself in her eyes. He was about to order when Tom Barr stopped at his table on his way out with Mr. Grant.

"Like to see you over at the store when you get a moment, Hughie. Got something to talk to you about."

O'Reilly was glad of the interruption, for it gave him the opportunity to act normal again. "All right, Tom. I'll be over right after breakfast."

When Tom Barr and the bank manager left, O'Reilly found Catherine Merrill was still waiting to take his order. Looking up at her suddenly, he was just in time to see a smile pulling at the corners of her mouth, which disappeared the instant she found him looking up at her. It brought the nervousness back to him.

"I'll have the usual, please . . . steak and two eggs."

"A hearty breakfast for a hungry man, Sergeant?"

O'Reilly grinned awkwardly. He would have liked to think of something witty or intelligent to say, but all he could conjure up was, "I guess it starts the day off right."

He watched her move quickly across the dining-room floor to the kitchen. The Chinese cook back there had been with Mrs. Merrill's husband for years, and after his death she had kept the old fellow on. O'Reilly didn't know much about the late Carl Merrill. It was he who had built the hotel, two years before the war broke out in South Africa. There had been speculation that Ottawa would declare the mountain country of the upper Palliser a national park, as had been done with Banff, west of Calgary, and develop it into a northern tourist resort, but the idea had lost favor because the country was too far from civilization and convenient transportation. So when word of the big gold discoveries in the Yukon seeped out the next year, precipitating the immortal Klondike gold rush of 1898, Carl Merrill had sought a shortcut to the gold fields by trying to cross the mountains from the North-West Territories into northern British Columbia and the Yukon, but perished in the attempt. That was what Tom Barr had told O'Reilly. Catherine Merrill had decided to stay on. She had been a widow four years now, and had turned the hotel into a viable operation by providing first-class accommodation for the Pacific & Western Coal Company's officials and engineers who often visited Coal City to inspect the mining operations, and by boarding Fort Determination's dozen bachelors.

Sipping his coffee, O'Reilly watched her over the top of his cup as she reappeared from the kitchen and busied herself cleaning the recently vacated tables. The two of them were almost alone, except for the three men in business suits sitting over in the corner.

She was a good-looking woman, O'Reilly thought. Tall and perhaps inclining toward the buxom side, but well formed, with the curves in the right places. There was a natural poise about her which drew and held a man's attention, yet she gave no indication she was aware of it. Her long wavy red hair she always wore the same, swept up from her neck and wound immaculately around on top of her head. O'Reilly knew nothing of the quality or styles of women's clothing, but her long skirts and neck-high blouses seemed both dressy and fashionable. He guessed her to be about thirty. He wondered how she felt about being the only white woman in the settlement. Almost the *only* woman for that matter, except for Marie Joussard, the métis wife of Bernard Joussard, a trapper living in a log cabin just up the street. It wasn't much of a life for a woman, and O'Reilly wondered why she didn't sell the hotel and go back to Ontario.

When Catherine Merrill disappeared inside the kitchen with a trayful of dirty dishes, O'Reilly's policeman instinct focused on the three strangers sitting at a corner table. Although dressed like dudes, their faces were weather-beaten, giving them an unmistakably outdoors appearance. Two were in their late thirties, while the third touched fifty. They talked quietly, and although O'Reilly strained his ears, he could not pick up more than an occasional word.

The moment Catherine Merrill returned to the dining room with a plate of steak and eggs in one hand and a coffeepot in the other, Sergeant O'Reilly lost interest in the trio.

"Here you are, Sergeant," she said, placing the plate in front of him and refilling his cup. Then, with the pot poised over another cup, she asked smilingly, "Would you mind if I joined you in a cup of coffee?"

O'Reilly started to rise. "Of course not."

Catherine Merrill put out her hand. "No, please don't get up, Sergeant." She poured herself a cup of coffee and sat down opposite him at the white-clothed table.

"Did you have a good trip?" she asked politely. "You were gone quite a while."

O'Reilly arched his black eyebrows. "The patrol? Yes, quite good, thank you. I enjoy getting away by myself. It gives a man the chance to think. Besides, I like the constantly changing scenery in the mountains. I can't think of anything more spectacular."

"Yes, they are beautiful, aren't they." She said that more as a statement than a question, and O'Reilly saw no need to reply. For that matter he couldn't think of anything to say in reply, so he knifed and forked a piece of his steak.

"Sergeant," she said when he had finished chewing his mouthful of steak. "I have something to ask you. Advice, really."

O'Reilly looked at her across the table. "I'd be honored to offer what advice I can, Mrs. Merrill."

"I'm planning a trip to Edmonton. I'd like to get away before the summer is over so that I can return by riverboat before the end of the navigation season."

O'Reilly cut another slice of steak. "That sounds like a fine idea, Mrs. Merrill. It would undoubtedly do you good to get outside to civilization for a while."

Even as he spoke, O'Reilly was surprised to hear these words coming from within him, for he felt a sudden sense of loss at the thought of Mrs. Merrill leaving Fort Determination, even if only for a few months. She had been here when he first arrived to take charge of the post two years ago, and all the time he had been coming to the hotel to eat his meals he had looked forward to seeing her, even though they exchanged little more than polite conversation. In fact, he hadn't even so much as danced with her at the two Christmas parties the settlement's residents had thrown during his two years there. He recalled with some chagrin that all the other bachelors had, especially Meecher. But not he! He had never learned to dance, and he'd been too sensitive to get up on the floor and make a fool of himself, and deathly afraid that he'd step on her toes.

"The problem is," Catherine Merrill's soft voice went on, "I need someone I can rely upon to look after the hotel while I'm gone."

He wondered what advice he could give her in that regard, but the answer was quick to follow.

"Constable Baxter recommended Simone Laboucan, over Black Town way. I'm afraid I don't know her very well, and I'd be grateful if you would tell me whether you think I should approach her, whether she would be reliable. It's more of a responsibility than it might appear, and I couldn't go away in peace if I had any doubts."

O'Reilly shrank back in horror, and he was going to have words with Baxter over this, but he tried not to show what he was thinking. In the most diplomatic tone he could summon, he said, "I would suggest you talk to Marie Joussard. She's much handier, living practically next door. And I'm sure she'd be just as capable as Simone Laboucan."

Catherine Merrill shook her head. "I've already asked Marie, but Mr. Joussard won't hear of it. He doesn't want anyone thinking he can't support his wife. Of course it's not a case of that, but I'm sure the extra money would be welcome."

"That sounds like Bernard. I'll have a word with him and see if he'll change his mind. I think if I could convince him he'd be doing you a favor, he might relent. Perhaps I could speak with Tom Barr. Bernard would listen to him."

Catherine Merrill smiled. "Thank you, Sergeant. I'd appreciate that. I gather you think it would be unwise for me to approach this Simone Laboucan if Marie can't help."

O'Reilly nodded. "I'm afraid so, Mrs. Merrill, and I'm surprised that Baxter would suggest her. I'll talk to him about that."

Concern showed in Catherine's green eyes. "Oh, please don't, Sergeant. I'm sure he was just trying to be helpful. I'd hate to see him in trouble over it."

O'Reilly paused. "He won't be in trouble, Mrs. Merrill. But if you'd rather I didn't, then I won't."

O'Reilly remained in the dining room another fifteen minutes before leaving and crossing the street to see Tom Barr. The settlement wasn't much—four buildings on one side of the street and three on the other, while at the bottom was the steamboat landing and the Palliser River. Closest to the landing stood the Northwest Transportation Company's warehouse and next to it the company's office. Then there was the

Hudson's Bay Company store, with Tom Barr's bachelor quarters at the rear. The fourth building contained the Canadian Bank of Commerce.

On the other side of the street was the Northern Lights Hotel, a pretentious double-story frame building glistening under a fresh coat of white paint. Just up from it were two trappers' log cabins, one of them occupied by Bernard Joussard and his wife, Marie. There was another building, a frame house, but it was boarded up. It had once been a brothel, catering to the miners over at Coal City, until the Mounted Police arrived at Fort Determination and closed it down, erecting their log barracks a hundred yards up from the small settlement.

Fort Determination didn't look like a fort. It got its name from the old fur-trading days when the North-West Company built a log fort and determinedly held it against constant attack by an intractably hostile tribe of Indians inhabiting the eastern slopes of the Rocky Mountains. When the Hudson's Bay Company amalgamated with the Nor'-Westers, they took over Fort Determination. All that remained of the old fort were a few feet of the once-formidable palisade, a dozen rotting logs stuck into the ground facing a stretch of poplars through which the Indians used to sneak to commence their attacks.

As he crossed the street, O'Reilly saw the three strangers, who had left the dining room ten minutes ahead of him, standing in front of the Northwest Transportation Company's warehouse with Meecher and Refflon Lasher, manager of the Pacific & Western Coal Company over at Coal City.

So, the big sergeant mused to himself, that's what

they are . . . coal company men, probably from Edmonton or Winnipeg, or perhaps Vancouver. Engineers, probably.

A moment before he pushed open the door of the Hudson's Bay store, O'Reilly saw both Lasher and Meecher glance over in his direction. Even in that brief interval, he couldn't miss the look of extreme dislike on Meecher's face. What the hell's the matter with him, O'Reilly wondered as the screen door slammed shut behind him.

"About time, Hughie," Tom Barr boomed gruffly from behind a counter. "I thought you'd forgotten. That's what happens when eligible young bachelors like you get talkin' to pretty widders like Catherine."

Blushing, O'Reilly laughed. "What did you want to have a word with me about, Tom?"

The white-haired trader stuck a thumb behind the wide elastic suspenders over his green-plaid wool shirt and squinted at the Mountie through watery blue eyes. "A piece back, you told me Mad Old Mike got himself killed in an avalanche last winter."

O'Reilly nodded. "A wandering band of Indians came in to the barracks and reported it."

"Did you investigate it?"

"Come on, Tom! He was reported buried under the damned avalanche."

"And I presume them Indians knew what they were talkin' about?"

"Look, Tom—" O'Reilly started to say, but the older man cut him short.

"They were wrong, Hughie. Mad Old Mike ain't dead. He's very much alive and up to his old tricks again. Jake Raff—"

This time it was O'Reilly's turn to interrupt. "I know. Corporal Rogers told me. Which reminds me, I should have a word with Raff over where he's getting his liquor. After all, this *is* prohibited territory."

"Pshw!" Barr snorted, shaking his head impatiently. "Jake knows when he's bein' shot at. And it ain't just Jake Raff. There's been a couple of others shot at just recently, too. Over by Surprise Lake. It's Mad Old Mike's brand of shootin'. Trappers are startin' to get scared. They reckon the police should stop him."

"He's never killed anyone!" O'Reilly retorted defensively.

Tom Barr unhooked his thumb from behind his suspenders and leaned forward over the counter. "But maybe he will. Maybe some day he'll just manage to miss comin' so close and kill somebody. I tell you, Hughie, you yellow-legs are goin' to have to do something about him."

O'Reilly sighed. "Maybe you're right, Tom. Maybe you're right."

When O'Reilly stepped out of the Hudson's Bay store some minutes later, he glanced down the street. Refflon Lasher was sitting on his buckboard in front of the Northwest Transportation Company's warehouse talking to Meecher, while the three strangers had changed into rough trail garb and had been joined by a fourth, who came out from behind the warehouse leading four saddle horses, a dozen pack horses, and three Indian handlers. As O'Reilly watched, Lasher finished his conversation with Meecher, waved to the four strangers, and drove off in the direction of Coal City.

31

"Hmmm," O'Reilly expressed half-aloud to himself. "Wonder where they're off to? Looks like a small expedition." Watching a minute or two longer, he put the matter out of his mind by telling himself, "Pacific & Western must be looking for new coal finds."

Then he looked past the transportation company's warehouse, across the blue-green water of the Palliser and on up the northern slopes of Mount Queen Victoria.

Over that mountain, somewhere on the other side, was Mad Old Mike.

Chapter 3

Bright red tunics ablaze in the dying rays of the setting sun, two trim young Mounties trotted their sleek brown horses through the grimy outskirts of the roughly-slapped-together log community of Coal City, or Black Town as they called it over at Fort Determination.

"I hate this bloody place," Constable Clyde Baxter remarked to the Mountie riding stirrup-to-stirrup beside him. "Look at it—dirty, dingy dump!"

Constable Harry Somers nodded in agreement. "It would help if they'd at least whitewash the buildings."

"They're too bloody lazy. When they're not down in their burrows digging coal, they're lounging around in these dank shacks getting drunk. Bloody coal company should divert a bit of its production time into beautifying the place." He laughed thinly. "*Beautify!* Hell!"

Constable Somers glanced around at the coal-blackened hills, stripped of most of their trees, beyond the crudely built log shacks. "Even Nature is against the place. Incredible how there can be so much difference between here and Determination, yet

33

they're only a dozen miles apart."

"It's this coal dust . . . It kills the plant life and trees—what trees they didn't cut down to build their bloody mine."

They rode along the blackened main street that wandered in a crooked line between two rows of log shacks. In their traditional scarlet and gold, with shiny brass buttons and polished leather belts and boots, the two Mounties looked out of place amongst these dirty surroundings. Yet not out of place really, because the long scarlet arm reached everywhere in the great North-West.

Sullen, hostile eyes peered out at them from the log shacks as they trotted by. Police meant trouble. Most of the miners came from central and eastern Europe, where they had been used to cruel and oppressive military-like police. Some had not yet learned that the jaunty Canadian redcoats, although strict, were neither cruel nor oppressive. Others, who had gotten to know them, realized that the Mounties did not have the same life-or-death powers of their European counterparts, and tended to push them when drunk or when having their fun interrupted because of some vague thing called *the law*.

It was Saturday night, and at the request of Refflon Lasher, the mining company manager, Corporal Rogers had drawn up a rotating detail of two men each Friday and Saturday night to ride from Fort Determination over to Coal City to patrol the mining town and keep the noise and revelry down to a dull roar.

"At least this isn't pay night for the miners," Constable Baxter said as he and Constable Somers bounced up and down in their saddles after the stiff

34

military style of the Mounted Police. "There won't be much money floating around tonight. The place should be fairly quiet. Maybe we can get the hell out of here before too long."

Constable Somers pointed down the street. "Let's look in on that honky-tonk dance hall. If there's anything doing tonight, that's where it'll be."

A moment later they reined to in front of a ramshackle log building with a false front and the sound of tinny music coming from within. Swinging down from their saddles, they hitched their reins to a long board protruding from a pile of lumber lying carelessly beside a rickety boardwalk.

Harry Somers looked down at it in disgust. "Some drunken miner is going to stagger out of this place one of these dark nights, fall over that, and break his neck."

Clyde Baxter laughed. "Ever known a drunk to hurt himself, Harry? Not bloody likely. Come on. Let's have a look at the action."

Spurs jingling, they sauntered inside. Despite the noise, there wasn't much action . . . half a dozen roughly dressed miners stomping across the crude board floor performing an eastern European dance that was completely at odds with the rattling music coming from a battered piano being banged by a cigar-smoking man with bowler hat and walrus moustache. Six of seven gaudily painted dance-hall girls stood around watching, with expressions ranging from boredom to mild amusement. One lit a cigarette, cast a provocative glance across the floor at the two Mounties, and flashed a lipstick-smeared smile. Constable Harry Somers smiled back.

"Hard-looking bitch," Clyde Baxter remarked.

"It doesn't hurt to be polite," Harry Somers countered good-naturedly.

"You've been in these mountains too long. You need a trip outside to Edmonton to see what women really look like. Come on, let's get out of here before some bastard steals our horses."

Outside they untied their horses and climbed back up into their saddles.

Constable Baxter wheeled his horse around. "I don't see any point hanging around Black Town any longer. Tonight will be dead. Let's ride out to Simone's place."

Constable Somers screwed up his face. "I don't know, Clyde. We're supposed to stay in town . . ."

"To hell with the town! Nothing's going to happen. It's not a pay night, so the miners don't have any money. We've already shown the flag. Come on."

He flicked his reins, tapped his spurs gently against his horse's ribs, and trotted the animal briskly back along the street. Somers sat watching him for a moment, then hurried his glossy brown after him.

"What if the sarge finds out?" Somers asked once he caught up with Baxter.

"He won't find out. Don't worry."

It was dark now, but not too dark for a pair of alert eyes to notice the two Mounties as they rode past a patch of light thrown from the Pacific & Western Coal Company's office window.

Refflon Lasher and his mine boss, Vince Strathman, were just locking up. Curious, Lasher

36

watched them ride on into the darkness beyond the town's outskirts, hearing the jingle of bit and bridle and the creak of saddle leather over the muffled thudding of the horses' hoofs.

"Where the hell are they going?" Lasher wondered aloud. "They're supposed to be patrolling right here in town, god damn it!"

Strathman had seen the two redcoats ride into town earlier and recognized Baxter. "That ain't too hard to figger out. One of them yaller-leg's sweet on that half-breed woman that lives alone in that cabin on the way to the Indian camp."

"Simone? Simone Laboucan?"

"Yeah. Bet you dimes to brass razoos that's where they're headin'."

"Is that so? Well, we're going to follow them and find out. Come on, I've got the buckboard just around the corner."

Lasher had no difficulty following the two police-men in the dark. It was simply a matter of staying on the trail until it forked to the north and headed toward Snake Valley. Two miles north on that trail, on the way to a camp of Stoney Indians, stood Simone Laboucan's cabin. When Lasher and Strathman sighted it, a square of yellow light in the blackness a hundred yards away, the two police horses were stand-ing riderless outside.

Lasher stopped the buckboard and sat looking. "So that's where our police protection is going. By God, I'll have something to say to O'Reilly about this."

Three impassive-faced Indians hunched together on

37

the back of a dilapidated wagon, while a fourth sat on the driver's seat, loosely holding the reins of a two-horse team. A shaft of yellow light beamed out through the window of the Pacific & Western Coal Company's store. Tinny music sounded from the dance hall up the street, while overhead pale green northern lights flickered across the crisp night sky. Mountain evenings were seldom warm even in the middle of summer, and the thinly dressed Indians shivered together.

Inside the store a tall young Indian stood at the counter watching a scowling clerk count the cost of two bags of flour, some tins of tea, tobacco, a couple of lengths of cloth, and a few other items. While he did so, a young Indian woman with large, doelike eyes browsed around the store, admiring a satinlike yellow dress that would be bought by one of the dance-hall girls. She didn't notice a hulking brute of a man with a massive jaw and an unruly thatch of sandy hair lounging on an upturned barrel in the corner of the store. Small, piglike eyes watched her every movement as he sucked on a bottle of whiskey.

"That'll be twenty dollars, Indian," the store clerk said, glaring across the counter at the Indian from beneath his green eyeshade.

Surprise marked the Indian's face as his dark eyes dropped from the clerk to the piled goods on the counter, where they remained momentarily before lifting back up to the clerk's mean countenance.

"What's the matter, Indian?" the store clerk snapped.

The Indian hesitated before answering. "Too much money. Not worth more than ten."

Pushing his eyeshade back, the store clerk leaned across the counter and waggled a pointed finger in the Indian's face. "Is that so? Hudson's Bay prices from over Fort Determination way, huh? Now you listen to me, Indian—if you don't like the prices here, you better haul your ass over to Determination and do your business with the Hudson's Bay Company. You savvy that?"

Taking advantage of the diversion at the counter, the hulking brute got up off the upturned barrel and ambled across the rough board floor to where the young Indian woman continued to admire the dress. "You'd look right purty in that bright yeller dress, Pocahontas. Why don't you slip off them skins you're wearin' and try it on?"

Her big brown eyes taking in the leering monster of a man, the Indian woman shrank back in fright. Still clutching his whiskey bottle, he threw out a huge hairy paw to touch her but, like a startled animal, she danced back beyond his reach. Displaying remarkable speed for a man so big, he sprang forward, his arm shooting out like a piston and grabbing her wrist. She screamed and struggled, knocking over the dress on its display stand. It landed on the floor with a hollow clatter.

At the counter the tall young Indian whipped his head around. Forgetting about his negotiations with the storekeeper, he leaped forward at the big man to free his pretty young wife's wrist. Snarling, the hulk tossed aside his whiskey bottle and met the Indian with an upraised arm, which he smashed down across the Indian's forehead, dropping him to the floor like a sack of potatoes.

The Indian woman screamed again, flailing with her small clenched fists and moccasined feet to get free. A case of tinned food was knocked over. The hulk grinned.

The storekeeper shouted in protest. "Hey, Zeke! The store, goddammit! Take it easy. There's breakables in here."

Big Zeke suddenly roared with laughter, then lashed out with a heavy-booted foot at a stack of packing cases standing beside one end of the counter, sending them flying. The storekeeper shouted again but his words were drowned out as the hulking monster erupted into further laughter. Next he turned his pig eyes onto the struggling young Indian woman as he pulled her to him. "How about a little kiss, huh?" he slobbered, thrusting his face down on hers.

But she spat in his face and jammed her pointed fingers into his eyes.

"*You bitch!*" he howled agonizedly, releasing her as he flung both hands up to his hurting eyes.

The Indian woman dropped to her husband's side as he was struggling to his feet.

"Go," he told her. "Quickly!"

"You too," she gasped urgently, grasping his arm and pulling him toward the door.

Scurrying around picking up the dress stand and rearranging the scattered cases, the storekeeper abruptly turned his attention to the two Indians. Spreading his arms, he herded them toward the door. "Get the hell outta this store, goddammit. You Indians are more trouble—"

Whatever else he was going to say was cut short by an enraged bellow that seemed to shake the entire store. Rubbing his inflamed eyes, Big Zeke lurched toward the door. The storekeeper reached it first and pulled it open to push the two Indians out, but before he could get it open wide enough, the hulking giant slammed his massive hairy arm against it with such jarring force that it almost broke. "You black bitch!" he roared, glaring at the Indian woman. "You're gonna pay for that!"

The storekeeper held up his hands in front of him. "Now, take it easy, Zeke," he pleaded. "Please! I don't want no damage done to the store. Mr. Lasher—"

"T' hell with Lasher and the goddamn store," Big Zeke shouted, making another grab for the Indian woman. She darted back and ran around behind the counter, Zeke lurching after her. Making the most of the opportunity, the storekeeper flung open the door and tried to shove the tall young Indian outside. But the Indian knocked the storekeeper's arms aside, bounded across the store, and leaped onto Big Zeke's back.

His face twisting in rage, Big Zeke reached behind him to drag the Indian off his back, but the Indian clung tenaciously on. Unsuccessful, Zeke fell backward across the counter, attempting to crush the Indian with his weight. The counter collapsed beneath them.

"Goddammit!" the storekeeper moaned, clapping both hands up to his head.

Big Zeke struggled up from the broken wood, sacks of flour, and scattered tins. The Indian was still on his back. This time the hulking brute took a run at the wall, at the last moment suddenly reversing himself to hurl himself backward against the wall's logs. The store shook from the impact, but the young Indian was knocked senseless, the wind driven from his body.

Running back around the smashed counter, the young Indian woman sprinted to the door and screamed for help from the four Indians sitting outside on the wagon. Led by the one sitting on the driver's seat, her brother Running Wolf, they jumped down from the wagon and surged toward the store's door. Her screams were also heard by half a dozen drunken miners swaggering up the darkened street on their way to the dance hall.

"Hey! Vhat's going on at der company store?"

"Don't know. Ve go look."

While the miners stumbled forward, the four Indians burst into the store but quickly came to a shambling halt when the found themselves staring at the hulking brute. Facing them, he crouched in a wrestler's stance, his booted feet planted firmly on the floor beneath him, his massive arms spread wide, his body leaning forward.

"More of youse stinking sons of bitches, huh!" Big Zeke snorted. "Well, come on. Come on to Big Zeke an' I'll break your goddamn backs."

Cowed, the four Indians hesitated until the woman screamed at them and Running Wolf threw himself at the giant. Big Zeke grabbed him and tossed him sideways into a shelf of canned food. The shelf collapsed and the cans rattled noisily to the floor.

"Goddammit, no!" the storekeeper muttered, shaking his head in despair.

When the remaining three Indians failed to follow up Running Wolf's attack, Big Zeke took the offensive and lunged at them. One leaped out of the way but Zeke's huge, bearlike arms wrapped around the other two. Merchandise went flying. Clambering over boxes and cans, the storekeeper made his way to the door, stood outside on the boardwalk, and yelled at the top of his voice.

"Police! Police, goddammit! Police!"

He had barely gotten the words out when the six drunken miners staggered up to the store. "Vhat's happening in dere?" one of them asked.

"A fight, goddammit," the storekeeper blurted. "Have you seen the goddamn police?"

"Dem two yaller-legs ain't around no more. Dey rode out of town an hour ago."

"Oh, great, goddammit! They're never around when you want 'em."

"Come on," one of the drunken miners shouted. "Let's haff a look at d' fight."

"It's Big Zeke," another shouted, peering in through the door. "Big Zeke's fightin' Indians."

"Let's help him," a third whooped.

"Yah! Ve show der Indians somethink. Ve show dem not to fool around wiff white mans."

Pushing through the door, a pair of miners fell upon the Indian who had eluded Big Zeke, While Zeke still had his huge arms around the other two. Running Wolf was picking himself up from the shelfful of cans Zeke had thrown him against. Two of the miners jumped on him before he was able to get all the way up. Over against the store's far log wall, the tall young Indian had regained his senses and was struggling dazedly to his feet. The remaining two miners, smelling like a brewery, stood covetously eyeing the

43

pretty young Indian woman.

In a moment the company store was turned into a whirlwind of hurtling bodies, kicking feet, and falling boxes and cans, punctuated by the sound of splintering wood and shattering glass.

Steadily squeezing the life out of the two Indians in his arms, Big Zeke looked around the store, his red-rimmed pig eyes searching for the Indian woman. As soon as he saw her, he threw the two bucks aside and lunged for her. But before he could reach her, her husband jumped in between them.

Big Zeke scowled. "You still lookin' for trouble, you stinkin' redskin? Well, goddamn you, I'll give it to you good this time."

With brutal force the hulking man drove his fist into the tall Indian's face. The blow sent the Indian hurtling across the broken counter, and he crashed into packed shelves behind it, bringing clattering to the floor the boxes, cans, and bottles that had survived the onslaught so far. Kicking what was left of the counter aside, Zeke leaned down, picked up the Indian by his collar, and yanked him to his feet. Zeke then smashed his fist into the Indian's face a second time. The Indian's head snapped back and he went limp. Big Zeke hit him a third time before letting him drop to the floor.

Behind the hulk the young Indian woman picked up a jar of pickles and was about to bring it down on the back of his head when two slobbering miners grabbed her. Twisting her head and kicking, she tried to bite one of them but he simply laughed and hung on to her.

Out on the dark street more miners were drawn to

the company store and they thronged around the door, gleefully watching the excitement and shouting encouragement to their drunken fellows as they beat upon the outnumbered Indians.

"Giff it to dem, boys. Damn rotten Indians!"

In the store two miners threw an Indian headfirst through the window, then stood back laughing as shards of broken glass crashed to the floor. Outside, two or three onlookers picked up the bleeding Indian and heaved him onto the back of the wagon.

"There, you red-skinned son of a bitch!"

"Let's give him a ride."

"Yah! Let's giff him a ride he won't forget."

Laughing, a miner climbed up onto the wagon seat and grabbed the reins. Helped by two others on the ground, he reined the team around until the horses were facing down the street. Then he snatched up the whip and cracked it over the horses' backs.

"*Güid-app!* Goddamn it, hosses. *Giddap!*"

The team broke into an instant gallop down the crooked, black street as the miner jumped wildly off, to the whooping and cheering of the other miners.

"That's the way to get rid o' them red-skinned bastards!"

"Yah! Let's look around town. Mebbe dere's some more ve can send packin'. Come on, boys."

Inside the wrecked store a laughing, bellowing Big Zeke looked around for more Indians to beat up. Running Wolf and one of his companions lay unconscious among a pile of cans and boxes. Three grinning liquor-stinking miners held a wildly thrashing Indian to the floor while one of their mates urinated on his face. Two more miners still held the Indian woman,

45

tears streaming down her face as she struggled and fought to reach her husband, who lay in a crumpled, lifeless heap beside the broken counter.

Turning his small, pig eyes onto the woman, Zeke wiped a hairy paw across his mouth and grinned lecherously. "Now, then, squaw, you've just seen what a *real* man can do. Now we're gonna spend a little time gettin' acquainted. Let 'er go, boys. I'm a-ready."

But a brittle voice from the floor stopped him cold.

"His neck's broke, Zeke," the store clerk said as he knelt beside the Indian woman's lifeless husband. "You killed him stone dead."

The monstrous hulk slowly turned his head and looked down. Fear glazed his red-rimmed eyes.

Refflon Lasher and Vince Strathman drove back into Coal City to find a mob of drunken miners armed with pick handles roaming up and down the darkened streets shouting and laughing.

"What the hell's going on here?" Lasher demanded.

"Indians!" shouted a miner. "We're lookin' for dirty, stinkin' Indians. We goin' drive 'em from whiteman's country."

"Good thing tomorrow's Sunday," Strathman grunted. "None of these johnnies will be fit for work."

"We better find out what caused this," Lasher said, flicking the horsewhip just as his team showed signs of balking at the prospect of further pulling when they thought they should be trotting home.

Lasher drove them up the winding street. When they reached the company store, a mass of noisy miners stood milling around. Jamming his foot down on the brake, Lasher jumped down from the buckboard. Strathman was right beside him. Together they pushed their way through the throng.

"Make way, you men," shouted Strathman. "Make way for Mr. Lasher."

The miners moved aside to allow the company manager through. As soon as he was inside the store, Lasher's eyes widened in dismay at the sight of the mess.

"My God! Was there a damned explosion in here or something?"

Looking around slowly, his eyes came to a stop when they reached the store clerk and at the store clerk's feet the crumpled, lifeless body of an Indian. The next instant the sound of a bottle being smashed came from the back room, and the huge form of Big Zeke Benders filled the doorway. In his hand he held a bottle of whiskey, the neck of the bottle broken off. The hulk fixed his eyes on Lasher for a moment, then he lifted the jagged neck of the bottle to his mouth and started drinking.

Lasher's eyes snapped onto the company-store clerk. "Well, Fisher?"

The store clerk opened his mouth to speak. Words babbled from it but they didn't make sense.

Her clothing in disarray, the pretty young Indian woman staggered out from the back room behind Big Zeke. She pointed an accusing finger at him. "He kill my husband!"

Strathman dropped onto a knee beside the Indian on the floor and examined him. He looked up at Lasher. "He's dead."

Glaring at Big Zeke Benders, Lasher snapped, "You damned fool!"

Zeke lowered the bottle and fixed Lasher with a baleful look. "You don't call me no damn fool again, Mr. Lasher."

Lasher showed no concern over the implied threat. He looked back at Fisher, the store clerk. "I'm in a firing mood, Fisher. And I'm going to start doing just that unless I get answers pretty damned fast. Now, how did all this start?"

"It was them stinkin' damn Indians," Big Zeke cut in.

"Yeah, that's right, Mr. Lasher," Fisher added emphatically. "The Indians started it."

"That's not true!" the young Indian woman sobbed. "We do nothing wrong."

Lasher looked from Fisher to Big Zeke, then to the Indian woman and back to Fisher. "Damned Indians," he muttered. "They shouldn't be allowed into town." Then he looked back at the Indian woman. "You better get the hell out of here. This is company property. I don't want to see you or any of your kind in here again."

"My husband—"

"I said *get!* His body stays until the police have a look at it."

"The police!" Big Zeke was visibly shaken.

Lasher glared back at the hulk with a measure of unconcealed delight. "Of course! The Mounties will want to have a look at him. You're facing a charge of manslaughter for your damned stupidity."

Big Zeke snorted. "He's just an Indian."

"That doesn't matter. The Mounties like Indians.

They'll take you over to Fort Determination and lock you up. It might teach you a lesson."

Glowering, Zeke raised the bottle's jagged neck to his mouth again. Taking a good swig, he spat on the floor and wiped his mouth with his hairy arm. "No damn yeller-leg is takin' me anywhere, 'specially not for killin' no stinkin' Indian."

Realizing the police would have their hands full with Big Zeke Benders, Lasher shrugged. "Anyway, if those two Mounties of O'Reilly's were where they should have been, none of this would've happened."

Chapter 4

The creak of saddle and harness, the occasional snorting of horses, and the muffled *clib-clob* of hoofs on the soft grassy ground were the only noises as the seven riders and their dozen pack animals made their way around to the south side of Mount Queen Victoria. When the mirror-top turquoise water of Surprise Lake spread in front of them, Lorne Hayden, the oldest of the three strangers who had sat in the Northern Lights dining room the other morning, reined to and looked around.

As Eric Nelson, one of the other two men, drew up alongside him, Hayden pointed toward Mount Queen Victoria. "We'll make a field camp over at the base of that mountain and look for samples."

The younger man nodded. "That's where that British syndicate did some exploratory work, isn't it?"

Hayden shook his head. "Nobody knows for sure. Leastways, nobody outside their syndicate. The rumor was they never did complete their exploration. Some lunatic scared them away by shooting at them."

"Rivals, maybe?"

Taking off his hat, Hayden ran a hand through thick gray hair. "Could be, I suppose . . . although nobody else has staked any claims in this area . . . or anywhere else in these mountains, for that matter. Which is just as well for us."

Turning in his saddle to look behind him, Hayden waved his hat to the riders moving up with the pack horses. "Hargreaves!" he shouted.

"Comin', Mr. Hayden," one of the riders shouted back, and legged his horse into a canter to join them. When he pulled up beside them, Hayden again pointed to Mount Queen Victoria.

"That's where we're heading, Hargreaves . . . over there to the foot of Queen Victoria. How long will it take us to get there?"

Touching fifty, Royce Hargreaves was the same age as Lorne Hayden, and his face, what there was of it showing between his gray beard and hat-brim, was burned almost black from a lifetime of exposure to sun and wind.

"There's a lot of timber 'atween here and there . . . won't make it afore sundown . . . have to camp somewheres like halfway . . . I'd say 'bout midafternoon tomorrow."

Hayden replaced his hat. "Good. Get your Indian handlers moving the pack horses in that direction."

"Sure thing, Mr. Hayden," Hargreaves replied, then swung his horse around and rode back to the pack train.

"How long do you think we'll spend over there, Lorne?" asked Nelson.

"Hard to say, Eric. It'll depend on what sort of samples we can pick up. Four or five days, I'd say.

51

Then we go back across the Palliser and push north to Snake Valley. Now come on. I want to get as far as we can before sundown."

They had just reached the shadows of the pine trees when Hargreaves caught up with them again.

"Mr. Hayden, the Indian handlers don't want to go no further. They reckon evil spirits live in among them pines, and they're plumb scared."

Lorne Hayden twisted around in his saddle to stare at Hargreaves. "Evil spirits! Come on, Hargreaves. That's sheer nonsense."

"It might be to you an' me, Mr. Hayden, but not to them. They've heard about the evil spirits what live in among them pines and shoots at anyone who comes near."

This time Hayden laughed. "Evil spirits don't shoot guns. Come on, Hargreaves. They're being paid well enough. Get 'em moving. We've got a lot of ground to cover and time is of the essence."

Royce Hargreaves sat in his saddle slowly shaking his head. "I don't know, Mr. Hayden. I ain't seen Indians scared like this afore. They just plain don't want to go in among them trees."

Hayden's brow tightened into a heavy frown. "I hired you for this job, Hargreaves, because you're a good trail man. Now, you know as well as I do that there's no damn evil spirits. You go back and convince them of that, and hurry. That sun's not going to stay up forever."

Crackling merrily, the campfire illuminated the night's darkness, throwing immense shadows against the black background of the surrounding pines as Lorne Hayden, Eric Nelson, and the third man, Ted Race, sat around drinking coffee and smoking. Royce Hargreaves sat a little away from them, staring moodily at another fire thirty yards away where the three Indian horse-handlers lay in their blankets.

"If we find what we're looking for in these mountains," Lorne Hayden was saying, "this whole Northwest will boom like crazy. They're sure to build a railroad up here from Edmonton to link up with Winnipeg and the East. And Ottawa is just as likely to reverse its earlier decision not to turn the upper Palliser into a national park. Tourists from all around the world would flock to this part of the country. They'd be able to see what Canada's great North-West is really like, without hardship and with all the comforts of civilization close at hand. Man, we could make ourselves fortunes in real estate and resort lodges, let alone mining. The key to it all, of course, is keeping the lid on what we're doing until we get back to Edmonton and set the legal machinery into motion. It's absolutely vital that no one gets wind of what we're looking for."

A doubtful expression covered Eric Nelson's face. "Well there's a dozen people back at Fort Determination who must be doing some wondering. You know how inquisitive people are in these remote northern settlements."

Lorne Hayden flicked his cigarette end into the fire. "The fact that they saw us with Refflon Lasher just before we left should settle their curiosity. They'd naturally assume we're with Pacific & Western Coal Company looking for more coal seams. They'd never dream we're really looking for silver."

"Are you sure we'll find silver in these mountains, Lorne?" Nelson asked. "It seems to me that if there's any around, that British syndicate should've found it."

Hayden leaned back contentedly against his saddle. "They didn't finish looking, Eric. You remember back in '97, the price of silver dropped—"

"*Collapsed* would be a better word for it," Ted Race interrupted.

"Right you are, Ted," Hayden continued. "They collapsed . . . the bottom fell right out of the market. Then word got out about the gold discovery in the Yukon, which led to the gold rush of '98. Right after that came the war in South Africa. The British diverted most of their interests to protecting what they had there, so that British syndicate never did complete their search." Laughing, Hayden added, "It wasn't some lunatic in these mountains shooting at them that stopped them. It was plain, simple economics. But now silver prices are pushing up again, and the time is ripe."

"But we've still got to find the stuff," persisted Nelson.

"We'll find it, Eric. The rock samples Lasher showed me looked pretty promising."

"The ones from Snake Valley?"

Hayden nodded.

"And that's where our problems start," said Race. "That valley, from what I've heard of it, is Indian country, and they don't take kindly to intruders."

Hayden turned to look at Race's face, highlighted by the flames from the campfire. "That's Lasher's

54

problem, Ted. He's assured me he'll look after that end of it."

It was just then, as his eyes shifted momentarily past Race to Royce Hargreaves, that Hayden noticed the trail boss was sitting bolt-upright, his eyes searching the blackness of the pines beyond the circle of fire.

"What's the matter with you, Hargreaves? You look like you've seen a ghost."

Hargreaves did not answer immediately, but when he did he kept his eyes glued to the shadows. "I've got me the damnedest feeling there's something out there among them pines watchin' us."

Hayden looked around, his eyes also probing the blackness of the pines. He saw nothing other than shadows. Then he burst out laughing. "You're seeing those evil spirits your Indian handlers are scared of, Hargreaves. Come on, man. You better turn in and rest your imagination. For that matter, I think we'd better all turn in so we can be fresh for an early start tomorrow."

Lorne Hayden woke up the next morning to find himself being shaken roughly by the shoulder.

"Wake up, Mr. Hayden. Wake up!"

Opening his eyes, Hayden looked up to see Royce Hargreaves bending over him. "What the hell's the matter, Hargreaves?" he demanded huskily.

"The horses and all our supplies—they're all gone!"

Hayden jerked himself up into a sitting position. "What the hell do you mean?"

"Someone's taken our horses. The whole damned

lot of 'em. And all the supplies as well!"

"Those damned Indian packers of yours," Hayden blurted angrily, struggling to his feet. "They must've got scared and lit out with 'em when we fell asleep."

Hargreaves quickly shook his head. "It weren't the packers. They're still here."

Nelson and Race were waking up also. "What's all the noise about?" asked Nelson.

Hayden ignored him. "Then, put your packers to work, Hargreaves. They're Indians, aren't they? Get 'em busy looking for tracks."

Again Hargreaves shook his head. "There ain't no tracks. Not a damned one! Them horses an' all our supplies have just disappeared into thin air. I reckon my Indian packers were right. There's evil spirits 'round here."

This time Hayden didn't laugh.

Chapter 5

The Sunday morning sun was rising high in the cloudless blue sky behind Constables Clyde Baxter and Harry Somers as they trotted their horses at a leisurely pace westward along the valley of the Palliser on their way back to Fort Determination. Baxter's good-looking face bore a contented smile, and his tan-colored Stetson was tilted at a rakish angle over his right eyebrow. But Harry Somers frowned.

"Don't you think we should have gone back to Black Town to make sure everything was all right?"

Baxter's smile widened. "You worry too much, Harry. You should be happy. You had a good feed and a good sleep. Better than if we'd patrolled Black Town all bloody night."

"Good sleep! On the damned floor? You're the one who had the good sleep. In a warm bed, with a soft body to keep you company."

Baxter chuckled. "Too bad Simone doesn't have a sister."

They rode on in silence for a mile or two, while Somers brooded and listened to the creak of saddle leather and the jingle of bridle and bit.

"What'll we put down on the patrol report?" Somers finally asked.

Irritation edged Baxter's reply. "Come off it, Harry! What do you think we'll put in the bloody patrol report? That we patrolled Black Town as we were supposed to and that nothing of any note occurred. I know the bloody drill."

"Well, I hope nothing happened."

"Of course nothing happened! Next Friday or Saturday night will be when it happens, right after those sods of miners get their pay. And fortunately, it'll be someone else's turn to police them. The only good thing about duty in that dump is I can slip away and see Simone."

Somers shook his head in a gesture of resignation. "You're a scheming dog, Clyde."

Baxter flashed a grin. "You have to be, in this outfit, Harry. They'd work a chap to death otherwise. Not that I'm not a staunch believer in rallying around the flag and all that sort of thing, mind you. I'm all for King and Country when I'm needed, but I'm also a firm believer in Mrs. Baxter's young lad, Clyde, having his share of fun."

Harry Somers didn't reply. He simply jogged along in his saddle as they rode toward Fort Determination. Clyde always made things sound so simple, but Somers didn't like being derelict in his duty. It wasn't the Mounted Police way.

The mood of Sergeant Hugh O'Reilly, DCM, was as black as his fierce, upswept moustache as he rode his dark bay at a steady trot along the banks of the pale green Palliser toward Coal City. Where the hell were Baxter and Somers? O'Reilly wasn't worried that something might have happened to them. He knew better—at least as far as Baxter was concerned.

No more than two hours had passed since once of the Pacific & Western Coal Company employees had driven into Fort Determination and reported to the Mounted Police what had happened in Coal City the night before. O'Reilly had lost no time saddling up and riding out.

He was halfway to the coal-mining town when he spotted two red dabs bright against the deep green of the pines almost a mile away. As they drew closer, the two red dabs firmed into Baxter and Somers. Riding easy, just like they were out on a Sunday jaunt. O'Reilly's mood blackened further.

O'Reilly was too damned angry to think, but the minds of the two oncoming Mounties were anything but blank. They were wondering themselves, and they were doing a great deal of fast thinking. The contented smile was gone from Baxter's face.

Sergeant O'Reilly reined to a dozen yards from the two approaching constables. "Where the hell have you two been?" he demanded savagely.

Baxter managed a weak grin. "Sorry we're a bit late, Sergeant. We patrolled until well into the morning and didn't manage to bed down until a couple of hours before sunup."

O'Reilly shot a critical eye at Baxter's rakishly tilted Stetson. "Straighten that hat, Baxter," he snapped. "Where do you think you are—in the Australian Light Horse?"

As soon as Baxter adjusted his Stetson to the regulation position, O'Reilly rasped, "You patrolled until a couple of hours before sunup, did you? *Where?*"

The grin had long since frozen on Baxter's face. "Why . . . ah . . . Black Town . . . where we were supposed—"

The big sergeant cut him short. "Then, you must have had your damned eyes closed and your ears plugged! Get yourselves back to Fort Determination immediately and report to Corporal Rogers. You're both under open arrest!"

Baxter's jaw dropped. Somers, fidgeting with his reins, looked thoroughly miserable. Baxter was on the verge of saying something more, of at least trying to get Somers out of trouble, but O'Reilly's fierce black moustache was standing straight out, an unfailing danger signal, so Baxter kept his mouth shut, other than to acquiesce to the sergeant's order with a muted, "Right, Sergeant."

Reining his dark bay off to the side of the trail to allow the two constables to pass, O'Reilly sat watching their retreating scarlet backs for a moment, then with undiminished anger he resumed his ride to Coal City.

Under the clear light of the morning sun, Refflon Lasher and Vince Strathman stood in the middle of

Coal City's crooked main street looking at the shambled remains of the company's store. Presently Fisher, the storekeeper, came out of the doorway and scurried toward them.

"Well?" demanded Lasher.

"He's still in there, Mr. Lasher," the worried storekeeper said. "Sucking on a bottle of whiskey. He says he won't leave."

"Did you tell him the Mounties are coming for him?"

Fisher nodded quickly. "He just smashed the head off another bottle of whiskey and said he's not goin' to let them take him for killin' no Indian."

"Damnation!" Lasher cursed.

"I don't see what you're worryin' about, Mr. Lasher," Strathman said. "Let the Mounties take him. That's the easiest way. At least, it is for us."

Lasher looked scornfully at the tall mine superintendent. "That's why you're only a mine boss while I'm the manager, Strathman. You've got no imagination. Can't you see? If the Mounties go in there and find Big Zeke Banders with a supply of raw whiskey, they're going to wonder where it came from. They might just start looking around." Then he added, his voice heavy with sarcasm, "This *is* prohibited territory, you know."

Lasher whirled viciously on the storekeeper. "And you, damn you, Fisher! Why the hell did you let that goliath in the back of the store like that? You know what he's like when he gets drinking. God, the man can soak up more liquor than a hundred miners. I should never have agreed to allowing liquor to be kept

61

in the back of the company's store."

Strathman shrugged. "It seemed the only place. The Mounties were suspicious of everywhere else. Hell, they even moved the rocks around up on the hills." He looked sideways at the storekeeper. "Anyways, Fisher can take the rap. It shouldn't make no difference to him. We pay the fine."

Lasher shook his head. "That's not the point. What bothers me is the reaction at Winnipeg if it gets back to head office that illicit liquor is being peddled from company premises. We don't want any adverse publicity, especially not now."

Pulling from his vest pocket a gold watch, Lasher opened the case and peered at the dial. "What the hell's taking the Mounted Police so long?" He snapped shut the case, returned the watch to his pocket, and turned to the storekeeper. "Fisher, get inside there and see what that monstrous moron is doing. Try and talk him into getting the hell out of there."

"But, Mr. Lasher," Fisher protested. "I already tried that."

"Try again. He'll listen to you."

Fisher reluctantly returned to the store. As soon as he was out of hearing, Lasher said to Strathman, "I hope we didn't make another mistake by taking him into our confidence. The more who know about our venture, the more danger there is. I don't have much confidence in him. He's as cocky as hell when everything's going well, but when things get a little bad, he gets shaky."

"There's only four of us," Strathman replied.

"You, me and Fisher, and Meecher over at Fort Determination. That don't seem like too many. And as far as Meecher is concerned, we need him to get our equipment and stuff in from Edmonton without anyone knowin' what it's for."

Lasher put his hand up to his mouth and nervously pulled at his bottom lip. "It's not Meecher who concerns me. It's Fisher. We could have got by without him. It would have meant extra work for you and me, but we could have got by without him."

Strathman thought to himself, What you mean, Mr. Big-Shot Lasher, is that it would have meant extra work for me, not you . . . and extra risks as well.

Sergeant O'Reilly clattered into Coal City. Riding directly up the main street, he saw Lasher and his mine boss standing together in front of the company store, while coming out of the doorway was Fisher, the storekeeper. Knots of curious miners clustered about, waiting to see what would happen.

"About time you redcoats showed up, O'Reilly," Lasher growled as the Mountie reined to. "But aren't there any more of you? You won't be able to handle this alone."

Looking down at Lasher from his saddle, O'Reilly said, "Your messenger said a man was killed during a brawl in the company store last night."

"I don't know about a man being killed," Lasher replied, inclining his head toward the store. "But there's a dead Indian in there."

O'Reilly's dark eyes bore into the mining-company

manager. "I don't think that's funny, Mr. Lasher."

"And I don't think it's funny the way your men police Coal City, O'Reilly. If they'd been doing their job last night like they were supposed to, none of this would've happened. Maybe I should send a bill to Ottawa for the damage to the company's store and merchandise, for the stuff stolen by those thieving Indians while all this was going on. I'm getting sick and tired of those damned Indians coming into this town and causing trouble. This is a company town, not a damned Indian powwow ground. If you Mounties would do your job properly—"

O'Reilly cut him off. "I had two men on patrol here all night."

Lasher laughed sarcastically. "Oh, no, you didn't, O'Reilly. They should have been here, but they weren't. But I can tell you where they were. They were shacked up with that half-breed woman, Simone Laboucan, over toward Thunder Hawk's camp."

"How do you know that?" O'Reilly asked sharply.

Leering triumphantly up at the Mountie, Lasher replied, "Because I followed them."

"Are you trying to make trouble, Lasher?"

"When I make trouble, O'Reilly, you'll know it. I've warned you about those damned Indians. I don't want them around here. You better move them out of these mountains. There isn't room for them and coal mines. And the mines are important to the country's economy, so it's pretty plain who has to go. As for those two constables, you better court-martial them. They're a disgrace to the uniform."

His brows spearing together in a fierce frown beneath the stiff brim of his crown-pointed Stetson, O'Reilly sprang down from his saddle, planted his feet firmly beneath him, and thrust his jaw two inches from Lasher's face.

"Don't tell me what to do, Lasher!"

Refflon Lasher was as tall as O'Reilly and a good twenty pounds heavier, but it was his self-importance rather than any courage that made him push O'Reilly.

"I've got political connections in Ottawa, O'Reilly. If you value your career in the Mounted Police, you better do as I say."

Barely managing to restrain himself, O'Reilly clenched his fists and dropped his voice so low that Lasher alone heard him. Not even Strathman, standing no more than three feet away, heard. But Lasher heard.

"If you threaten me again, Lasher, I'll break your bloody neck."

Lasher went white. Whirling around, O'Reilly almost pushed Strathman out of his way as he started for the store. "Watch my horse, Strathman," O'Reilly said over his shoulder.

In a few angry strides, O'Reilly reached the store. "Is the body of the dead Indian still in there?" he asked Fisher, who was still standing by the broken door.

Fisher nodded, and O'Reilly stepped inside.

Back in the middle of the street, Lasher watched O'Reilly's red-coated figure disappear through the doorway. "*If* you walk out of that place in one piece after tangling with Big Zeke Banders, O'Reilly," he muttered to himself, "I'll fix you. So help me, I'll fix you."

Holding O'Reilly's horse, Strathman turned his head. "What was that, Mr. Lasher?"

"Nothing!" Lasher snapped back at him.

Chapter 6

Spur rowels jingling lightly with each step, O'Reilly moved through the littered mess that was the inside of the company store. He could see there had been a hell of a fight. Scattered boxes, cans, tobacco, clothing, blankets . . . all covered by a powdery white blanket from torn flour sacks. Here and there on the floor were patches of blood.

Then he saw the crumpled body of an Indian lying on the floor.

At the end of the broken counter Big Zeke Banders sat on the upturned barrel, watching O'Reilly through his little pig eyes. One huge paw held a broken-topped whiskey bottle, the other a blood-smeared pick handle. O'Reilly recognized him instantly. They had held him in the cells at Fort Determination last year for nearly killing a fellow miner in a fight. It had taken four Mounties to bring him in. O'Reilly realized he should have brought someone with him. George Bailey, for instance. George would have been a good man to have along in a situation such as this.

Keeping a wary eye on the giant, O'Reilly knelt down beside the body of the Indian. Turning him over, he looked into the battered face of Johnny Blue Sky, a damned fine Indian. The way his head hung, it looked as though he had died of a broken neck. His pretty little wife would be devastated.

Slowly O'Reilly rose, his dark eyes glinting hard like two polished stones, glaring accusingly, almost hatefully, at the big man. When he spoke, his voice was so low it was barely more than a hiss.

"You must feel damned proud of yourself."

The huge man glowered back at the Mountie. He looked mean and dangerous, his mouth drawn in a hard, tight line across his face, his massive jaw hanging low toward his chest, like a great buffalo bull about to charge. The pick handle swung menacingly backward and forward. Instead of answering, he swept the whiskey bottle up to his lips and poured half the contents down his throat, seemingly immune to the bottle's jagged glass neck. Then he slammed the bottle down hard on what was left of the counter with a bang that would have startled a man with less nerve than the big, black-moustached Mountie.

"I'm taking you in to Fort Determination," O'Reilly told the giant quietly.

"For killin' an *Indian*?" Big Zeke spat out the words.

"For killing a *man*!"

"You ain't takin' me nowhere, yaller-leg. Specially not for killin' no goddamn Indian." The hulking giant picked up the bottle again to take another swig, evidently thought better of it, and slammed the bottle down hard on the counter again, with a sharper bang than before.

"I'm taking you in, Banders," O'Reilly replied evenly. "One way or the other. You might as well make it easier for yourself."

Big Zeke got off the barrel and faced O'Reilly. "Easier for you, you mean—*yaller-leg!*"

O'Reilly shrugged. "Easier for both of us. Now come along quietly."

Suddenly the giant let out a terrifying bellow, raised his left arm, and swung the pick handle viciously at the Mountie's head. O'Reilly threw up his right arm and blocked the giant's swing, at the same time driving a hard left into Big Zeke's bulging stomach. It was like hitting rock.

O'Reilly tried to step back, but Big Zeke was too close. Still grasping the pick handle, he wrapped his huge arms around O'Reilly's body and tried to squeeze the life out of him, using the pick handle to gain leverage, then working it so that it ground up and down against the Mountie's spine.

Hugh O'Reilly could feel the life being crushed out of him, while pain darted up and down his back. He struggled with his arms to break the giant's bearlike embrace, driving his fists into Big Zeke's kidneys, but all he managed to do was encourage the brute to tighten his terrible grip. O'Reilly grunted in anguish as stars circled before his eyes. He was on the verge of blacking out. Then he remembered something George Bailey had done in a barroom brawl in Regina years earlier, something that had resulted in George appearing in front of the depot adjutant on an orderly-room charge of being improperly dressed by wearing a Stetson hat instead of the little, round pillbox forage caps they were supposed to wear for *walking out* in those days. O'Reilly drove his head forward so that the board-stiff brim of his Stetson cracked sharply across the bridge of Big Zeke's nose.

The blinding pain was excruciating. Instantly releasing his grip, Big Zeke howled in agony and dropped the pick handle as both his huge paws flew up to his face. Staggering free of the giant's clutches, O'Reilly paused to regain his breath, while Big Zeke nursed his tender forehead.

Both men recovered at about the same time.

Glowering at O'Reilly, Big Zeke snarled. "You yaller-striped son of a bitch! I'll tear you apart for that." Then he charged.

O'Reilly met him with a hard straight left that cut the bigger man's lips, then danced back out of the way as the monster hurtled harmlessly by.

Roaring like an enraged wild bull, Big Zeke stopped, swung around, and rushed back at O'Reilly. This time the Mountie turned sideways, caught Big Zeke's arms, threw his right hip into him, and pivoted, sending the hulk of a man sailing across the littered store to land with a jarring, skidding thud among some boxes at the far wall.

"Are you ready to come along peacefully now?" O'Reilly asked

Big Zeke spat violently at the floor, struggled to his feet, and kicked boxes and cans out of his way. "Like I told you, yaller-leg, you ain't takin' me nowheres."

He advanced on O'Reilly again, but this time

without haste, cautiously, arms spread wide to grapple. O'Reilly realized he would have to beat the brute, knock him senseless. There was no other way. He knew he could not subdue him long enough to lock handcuffs around his wrists. He would have to whip him completely. It did not occur to him to draw the big Enfield holstered high on his right hip. That was not the Mounted Police way.

As Big Zeke came on slowly, O'Reilly suddenly darted in and cut him with two stinging left jabs to the face. Before Big Zeke could close his arms, O'Reilly had danced back out of reach. An instant later he stepped forward again and swung a right cross to Big Zeke's face, rocking the brute's head back on his neck. The riding gauntlets covering O'Reilly's fists made a distinct smacking noise as the leather contacted with the skin of Zeke's face.

Momentarily dazed, Big Zeke shook his head to clear it, then his eyes widened in rage and he rushed at the Mountie, swinging his fists wildly. O'Reilly ducked in under Big Zeke's flailing arms and drove a straight right directly from the shoulder. It connected with Big Zeke's nose with a sickening crunch. The huge man went flying backward, fell over the broken counter, and landed upside down on his head on the other side.

Seizing upon an opportunity, O'Reilly whipped a pair of blued-steel handcuffs from his breeches pocket and swung over the counter to land on top of the big man. Quickly O'Reilly grabbed a hairy wrist and clapped a handcuff around it, trying to turn the key in the lock. But his fingers fumbled the key and Big

Zeke jerked his arm free, rolling over onto his side and aiming a vicious kick at O'Reilly's head as he went. O'Reilly threw himself in the opposite direction. Big Zeke's boot missed O'Reilly's head but caught the brim of his Stetson and sent the hat flying.

Both men sprang back upon their feet at the same time. Blood pouring from his nose, Big Zeke dived at O'Reilly's midriff, driving his massive head into the Mountie's stomach just above the buckle of his Sam Browne belt. Driven by the force of Big Zeke's rush, O'Reilly staggered backward, losing his balance. They went down with a jarring crash, Big Zeke on top. O'Reilly smashed his elbow into Zeke's thick neck and struggled to get out from under him. But Big Zeke hung on. O'Reilly managed to get his left knee free and rammed it into Zeke's side, once ineffectually but then twice with telling force. Zeke grunted as wind was knocked out of him. O'Reilly twisted and rolled out from under the giant, but Zeke's arm shot out and grabbed the Mountie by the back of his Sam Browne shoulder brace. Like a rubber ball Big Zeke bounced up onto his feet, yanked O'Reilly up, then swung him free of the floor. Next the giant whirled around and around on his feet, swinging O'Reilly around him in a flying circle. O'Reilly was completely powerless. Big Zeke meant to let go so that the Mountie would crash headfirst into the wall and be knocked senseless, but Zeke miscalculated. He let go an instant too soon, and O'Reilly's red-coated figure sailed cleanly through the window that had been broken the night before.

Fortunately for O'Reilly, he landed amongst a

group of miners watching the fight through the broken window. They all landed in a tumbled mass on the ground outside. O'Reilly had the wind knocked out of him, but that was all. He was just staggering to his feet when Big Zeke, with an enraged bellow, kicked the remains of the front door out of his way and rushed the Mountie.

O'Reilly dropped to a knee just as Big Zeke reached him. The giant stumbled over O'Reilly and went sprawling in the blackened dust of the street. The momentum of Big Zeke's rush had rolled O'Reilly over also, but O'Reilly hip-swiveled on the ground, and as Zeke was about to get up to lunge at him, O'Reilly kicked. His spurred boot smashed into Big Zeke's face, adding to the damage to his nose that O'Reilly's fist had already done. Big Zeke screamed with pain as both his hands flew up to his shattered, bloodied nose. Before the giant could get up from his knees, O'Reilly followed with a swinging right that caught Zeke on the side of the head. Zeke toppled.

Amid the crowded spectators—Lasher, Strathman still holding O'Reilly's horse, Fisher, and several dozen miners—O'Reilly, his deep chest pulling in great draughts of air, staggered back into the store, to return a moment later dangling his handcuffs.

Big Zeke lay on his back in the street's black dust, his head to one side, blood pouring from his nose. Leaning over the hulking form, O'Reilly rolled him over on his stomach and handcuffed his thick, hairy wrists behind his back. Then the Mountie stood up and started slapping dust and dirt from his red coat and yellow-striped blue breeches. It was then that

Lasher spoke, his voice a harsh indictment that stung O'Reilly to the raw.

"You're a disgrace to the king's uniform, O'Reilly—brawling in the street like that. And you didn't have to beat Mr. Benders up like that. That's what I call excessive force and needless brutality. Your headquarters at Regina is going to hear about this!"

Chapter 7

Walking up the winding street toward the Pacific & Western Coal Company's offices on the outskirts of Coal City, Vince Strathman looked twice when he saw Refflon Lasher about to leave. His boss was dressed in his best striped suit and brand-new derby.

Lasher cursed when he saw Strathman approaching, and wished he had left ten minutes sooner. He knew Strathman would wonder why he was dressed up. He didn't want him—or anyone else—knowing where he was going, or even suspecting where. Deciding not to allow the tall mine superintendent the chance to ask questions, Lasher set about giving him something else to think about.

"Glad you came along, Vince. I would have had to go looking for you if you hadn't. A permit came in today's mail packet authorizing us to sell liquor to mine employees from company premises. It's all legal now, signed by the lieutenant governor himself at Regina. That's one of the advantages of my political connections in Ottawa. Winnipeg head office has given its blessing. The chief general manager realizes all too well that we've lost more than enough production through having half our miners regularly disappearing downriver to Edmonton or across the border into British Columbia for a month-long drunk every time they manage to save three or four pays."

Strathman's long face showed no reaction. "That ain't going to matter to you and me too much, Mr. Lasher. When our silver mining gets going, this coal company can go suck eggs."

"I know that, Vince," Lasher replied, trying to conceal his impatience with the mine boss at this particular moment. "But until that comes on stream, we have to pay lip service to Winnipeg."

"When'll we know about the silver, Mr. Lasher?"

"As soon as Lorne Hayden gets back from the Snake Valley," Lasher replied, glancing up at the darkening sky. The long summer day was drawing to a close and he was anxious to be on his way. "But right now I want you to organize a place to sell the liquor from. A big tent will do until we can get a building put up. Maybe even part of that dance hall. Get Fisher to help you."

As Lasher talked, Strathman sniffed the air. However, it wasn't the summer air he could smell. It was perfume or cologne. And it was coming from the mine manager. When he left Lasher a few minutes later to return to the center of the coal-blackened mining town, Strathman was more than curious to know where his boss was going.

Lasher hurried around to the rear of the offices, and

a few minutes later drove out of town in the company buckboard. It was almost dark enough now so that no one would see him, but he glanced back over his shoulder twice to make sure he wasn't being followed.

He had no trouble finding his way in the dark. He had been this way a month before when he and Strathman had followed the two Mounties to Simone Laboucan's cabin. All he had to do was stay on the trail until it forked toward the Snake Valley, then two miles north . . .

There it was . . . the patch of yellow light in the darkness that was the log cabin where Simone lived alone. Lasher's pulse quickened at the thought of what lay ahead . . . the pleasures and joys that would be his. Simone should be willing, especially now that O'Reilly had confined that Mountie—what was his name? Baxter—to barracks at Fort Determination. In fact, she would probably be hungering for a man right now. And Refflon Lasher was just the man. At least, he thought so. And why not? he asked himself. He could provide her with things that no Mountie could afford on a redcoat's meager pay.

Reaching Simone's cabin, Lasher climbed down from the buckboard, straightened his derby, and sauntered jauntily to the door. Grinning, he rapped softly.

"'Oo is it?" a woman's voice called from within.

Lasher's hand went up to adjust the knot of his silk necktie. "A visitor," he called in reply.

There was a moment's wait, then the door opened, just a fraction at first, then wider. Sultry dark eyes looked out from a dusky, attractive face. Long black hair shone against the yellow background, and a tall, willowy figure with a small waist and full breasts instantly aroused the mining company manager.

Taking off his derby, Lasher smiled broadly. "Good evening, Miss Laboucan. I . . . ah . . . guess you know who I am?"

She looked at him for a moment, but no expression crossed her face. "You d' big boss at d' mine in Coal City. What you wan'?"

Lasher's smile grew even broader. "May I come in?" he asked expectantly.

"What for?" she asked, holding the door steady.

The smile froze on Lasher's face. Her unmistakable disinterest caught him flatfooted and he didn't know how to handle it. He never really had been a lady's man. "Well . . . I . . . er . . . I just thought . . . "

"Go 'way," she replied, and went to shut the door in his face.

But Refflon Lasher's passions had been aroused. He'd wanted a woman for a long time, but the opportunity had not presented itself—except for those whoring dance-hall girls back in Coal City, and no matter how badly he might have wanted a woman he wouldn't have dared touch one of them. With Simone it would be different. Being half-French half-Indian, she would be hot and desirable, he reasoned, and that Mountie wouldn't have been playing around with her if she weren't clean.

Lasher flung out his arm and caught the door before the half-breed woman could shut it. Giving it a mighty push, he shoved it open and stepped inside. Simone quickly slunk back.

Grinning, Lasher held out his hand. "You don't have to worry about me, Miss Laboucan. May I call you Simone? I'm just here on a sociable visit. You must be real lonely here all by yourself, since that . . . ha ha! Well, you know what I mean."

Lasher's hungry eyes darted around the one-room cabin. Over in the corner was a bed, neatly made up, and his lust sharpened. Lunging, he grabbed at the half-breed woman. She darted back but not fast enough to escape Lasher's hand. It closed around her wrist and he dragged her toward him. With catlike agility she twisted her wrist free and sprang back around behind the flimsy protection of a table.

For perhaps sixty seconds they stood glaring at each other across the table. Then Lasher grinned again.

"There's no need to carry on like this, Miss Laboucan. I don't mean you any harm. I'd just like to get to know you better. I can offer you a lot more than that Mountie can. I can give you jewelry, pretty dresses, expensive perfume . . . all kinds of nice things. That Mountie . . . why, he can't even come and see you any more."

Simone tossed her head haughtily. "Hah! Dat beeg sergeant, 'e no keep Clyde in barracks forever. Den Clyde, 'e come back to see me."

"But think of all the things I can give you. This time next year I'll be rich. I can even take you places you've only heard about . . . Vancouver, San Francisco, even London and Paris. You'd like that, wouldn't you?"

But Simone kept watching Lasher warily, poised for instant movement the second he tried to get around the table.

Still grinning, Lasher said, "Wouldn't you like all that?"

"You better go 'way," she told him huskily. "You go 'way before I call police."

"The police! Ha ha! That's good. They aren't even around tonight. Come on, Simone. You be nice to me and I'll make you happy."

"Go 'way," she repeated.

"Damn your hide!" Lasher exclaimed. "You aren't going to reject me. You think I'm not as good as that Mountie? Well, I'll show you!"

Suddenly Lasher hurled himself at her, smashing the table aside. She tried to dart around him but his arms caught her.

"Got you, my beauty! Now, how about a little loving?"

Lasher thrust his mouth down on Simone's face. She twisted her head and instead of her lips he got the side of her face. Undeterred he pushed her toward the bed in the corner. They crashed heavily onto it, almost breaking it. Lasher's weight knocked the wind out of Simone and she lay unresisting beneath him as he pressed his lips to hers. The next instant, fully aroused, he thrust his hand under her tight buckskin skirt. The touch of her bare skin almost sent him into a frenzy, and his hand slid higher along up her thigh.

Suddenly Simone began to struggle. She snarled

and twisted and screamed and fought. She kicked and scratched, leaving deep, vivid furrows of blood streaming down Lasher's face. But woman-starved Refflon Lasher just laughed.

Until a hand of steel fell across his shoulder!

At first Lasher didn't notice the hand. Not until he felt himself being jerked off the half-breed woman and hurled halfway across the cabin. He landed in a heap on the floor and found himself looking up at the copper-hued, hawklike face of an Indian.

The Indian glared broodingly down at Lasher from a height of more than six feet. Fierce black eyes burned into the very depths of Lasher's soul. The Indian was unarmed except for a knife at his belt.

Flinging out a buckskin-covered arm, the Indian pointed at the door. "Go," he commanded in a rumbling, thunderlike voice.

Lasher climbed slowly to his feet. Even though he was a big man himself, and one not inclined to brook having a hand laid on him by another man, especially not an Indian, Lasher wasn't going to argue with *this* Indian. Although he had never laid eyes on him before, Lasher knew very well who he was. The brooding, hawklike face was identification enough.

As soon as he entered the coal company manager's office, Lorne Hayden's eyes widened. Almost speechless, he stood open-mouthed in the doorway staring at Refflon Lasher's face. "What the hell happened to you? You tangle with a mountain lion or something?"

Lasher glared back at the mining engineer from behind his desk. "Never mind my face! You've sure taken your sweet time. You should've been back from that exploration trip a week ago."

Sweeping his hat from his head, Hayden sat down on a chair opposite and ran a big hand through his gray hair. "God damn it, Lasher. We're lucky to be back at all. We damn near got killed over at the base of Queen Victoria. The first night in, some damn spirit or something took all our horses and gear—everything!"

Lasher scowled. "A *spirit*? Are you trying to faze me, Hayden?"

"No, damn it all! I know what you're thinking. I thought the same when our Indian packers didn't want to go near the place because they were afraid of evil spirits. But, damn it all, our horses and all our gear disappeared. Clean as a whistle! No tracks or anything."

"Evil spirits—*hell*! Must've been Indians. They'd steal anything. Why didn't you go after them?"

"Like I told you, Lasher, they left no tracks. Nothing! It was just like the horses disappeared into thin air. Anyway, we walked back to Fort Determination to get another outfit. When we returned to the south side of Queen Victoria we approached it from around the other side of Surprise Lake. Now, I want to show you something."

Hayden got to his feet, stepped over to the office door, and called out. In a moment Eric Nelson and Ted Race walked into the office, and a few seconds behind them Vince Strathman.

"I knew you were busy, Mr. Lasher," Strathman said, "but when I saw these two men going to your office, I reckoned you might want to see me too."

Lasher nodded and Hayden continued.

"When we got close to the trees separating Surprise Lake from the foot of the mountain, damned if someone didn't open up on us with a rifle. Damned near killed us. Look at this." He held up his hat and poked a finger through a hole in the crown. "That's a bullet hole." He looked around at Eric Nelson and Ted Race. "Show Mr. Lasher your hats, fellas."

Nelson and Race took off their hats and poked fingers through identical holes in identical places.

"Not only the three of us," Hayden continued, "but Royce Hargreaves and the three Indian packers as well."

"Spirits don't use guns," Lasher countered sourly.

"Maybe not," Hayden replied. "But I've never yet seen a marksman who can put seven shots into exactly the same place in seven hats in as many seconds. No mortal can fire a rifle like that."

Lasher scoffed. "That's no spirit. There's some crazy trapper or something up on that mountain who scares intruders off. Anyone at Determination could've told you that."

"And shoot like that?" Hayden shook his head. "Well, I'd like to meet him—on favorable terms, of course."

"What happened next?" Lasher prodded impatiently.

"Well, there was no point hanging around there and running the risk of getting killed, so we turned back and hit out for the Palliser, crossed over, and headed north for the Snake." Hayden grinned broadly. "And that's where things started looking good. We found a vein of ore three feet wide in one place, and four more ranging from ten to twenty inches wide in other locations. And just about everywhere else we looked we found excellent showings of silver and galena. There's no doubt that there's enough silver and lead along the Snake to make a very profitable mining venture."

Refflon Lasher moved excitedly to the edge of his chair. "How much working capital do we need to get started?"

Lorne Hayden thought about that for a moment. "Three hundred thousand."

"We can raise that much. Now all we have to do is stake claims and register them with the Dominion lands office in Edmonton before that British syndicate decides to come back to Canada now that the war in South Africa is over."

Ted Race stepped forward. "There's one other thing, Mr. Lasher."

Lasher looked hard at Race's unsmiling face. "And what's that?"

"Indians!" Race replied. "They watched us all the time we were in the Snake. Didn't come near us, but they watched. From what Hargreaves told me, they're Stoneys, an offshoot of the Sioux a long time back. For generations they hunted along the eastern Rockies all the way from Montana to the Valley of the Snake. The main tribe settled by the Bow a couple of hundred miles south, but this band liked the Snake well enough to stay. That was before white men started moving into these mountains. Their chief is quite a man . . . name of Thunder Hawk, I think Hargreaves said. Fella in his late thirties, physically as tough as nails, and clever to boot. He seems to think all of the Valley of the Snake belongs to the Stoneys. He's supported in that view by the Hudson's Bay Company trader over at Fort Determination, Tom Barr. Hargreaves said it was the Stoneys who drove off a troublesome tribe of British Columbia Indians that kept attacking the old fur-trading fort back in the days before Confederation. Now, as long as these Stoneys are around, we're going to have trouble mining silver in the Snake."

At mention of the name Thunder Hawk, Lasher's scarred face took on a hateful expression. Before he could reply, Vince Strathman spoke.

"Mr. Lasher tried to get his political friend at Ottawa to have the Indian Affairs Department move them right out of the area, but his friend don't have no pull with Indian Affairs because the minister that looks after that department don't like him. Mr. Lasher tried to get the Mounties to move 'em, but O'Reilly—"

Lasher impatiently waved Strathman to silence. "All right, Vince. I'm not mute."

Hayden looked concerned. "Race is right, Lasher. It's essential to get those Indians out of that valley before we can start. If the government or the police move them, so much the better. Otherwise, we'll have to try it ourselves, and if this Thunder Hawk is half the chief Hargreaves says he is, he won't be interested in moving peacefully or for a payoff."

Refflon Lasher ran a hand over the long red scratches on his face. "I've already got that matter in hand, Hayden. Believe me, I have."

Chapter 8

Standing at the *Northern Voyager*'s upper deck railing as the sidewheel river steamer cut through the pale green water of the Palliser, Inspector Wolsley Wellington Kerr watched Fort Determination grow larger on the north bank, a cluster of white frame and log buildings, with red or brown roofs. He could not locate the Union Jack that would identify the Mounted Police post because it was further back from the settlement and was screened by a grove of tall deep-green pines.

He was not impressed by what he saw, not even by the undeniable beauty and grandeur of the mountains. There was too much a sense of isolation about them. However, it could have been worse, he told himself. Herschel Island, in the Arctic Ocean, for instance . . . or Hudson Bay. Calgary or Lethbridge would have suited him much more. It was relatively civilized down south there, with reasonable social amenities and a pleasantly bearable climate.

The *Northern Voyager* slowed as it neared the landing. Inspector Kerr could see no flash of scarlet among the three or four waiting people, no member of the detachment to meet the riverboat if only to see who might be traveling on it. He would have something to say to the NCO in charge about that.

When the river steamer tied up and still there was no sign of anyone from the detachment, Inspector Kerr did not disembark. Instead he requested the steamer's captain to send one of his crew with a message to the Mounted Police post. Then he waited impatiently until a visibly surprised sergeant and two constables hurried down from a height of land beyond the settlement. He listened to the thud of their boots as they tramped onto the landing and watched the morning sun's reflection on their polished brown boots and dazzling brass badges and buttons. At least they were well turned out, he had to admit.

The sergeant, a deep-chested man with an upswept black moustache, stepped onto the gangway and alighted onto the steamer's deck, leaving the two constables on the landing. As the sergeant halted in front of him and snapped off a smart salute, Inspector Kerr noted with envy the red and blue ribbon of the Distinguished Conduct Medal beside the orange-blue-red of the South African Medal above his tunic pocket.

So this was Sergeant O'Reilly! For a moment Inspector Kerr felt himself tremble.

O'Reilly held his salute until the inspector thrust his riding crop under his left arm and returned the salute. During that brief moment O'Reilly took in the officer's impeccably tailored blue tunic and breeches, his superbly shined Sam Browne, the rich gold of his buttons, the single gilt star on his shoulder straps, the

South African Medal ribbon above his left breast pocket, and the elaborately embroidered cap badge with its silver bison head, gold maple-leaves wreath, and red and gold crown. All new. None of it showed any sign of field service. No inevitable darkening on the insides of the fitted brown riding boots, no tell-tale weather stains on the yellow band around his blue cap or on the wide yellow cavalry stripes down the sides of his breeches, no tiny nicks on his leather-bound riding crop.

Instead of identifying himself to the more-than-curious O'Reilly, Inspector Kerr asked, "Don't you have a democrat, Sergeant?"

O'Reilly shook his head. "No, sir. Not much need for one in these mountains."

"Then, your two constables will have to carry my baggage. I have two large bags and a trunk. They will have to make two trips. In respect to your rank, I will not expect you to carry anything."

Two large bags and a trunk! O'Reilly repeated to himself. *Who* is this officer . . . and what the hell is he doing here?

Together they walked from the deck down the gangway to the landing. Tom Barr and Catherine Merrill were on the landing, together with Barr's assistant and Meecher, the Northwestern Transportation Company manager. Their eyes were on Inspector Kerr. Commissioned officers of the Mounted Police were not often seen in remote places like Fort Determination, and their sudden appearances were just as likely to mean that the NCO in charge of the local post was in some sort of hot water. Tom Barr was on the verge of stepping forward and introducing himself, but something about the inspector's face changed his mind.

O'Reilly instructed the two constables to collect the inspector's baggage, then he and the inspector commenced walking up what passed for Fort Determination's main street toward the barracks.

"Don't your men meet the riverboats when they arrive, Sergeant?" Inspector Kerr asked. "Otherwise, how do you know whether or not a dangerous criminal or a wanted person has entered your area?"

"We usually meet them, sir. There's generally only the one, the *Northern Voyager*, although occasionally the *Indian Princess* takes her place. Meeting them helps relieve the monotony in a place like Fort Determination, a bit of a minor social—"

Inspector Kerr cut O'Reilly short. "Then, why didn't one of you do so today?"

O'Reilly didn't like the officer's manner. "Because we were engaged in our monthly drill parade, and I don't let anything short of an emergency interfere with that."

"Not even the arrival of a commissioned officer?"

"I wasn't informed you would be arriving, sir. As for the matter of dangerous criminals—"

For the second time Inspector Kerr cut O'Reilly short. "I'm not interested in excuses, Sergeant."

"I'm not giving excuses, sir. I'm trying to explain."

Inspector Kerr impatiently flicked his riding crop in an unmistakable gesture for silence. O'Reilly angrily clamped his mouth shut.

The North-West Mounted Police post was five

hundred yards from the steamboat landing, on a slightly rising incline. O'Reilly could hear the inspector's breathing as they walked together, the breathing becoming noticeably heavier the further they went, as though the officer was not in shape. So the long-legged O'Reilly increased the pace, forcing the inspector to walk faster. The officer was not happy to be walking at all.

The two constables collecting the inspector's baggage back at the riverboat landing were even less happy.

"Christ! Look at the size of that trunk. Do we have to lug that?"

"Apparently so, dear chap. Unless you can think of another way to get it up to the post."

"Well, I didn't join this outfit to be lugging officers' baggage. Who is he, anyway?"

"Don't know, but judging by the size of his gear, he's here for a lengthy stay."

"Boy, oh boy! The sarge is really going to like this."

Up at the post, Sergeant O'Reilly led Inspector Kerr into his office. The inspector glanced around approvingly. He pointed to a closed door leading from the office. "What is in there?"

"My quarters, sir."

"I would like to see them."

O'Reilly stepped over to the door, opened it, and stood aside for the officer to enter. Inspector Kerr went in and looked around as he had done in the office, only taking longer this time.

"These will do, under the circumstances," he said.

"Sir?"

91

The inspector turned an unsmiling face to O'Reilly. "I said, these will do . . . for my quarters. I'm taking command of this post as of now."

O'Reilly reeled from the shock. *Taking command!* Of *his* post? "I don't understand, sir . . . am I being relieved?"

Inspector Kerr walked back into the office, took off his cap and gloves, and laid them, together with his riding crop, on O'Reilly's desk. O'Reilly followed him. The inspector turned to face him again.

"Relieved?" he repeated. "No . . . you will continue as NCO in charge of the detachment, except that nothing will be done without my approval. You see, Sergeant . . . headquarters at Regina is not satisfied with your performance of your duties here. You have failed to initiate prompt action, or any action at all, in several recorded instances which have resulted in complaints reaching the commissioner's desk. And you have failed to maintain a suitable level of discipline. For instance . . ." The inspector unbuttoned a tunic pocket and produced two sheets of paper, which he unfolded and commenced to read aloud from.

"Despite complaints from residents of the community, you have failed to take any action to apprehend a mysterious, deranged person inhabiting the area around the southern foot of Mount Queen Victoria, who shoots at all and sundry who venture too near to what he evidently considers his exclusive domain. In view of the threat to human life posed by this person, your failure to even attempt to apprehend him can only be considered a grave dereliction of duty." Hard, buttonlike eyes lifted from the paper a moment to look briefly at O'Reilly before returning to the paper. "This even poses the unpleasant question of whether you and your men lack the nerve to tackle what might be considered a dangerous undertaking."

Coloring, O'Reilly opened his mouth to say something, but he quickly closed it as the inspector resumed reading aloud.

"Despite requests from the manager of the Pacific & Western Coal Company at Coal City for police protection to that community, you have failed to provide adequate protection, resulting in at least two riots, an undetermined amount of damage to property belonging to the coal company, and the death of an Indian male person in a fight. Further, despite requests from the said manager of the said coal company, you have failed to take action to move a troublesome band of Indians from the Snake Valley, from where they repeatedly convergé upon the coal-mining community and wreak havoc through riotous behavior and drunkenness, to another region far enough away so that they will not be able to continue the said acts."

Inspector Kerr turned over the page and read aloud from the second page. "Additionally, you have failed to maintain a cordial level of cooperation and liaison between the Force and Mr. Refflon Lasher of the Pacific & Western Coal Company who, as manager of the said company, is the leader of a civilized community, and by such failure you have allowed to develop a deplorable situation resulting in lawlessness and apprehension, whereby law-abiding miners are afraid to go about their employment because of the danger of harassment by the afore-mentioned Indians, thereby causing an interference with an industry considered vital to the development of the Rocky Mountain region of the North-West Territories and of overall benefit to the economy of the Dominion of Canada."

Hugh O'Reilly wanted to sit down. He could take a barroom brawl in his stride, or a manhunt, or an attack by a Boer commando, but this sort of thing was something entirely different. He had never had to defend himself against an assault on his competence as a Mounted Policeman, and he didn't quite know how to handle it. Nor was it yet over, for there was more to come, as Inspector Kerr gave him a cold stare across the top of the paper and continued.

"With regard to discipline . . . two of your constables, who were supposed to be on town patrol at Coal City, absented themselves from their duty and spent the night in the cabin of a half-breed woman of ill repute living on the way to the troublesome Indian camp in Snake Valley. This was drawn to your attention, but you failed to take any disciplinary action against the two constables other than to confine them to barracks for a month, despite the fact that they, by so absenting themselves from their duties, indirectly contributed to the outbreak of a riot resulting in considerable damage to private property and the death of an Indian male person."

Inspector Kerr folded the paper and returned it to his pocket. "Not very impressive, Sergeant. Not very impressive at all. Obviously you are not capable of functioning as NCO in charge of a detachment without yourself being supervised. Colonel Perry has therefore sent me here to provide the necessary supervision while at the same time enquiring into these complaints."

With mounting impatience, O'Reilly stood before the inspector waiting to be allowed the opportunity to say something in his own defense, but the officer seemed uninterested in hearing what he had to say.

"Now . . . I have some other matters to discuss. First of all, I want a review-order mounted parade for tomorrow morning at ten o'clock, when I will inspect the detachment. Then I —"

"Excuse me, sir," O'Reilly interrupted, unable to contain himself any longer. "Don't I get a chance to say anything?"

Inspector Kerr raised an eyebrow. *"Anything?"*

"Yes, sir . . . about these allegations . . . these complaints."

"I told you before, Sergeant—I'm not interested in excuses. Now . . . I would like to settle in to my new quarters. If you would be so good as to collect your things and move out immediately . . . Oh, and those two constables down at the river steamer, kindly direct them in here with my trunk and baggage. That will be all, Sergeant."

Less than ten minutes later a fuming, red-faced Sergeant O'Reilly stalked out of the building, kit bag over his shoulder and rifle and saddle bucket in his hand. He loved the Mounted Police and he loved this post. He had worked hard during the two years he had been in charge, and he was sure he had done a good job, good enough to satisfy his superior, Major

Cavannagh, the officer commanding G Division down at Fort Saskatchewan. That in itself was an accomplishment, for Major Cavannagh, a legend in the Mounted Police second only to Colonel Sam Steele, was not an easy man to satisfy. O'Reilly would not have minded so much if it were the major up here dressing him down. Then he would at least feel he had it coming. But not from this upstart inspector, whose spotless, expensively-tailored uniform all too clearly pointed to his headquarters origin. It was a fact that O'Reilly himself aspired to commissioned rank. For eleven years he had served the Force with dedication and loyalty, from Blackfoot country in the southwest corner of the Territories to the Yukon gold fields, from South Africa back to the Rocky Mountains. Now to have *this* happen to him, these complaints sent to the commissioner at Regina. They were grossly exaggerated and lacking much foundation, but they were enough to ruin his chances of being recommended for a commission unless he could completely clear himself. Confronted by an officer with an attitude such as Inspector Kerr's, how could he possibly clear himself? The man wouldn't even give him an opportunity to say anything.

Out on the grass parade ground between the rambling detachment building and the barracks, Corporal Rogers had the men, still in full review order the way they had been for the monthly drill parade, waiting for Sergeant O'Reilly's return. The slim, dark-haired corporal tossed an enquiring glance at his sergeant, especially noting the kit bag over his shoulder. He could tell by O'Reilly's face and the way the big black moustache stood straight out that it was not wise to ask questions, however. When Hugh was ready to tell him, he would.

Before storming into the men's barracks, O'Reilly looked over and barked in a drill-square voice. "Break the men off, Corporal! Attend to stables, then have them clean saddlery and polish kit."

In a no-nonsense voice, Dusty Rogers shouted back. "Very good, Sergeant!"

O'Reilly's mood was communicated to the men in those few words, and because shortness was unlike him, they became uneasy. They did not know what was wrong, although they had glimpsed the blue of an officer's uniform from where they were lined up on the parade ground. They knew nothing else. However, it did not take long for the word to get around, the word that the officer, whoever he was, would be with them for some time. It took only long enough for the two constables carrying the inspector's baggage from the river steamer to join their comrades polishing kit in the barracks.

"Do you know what his name is? Wolsley Wellington Kerr, if you can imagine. Painted right across the top of his trunk in fancy white lettering."

One of the men laughed. "Wolsley Wellington! His mother must've had great aspirations for him, naming him after two bloody generals."

"Sounds like a bloody Imperial! Probably have us mounting the guard at *reveille*."

"Sounds like one of Baxter's relatives. You should go pay him a visit, Clyde. Tell him you're one of his neighbors from the Old Sod."

Baxter snorted. "Not me, old man. I'm too low down on the totem pole to mix with officers."

"Don't give us that, Clyde. We know you're the bastard son of the fifth Duke of Coldcock sent out from the old country to teach us backwoods colonials how to eat off plates."

The constables, including Baxter, laughed.

"One thing . . . Sergeant Hugh isn't very happy."

"Lord, no. I've never seen him like that before. Did you see the way he looked when he left here? He was spitting bloody nails."

"Tone it down, you fellows," cautioned George Bailey, glancing out the barracks doorway. "Here comes Hugh now."

A moment later O'Reilly stamped into the barrack room. Without a word to the half-dozen constables standing around their beds polishing boots, belts, and bridles, he stormed down the aisle between the beds to the corporal's room at the far end and slammed the door shut behind him. The men exchanged glances, then silently resumed polishing.

They had barely brushed another dozen strokes when Corporal Rogers arrived at the barracks from the stables. O'Reilly's mood had hit him too, for he gave Baxter a withering glare.

"You missed grooming your horse's belly, Baxter. If you're looking for another thirty days confined to barracks, that's the way you're going to find it."

The slim, dark-haired American walked on down the barrack room to the corporal's room, opened the door, and went in. O'Reilly stood glaring out the window at the mountains beyond. He had dragged a spare bed in from the men's room and piled his uniforms and equipment onto it.

"You want me to move in with the men?" Rogers asked.

O'Reilly took a moment before replying. He finally turned away from the window. "No, Dusty. There have to be some privileges with rank . . . although from what I've seen today the privileges belong to the officers. This room is big enough for the two of us— for the time being, anyway."

"What's that supposed to mean?"

"Remember that rumor about Ottawa being on an economy kick and the Force offering free discharges? If it's true, I might take them up on it."

Dusty Rogers could hardly believe what he was hearing. "Hey, Hugh . . . that doesn't sound like you. What's going on, anyway?"

"You must have seen the officer who arrived on the *Northern Voyager*. He's taken command."

"*Taken command!* What the hell . . . ? This isn't a sub-district headquarters. Who is he?"

"Inspector Kerr."

"Never heard of him."

"Neither have I, and I thought I knew the name of every officer in the outfit. He's come from Regina. Must have been riding a desk down there. Certainly not horses. Those boots he's wearing have never straddled horseflesh. Anyhow, you'll meet him soon enough. He's ordered a review-order mounted parade for tomorrow morning."

At that moment a knock sounded on the door. Dusty turned his head. "Come in."

When the door opened, George Bailey's husky form filled the space. His eyes sought O'Reilly. "You want me to sound *retreat* at sundown, Hugh?"

O'Reilly looked at him for a moment before answering. "Sure . . . why not, George? Can't do any harm. Might even make the inspector feel more at home."

George made a face. "Speaking of him . . . is it all right if I tag along with you fellows as usual when you go down to Mrs. Merrill's for supper? If he's just come up from Regina, he mightn't appreciate you NCOs mixing with the men. Not that I mind incurring the displeasure of an officer. It wouldn't be the first time, but I don't want to see you two getting on the wrong side of the brass. You know how regimental they can be down there at the depot."

The three of them went to dinner together anyway, and when they arrived at Mrs. Merrill's dining room they found Inspector Kerr was already there. The inspector paid them no attention whatever, for he was too busy charming the attractive red-haired widow, which Hugh O'Reilly was quick to notice, and during dinner Dusty and George observed that the big Nova Scotian was broodingly silent.

The next morning Inspector Kerr conducted his inspection of Fort Determination Detachment, lined up on their horses in front of the flagpole. Unlike every other Mounted Police inspecting officer Sergeant O'Reilly had ever encountered, Inspector Kerr did not examine the horses, nor did he examine the bridles, lanyards, saddles, or stirrup leathers, although he closely scrutinized the men to see whether their scarlet tunics were clean and fitted properly and that their belts and boots were polished to perfection and their brass badges and buttons burnished to brilliance.

When the inspection was over, Inspector Kerr and Sergeant O'Reilly walked toward the rambling detachment building, which contained the police offices, guardroom, armory and—now—the inspector's quarters. Holding his leather-scabbarded sword steady on his Sam Browne belt, Inspector Kerr glanced sideways at the medals on Sergeant O'Reilly's scarlet tunic.

"CMR, Sergeant?"

"No, sir . . . Strathcona's Horse."

"I was Royal Canadian Regiment, although in South Africa I was seconded to the Imperials—Lord Roberts's staff."

The inspector's tone was one of haughtiness, or perhaps feigned nonchalance, as though he was waiting for the sergeant to make some comment indicating that he was impressed. But O'Reilly wasn't impressed, for the inspector had merely confirmed what the big sergeant already suspected, that he hadn't worked his way up through the ranks. When Inspector Kerr glanced sideways again, O'Reilly's ruggedly handsome face bore an expression of studied indifference.

As they mounted the veranda steps, Inspector Kerr's eye caught the carved sign *Fort Determination Detachment*. Pointing a gloved finger, he said, "I don't like that name. It's too cumbersome. I think I'll change it . . . Fort Palliser Detachment, I think. That sounds quite appropriate, seeing that it's on the

Palliser River."

O'Reilly shook his head. "You can't do that, sir. The name's gazetted. Not only by the Mounted Police, but by the Post Office Department as well . . . not to mention the maps."

Inspector Kerr paused in front of the sign. "Hmmm . . . I suppose you're right . . . although to my knowledge Palliser was never this far north."

It went through O'Reilly's mind that Inspector Kerr probably hoped to show him up by pointing to a possible inadequacy in his knowledge of history. If that was so, then O'Reilly was pleased to be able to disappoint him.

"No," he said, "but Dr. Hector and two others of the Palliser expedition struck over this way from Rocky Mountain House. They named the river in honor of Captain Palliser."

"Hmmm," Inspector Kerr murmured, and they passed on inside the building, turning into the office that had, until the day before, been Sergeant O'Reilly's. A stab of anger shot through the black-moustached Nova Scotian's big frame.

Inspector Kerr walked around behind the desk and stood there, carefully pulling off his expensive brown leather gloves, one finger at a time. Sergeant O'Reilly stood at attention in front of the desk. The inspector had ordered him to accompany him to the office, and now O'Reilly waited to hear what he had to say. He didn't expect he would like it.

"I intend to institute a weekly review order inspection parade, Sergeant . . . every Friday morning at ten o'clock."

O'Reilly hesitated before replying. "You realize, sir, that there will be Fridays when the parade might consist of no more than two men."

Inspector Kerr raised his eyebrows. "Oh! And why is that?"

"Normal police duties, sir. This detachment has a pretty large area to patrol. It's not uncommon to have only two or three men on the post at any one time."

"Then, arrange the patrols so that all the men are back by Thursday evenings."

"That's not possible, sir. Some patrols take up to a month or six weeks. Occasionally longer."

"Nothing is impossible for the staff-trained military mind, Sergeant . . . as we showed the Boers in South Africa. Draw up a list of the patrol routes, together with mileages, and I will schedule the patrols myself." Inspector Kerr unfastened his cased sword from his Sam Browne and laid it across the desk, then took off his cap and placed it beside the sword. He looked across at O'Reilly. "Now . . . I shall want a constable detailed as my servant. Who would you recommend?"

"*Servant*, sir?" O'Reilly wasn't sure he had heard right. "We don't have the manpower to spare a constable for servant's duties."

"Why not? You have a bugler."

Immediately O'Reilly realized it had been a mistake to have allowed George Bailey to sound *retreat* at the lowering of the flag the previous evening. "The rank is *trumpeter*, sir. We don't have *buglers* in the Mounted Police, unless they've just changed it again. And Constable Bailey, whom I presume you're referring to, *used* to be a trumpeter at Regina, but that

103

was thirteen years ago."

Inspector Kerr's tone was pure acid. "Watch your tongue, Sergeant! Don't try any impertinence with me, or I'll break you. I know all about your reputation."

Flashing dark eyes glaring back at the inspector, O'Reilly stiffened to rigid attention in an effort to control his rising temper.

"And don't stare at me like that, Sergeant—or I'll charge you with dumb insolence. Now, give me the name of a constable suitable for servant's duties."

"I can't do that, sir."

"That's an order, Sergeant!"

"It's not a lawful one, sir. If you care to consult *NWMP Regulations and Orders*, you'll see that constables may only be employed as officers' servants at those posts where there are sufficient numbers available to perform all regular police duties. We have just enough men here to do that. The loss of one constable would mean we wouldn't."

Now it was Inspector Kerr's turn to glare. The knuckles of his hands whitened as he clenched his fists in impotent rage. When he spoke his voice almost shook. "You think you're very clever, don't you, Sergeant! Well, mister, don't think I can't handle you. Your Distinguished Conduct Medal means nothing to me. The only thing that counts is *this*!" His pointed finger stabbed at the single gilt star on his shoulder strap. "And I'm wearing it!"

Fixing his eyes on an imaginary spot on the log wall just above the inspector's right ear, Sergeant O'Reilly remained at rigid attention as though he were outside on the parade ground. He didn't open his mouth and the expression on his face showed absolutely nothing, and certainly not the slightest indication of awe or concern. Which only served to heighten the officer's feeling of impotence.

"Have I made myself understood, Sergeant?"

O'Reilly's eyes didn't move from the imaginary spot. "Yes, sir."

"Very well. Carry on!"

"Sir!" O'Reilly snapped off a crisp salute, spun around on heel and toe, and marched out of the office. The moment his spurred boots touched the veranda floor outside, he reached up to the medals on his tunic, unclasped them, and thrust them into his breeches pocket. All around him deep green forests of pine swept up the sides of towering gray or brown mountains, while above the sky was a brilliant blue.

O'Reilly left the post and strode down toward the settlement.

Chapter 9

An angry Hugh O'Reilly found Tom Barr in the back of the Hudson's Bay trading post. He wasted no time on cordiality.

"That complaint to Regina was below the belt, Tom. If you had to complain, you should've written to G Division headquarters at Fort Saskatchewan instead of the commissioner's office at Regina. Major Cavannagh would've looked into it a hell of a sight more thoroughly than that tin soldier Regina sent here."

The white-haired trader took the pipe out of his mouth and stared blankly at O'Reilly. "What d' you mean, Hughie . . . complaint to Regina?"

"That officer who arrived yesterday came from Regina to investigate why I haven't brought in Mad Old Mike, among other things. He even suggested I haven't done so because I don't have the stomach for it. I haven't brought him in because, in my opinion, Mad Old Mike shoots to scare away intruders. He won't kill anyone."

"How can y' say that, Hughie? How d' you know

he won't kill somebody some day?"

"Because I know h—" O'Reilly caught himself just in time. "I just don't believe he will. I realize you feel differently, and that's your right, especially you being the local justice of the peace. But if you had to write a letter of complaint about it, you could at least have sent it to Major Cavannagh, not the commissioner."

Tom Barr stuck the pipe back in his mouth and talked around the stem. "Anyway, Hughie, you're daft. I didn't write any letter of complaint. And if I had, I would've told you about it first."

O'Reilly stared hard at the trading post manager. "Well, somebody did. Who else would have?"

The trader took the pipe out of his mouth a second time and looked steadily back at O'Reilly. "Are y' calling me a liar, Hughie?"

The big red-coated Mountie dropped his eyes. "No, of course not. I know you better than that. But the thing's got me stymied, Tom. Who else would be upset enough about Mad Old Mike? Except maybe someone he shot at, and I doubt that. Jake Raff can't even sign his name, let alone write a letter. I know Refflon Lasher wrote to Regina or Ottawa. He threatened he would, but I doubt he'd have even thought about Mad Old Mike."

"How about Meecher? He's not what I'd call one of your admirers. He's got his eye on Catherine, and he's jealous of you on that account."

"Jealous of me? There's nothing between Catherine Merrill and me."

"Haw! Maybe you don't see it, Hughie boy, but I do. The way she looks at you. I think she's in love with you."

"That's nonsense!"

The older man nodded wisely. "I've known Catherine a mite longer than you have, Hughie. I can see it when she looks at you. And a right-fine-looking couple you'd be. Y' should consider poppin' her the question. Young fella like you should be thinking of marriage. Even Mounted Policemen marry. Catherine's the kind of woman who'd follow the right man anywhere, even some of the places you yellow-legs get sent to."

O'Reilly reddened a little and changed the subject. "I can't see Meecher writing to Regina. He knows I come under Fort Saskatchewan. If he had written a letter of complaint about me, he'd have sent it there."

Tom Barr struck a match and held it over his pipe. "You mentioned Lasher. You know him and Meecher are pretty thick." He looked shrewdly at O'Reilly through clouds of bluish tobacco smoke.

O'Reilly nodded. "I've seen them together a time or two . . . probably because Pacific & Western use the transportation company's riverboats to ship in materials and supplies and haul out their coal."

"I think it's a little more than just that, Hughie," Tom Barr replied sagely.

"What do you mean?"

"Don't know . . . but I think they're a wee bit deeper than that."

O'Reilly frowned under his Stetson. "You mean you think Lasher might have put Meecher up to writing to Regina?"

"I wouldn't know, Hughie. I've got enough of the company's business to occupy my thoughts with, but y' might just bear in mind what I told you. It might come in handy someday."

Inspector Wolsley Wellington Kerr had been in command of the North-West Mounted Police post at Fort Determination little more than twenty-four hours when Refflon Lasher drew up his buckboard outside and stepped into Inspector Kerr's office.

The inspector looked up from his desk with undisguised annoyance at this unannounced entry.

"You must be Inspector Kerr," Lasher grinned, walking toward the desk with outstretched hand. "I was informed you arrived yesterday on the *Northern Voyager*. We have a mutual friend."

Inspector Kerr remained seated and eyed Lasher coldly. He resented the interruption and would have preferred this man, whoever he was, to have made an appointment. He must select a constable to act as his orderly, who would screen callers like this. "Oh . . . and who might that be?"

"The Honorable Wilbur Roget, Minister for Mines and Minerals in Prime Minister Sir Wilfred Laurier's cabinet."

A smile leaped to Inspector Kerr's face and he sprang to his feet and shook Lasher's hand. "Oh, yes . . . the Honorable Wilbur Roget . . . of course."

"In fact," Lasher said, "the Honorable Wilbur Roget is my uncle. My mother was a Roget."

"I see," replied Inspector Kerr agreeably, waving his arm to a chair opposite the desk. "Please sit down, Mr. . . . "

"Lasher . . . Refflon Lasher. I manage the Pacific & Western Coal Company over at Coal City. Uncle

Wilbur wrote and told me you would be arriving. In fact, his letter arrived on the same river steamer that brought you here. I got it last night and rode over here today to welcome you to your new post."

"Very kind of you, Mr. Lasher . . . very kind indeed. Can I offer you a cigar and brandy? I have some excellent brandy, as a matter of fact. Brought it with me . . . securely packed in my trunk, of course. Oh, no worry . . . we won't be breaking the territorial liquor ordinance. I have a special permit signed by the lieutenant governor."

Lasher sat down in the proferred chair, crossed one leg over the other, and made himself comfortable. Very comfortable, for he knew this had been O'Reilly's office and correctly deduced that the inspector had kicked O'Reilly out. Lasher grinned to himself as he thought of the expression that would be on O'Reilly's face if the big sergeant could see him in there now. But he was just as glad O'Reilly couldn't, for he had important matters to discuss with the pompous, blue-uniformed pawn sitting behind the desk opposite him, business that he didn't want O'Reilly knowing about—not yet, anyway. And Refflon Lasher would get down to brass tacks as soon as the softening-up preliminaries were dispensed with.

Over the brandy and cigars Refflon Lasher seemingly very casually let the Mounted Police inspector know that he was his uncle's favorite nephew, information that Wolsley Wellington Kerr was quick to absorb. Although he had only met the Honorable Wilbur Roget once, Inspector Kerr had in his tunic pocket a letter from him saying that any favors the inspector might be able to extend to the honorable gentleman's nephew would not pass unnoticed and would certainly not be forgotten. And, as Wolsley Wellington Kerr realized full well, a friend in high places, most particularly one in Sir Wilfred Laurier's cabinet, could work wonders in advancing a Mounted Police officer's career.

"The Honorable Wilbur Roget—my uncle," Lasher smilingly added, "has a profound interest in these mountains, and he has watched with keen interest the growth of the coal-mining industry, which is understandable considering his ministerial portfolio is mines and minerals. I know he is deeply concerned over the threat a certain band of Indians led by one Thunder Hawk poses to the continuing economic development of the coal-mining industry, so much so that he is seriously considering taking official action through the Department of Indian Affairs to have them moved back to the prairies where they came from. Unfortunately Uncle Wilbur and his colleague, the Minister for Indian Affairs, don't always see eye to eye, and Uncle Wilbur will probably have to initiate this action through the Prime Minister personally."

Eying the burning end of his cigar, Lasher cunningly chose his next words. "If it should so happen that the Mounted Police under your command took the . . . er, necessary action of their own initiative and moved these Indians, shall we say . . . Uncle Wilbur would be spared both the time and effort of having to bother Sir Wilfred personally, and he would be free to devote his attention to other matters. It shouldn't be too difficult for your men, really. After all, it's well known that the Mounted Police, ever since they first arrived in the West, have moved Indians around. They seem better suited to it than the Indian Affairs officials. The Indians seem to pay more attention to the police. It's all part of their respect for the red coat. And I happen to know that Uncle Wilbur would look upon such action as a great personal favor rendered him by you, and he would assuredly see fit to express his appreciation by whispering the appropriate words into the right ears."

There was a slight inflection in Lasher's speech as he voiced these last words, and he paused to let the implication sink in, watching the inspector closely through cigar smoke. He could see the blue-uniformed man's mind working.

As for Inspector Wolsley Wellington Kerr, a superintendent's crowns were already beginning to form on his shoulder straps.

O'Reilly walked down to the Northern Lights a little later for dinner that evening because he wanted the opportunity to talk alone to Catherine Merrill. Tom Barr's words of earlier in the day about Catherine being in love with him had stirred the Nova Scotian's heart. After all, he certainly had feelings for her, too. He had been aware of them for a long time, if only vaguely. However, he wouldn't have been so rash as to label them love, for what did he know about love? But there was definitely something, and tonight he intended finding out.

The moment he stepped into the dining room everything changed, for seated at a table against the far wall were Catherine and Inspector Kerr. Catherine had her back to the door, and she neither saw nor heard O'Reilly, while Inspector Kerr was so engrossed in charming the attractive, red-haired widow that he failed to notice the sudden presence of the sergeant.

O'Reilly didn't give them the opportunity to realize he was there. Instantly he wheeled around and pushed through the door back outside, and in long, angry strides he charged up the slope to the barracks, where he threw a saddle onto his dark bay and rode off into the pines.

It was almost dark when O'Reilly returned his horse to the stables. Dusty Rogers looked up from his bed in surprise when O'Reilly walked into the room they now shared.

"Hey, where've you been, Hugh? George and I were reckoning on going searching for you."

"I went for a ride," O'Reilly replied simply.

"Inspector was looking for you."

"Oh! I'm surprised. I thought he was too busy."

Dusty didn't know what O'Reilly meant by that, and the expression on the big sergeant's dark face didn't lead him to risk asking.

When Sergeant O'Reilly entered the detachment building the next morning, it wasn't because Inspector Kerr had been looking for him the night before. It was simply that, as he was still in charge of the detachment and his duties were partly administrative, he had to have office space to attend to them. With the inspector having taken over his office, O'Reilly had no alternative but to occupy the general office across the hallway from the inspector.

O'Reilly had barely taken off his hat when Inspector Kerr called him into his office.

"You broke barracks last night, Sergeant!"

"*Broke barracks!*" O'Reilly was incredulous.

The inspector looked at him from a pale, stonelike face. Only the mouth moved. "You must be aware that *Regulations and Orders* stipulate quite plainly that all single men are required to be in barracks no later than half an hour before *lights out* unless they're in possession of a pass. I have not signed any passes since I've been here, so quite obviously you didn't have one."

"But, sir . . . we don't follow post routine like they do at the depot or divisional headquarters. No detachment on outpost duty does. It's not practical, not practical at all."

Inspector Kerr was unimpressed. "The book of *Regulations and Orders*, which you referred me to yesterday, does not specifically exclude detachment posts from that routine."

O'Reilly thought it did, but he didn't know where to immediately find it, and he realized it would be pointless to argue with the inspector unless he was sure of his grounds.

"The laid-down post routine will be followed here," Inspector Kerr continued. "I shall issue a local order to that effect. In the meantime, Sergeant, I would like an explanation as to where you were last night."

"Exercising my horse," O'Reilly almost snapped back.

From his desk the inspector stared up at O'Reilly for a moment. O'Reilly stared unblinkingly back. Finally the officer shifted his eyes. "Very well. In deference to your rank I will accept that explanation,

114

but I trust from now on you will ensure my wishes in this regard are observed by *all* members of the post, including NCOs. Is that understood?"

"These men are policemen, sir—not toy soldiers. You'd get better results—"

"Do you *have* to argue about everything, Sergeant?" Inspector Kerr interrupted sharply.

O'Reilly squared his shoulders. "No, sir."

"Very well. Now, I have other matters to discuss. First of all, I want Constable Baxter as my orderly." The inspector sneered. "I presume there's nothing against *that* in *Regulations and Orders.*"

O'Reilly guessed the inspector had already looked it up in the blue-covered Mounted Police bible. "I don't believe so, sir."

"Good. Adjust your duties roster accordingly. Now . . . I have been going over these patrol routes you gave me." He moved some paper sheets on his desk and ran a finger down one of them. "I have consulted a map and I do not find myself in agreement with your mileage estimates." Then he looked up at O'Reilly. "I think you grossly exaggerated them in order to try to win the point you were attempting to make yesterday. I suggest you redo them."

O'Reilly felt his temper rising, but he took a deep breath. "Between the two of us, Corporal Rogers and I have ridden over each one of those patrol routes. We gave careful consideration to the mileage figures and I would say they're no more than ten percent out, which is about as accurate you'll get without odometers."

"Not according to the maps."

"I don't know what maps you've been looking at, sir, but only part of these eastern ranges have been surveyed, and our patrols cover a lot of territory that hasn't been surveyed at all. And even if they had, you can't measure distances in mountain country by looking at maps."

At that moment the two men were distracted by the sound of bootsteps on the veranda outside. Tom Barr appeared in the hallway. Seeing O'Reilly in the inspector's doorway, the Hudson's Bay man beckoned.

"Could I have a word with you, Hughie . . . outside?"

O'Reilly nodded. "If you will excuse me, sir." He followed the white-haired trader outside the building.

"Mad Old Mike's been at it again," Tom Barr said, fixing his watery blue eyes on the Mountie sergeant. "Jake Raff just came in from across the Palliser. There's a government survey team that's been workin' its way up from Rocky Mountain House, and when they got near the foot of Mount Queen Victoria, Mad Old Mike opened up on 'em. Didn't hit anyone but he sure as hell scared the daylights out of 'em. It'll take 'em a couple of hours to reach the settlement, but when they do they'll be comin' right up here to the barracks to report what happened. I figured I better warn you, especially seein' as how you've got that inspector on your back about it. You know, Hughie . . . I warned you about this."

"I know, Tom . . . and thanks for the information."

Leaving the trader to walk back down the slope toward the Hudson's Bay store, O'Reilly returned to the police building. Inspector Kerr stood waiting in his office doorway.

"What was that about, Sergeant?"

"The recluse who people around here call Mad Old

116

Mike shot at a government survey party on the other side of Mount Queen Victoria. I'll ride over there and bring him in."

"No, you won't. Your responsibility is to remain at the post and administer the detachment, not chase gunmen around the mountains. You have a corporal and six men to do that."

O'Reilly felt his temper rising again. "They won't be able to bring him in. I can."

Inspector Kerr sneered. "Come now, Sergeant. I know you won the Distinguished Conduct Medal in South Africa and cleaned up the Yukon practically single-handed, but I'm sure there are other men in the Mounted Police capable of bringing in some decrepit old lunatic who fancies himself as some sort of Canadian Buffalo Bill."

O'Reilly had the strongest urge to smash his fist into the inspector's sneering face. "That man is no decrepit old lunatic," he replied hotly. "He's a crack marksman who would have given Buffalo Bill a run for his money."

"You seem to know a lot about him, Sergeant," the officer smirked. "If you're so sure you could bring him in, why haven't you already done so?"

"Because he's never harmed anyone."

"I realize I haven't been a policeman very long, Sergeant, but I am aware that under Canadian law, and I would think under the laws in most civilized countries, it's an offense to go around shooting at people except in self-defense."

There was nothing else that O'Reilly could say, so he fell silent.

"Under the circumstances, you may send two men."

O'Reilly walked over to the barracks and told off Dusty Rogers and George Bailey.

"I'm sending you two because you're the most experienced on the post. But be bloody careful."

He stood watching them ride off into the distance, until their scarlet tunics were nothing more than two bright-red dabs merging into the deep green of the pines. He should have ordered them to wear brown duck instead of the eye-catching scarlet, he told himself, but then just as quickly he realized it wouldn't make much difference what they wore. Old Mike's eyes were eagle-sharp . . . he'd spot them no matter what they wore. They could be invisible and he'd still spot them.

Apprehension gnawing savagely at his guts, O'Reilly turned and walked back to the detachment building.

Chapter 10

Inspector Kerr was furious!

"By what right did you take it upon yourself to send the corporal to bring in that lunatic?"

"You authorized me to send two men," O'Reilly replied. "So I sent Corporal Rogers and Constable Bailey."

Inspector Kerr slammed his crop hard on top of his desk. "In His Majesty's Forces, which includes the North-West Mounted Police, we have officers, NCOs, and men. I said two *men* and that was what I meant—two constables, *not* an NCO and a constable. It was my intention to send Corporal Rogers with a four-man detail to the Snake Valley to escort Thunder Hawk's Indians back to the prairies."

"So that's what Lasher was doing over here yesterday! I might have known!"

The inspector's tone was instantly defensive. "What Mr. Lasher was doing here yesterday is none of your business. If you had been doing your job all along, his visit wouldn't have been necessary."

"Lasher is a troublemaker," O'Reilly said, striving to contain his growing anger. "Anyway, you won't need Corporal Rogers."

"Why not?"

"Because we have no reason to interfere with Thunder Hawk's Indians. They're no trouble."

"That's not what Mr. Lasher says."

"Lasher's a damned liar! The only time there's trouble with Thunder Hawk's band is if Lasher or his miners start it."

Inspector Kerr's face purpled with rage. "I'm not asking for your opinion, Sergeant! Your job is to obey orders, and I'm going to give you one right now. Tomorrow morning you will lead a detail of four constables to the Snake Valley and escort those Indians out of the mountains and onto the prairies."

"We can't do that," O'Reilly protested. "They're not treaty."

"Confound it all, Sergeant! I'm tiring of arguing with you. I have given you an order. If you care to dispute it, think how an orderly-room charge will look on your record when it reaches the commissioner's desk."

Disregarding military protocol, O'Reilly leaned forward over the desk that had been his until three days ago and locked blazing dark eyes onto the inspector. "And you think about this, sir: if you initiate any action to move a band of Indians that are the responsibility of the Department of Indian Affairs—if they're anyone's responsibility at all—you'll stir an interdepartment tempest between Ottawa and Regina that will land you in twice as much hot water as any

120

orderly-room charge you can throw at me. The old days of the Mounted Police moving Indians around are long gone, and even then they only did so when absolutely necessary or upon Ottawa's instructions, but never on the unsubstantiated complaint of a civilian. The Mounted Police enjoy a good reputation out here in the Territories, not only with the inhabitants but with other departments of government as well, and in case you haven't been in the outfit long enough to know, Colonel Perry is very jealous of that reputation. He takes a decidedly dim view of anything done by any member that tarnishes it, especially by an officer, because officers are supposed to know better."

A frown creasing his forehead, Inspector Kerr pushed his chair back from the desk, back from O'Reilly's flashing dark eyes, and sat silently. He didn't know whether O'Reilly was telling him the truth, but he could hardly afford to take the chance. He wanted very much to accommodate the honorable Wilbur Roget, for he wanted the promotion that Refflon Lasher has assured him would follow, but he was more afraid of incurring the displeasure of the proud, aloof Mounted Police commissioner.

Damn this man O'Reilly!

O'Reilly worried about Dusty Rogers and George Bailey for the first three days, but when they weren't back by the fourth, he grew really concerned. It would have taken them a day to get around to the south side of Mount Queen Victoria and another day to get back. Then a day to apprehend Mad Old Mike—*if they could*! And that was the nub of O'Reilly's concern.

He voiced his concern to Inspector Kerr, requesting permission to ride out and see what was happening, but predictably the officer refused.

Then on the fifth day a riderless police horse trotted into the post. Corporal Rogers's horse. O'Reilly hurried to the inspector's office, but the inspector was not there.

"Where the hell is he, Baxter?" O'Reilly demanded.

Baxter shrugged. "I don't know, Sergeant. He might be down at the Northern Lights visiting Mrs. Merrill."

That was all O'Reilly needed. Damn Kerr! He should be on the post. Damn her, too. Obviously an officer was a better catch than a sergeant. Besides being eligible, Kerr was relatively young—a year or two older than O'Reilly—and not bad looking if one liked the trim, dapper type. Probably had a private income as well.

Hurrying over to the barracks, O'Reilly loaded his rifle, strapped his bedroll, and collected his saddle wallets. Stopping at the stores building long enough to grab rations, he then doubled over to the stables.

Two minutes later he rode out of the post and headed down to the bank of the Palliser, swung west, and moved up along the valley. After several miles he reached a point where the river narrowed, cascading in a rush of foam and spray over boulder-size rocks from the melting icefields higher up. There the first detachment of Mounted Police in that part of the country had built a bridge over the river, and O'Reilly's dark bay thundered across.

He rode as far as he could before nightfall forced him to camp. Before first light the next day he was back on the trail, and by midmorning he reached Surprise Lake. He had barely reined to when he heard a rifle shot rolling across the turquoise, mirror-top water. A Winchester! Whose? Mad Old Mike's, or the police? Well, at least someone was still alive.

Taking a pair of field glasses from his saddle wallet, O'Reilly swung down from his horse, took off his hat and tunic, and climbed up into a pine tree. From as close to the top as he could get without his weight tilting the pine, he swept the timber over toward the mass of rust-colored Cambrian and Precambrian quartzite that a patriotic and Imperial-minded government had named Mount Queen Victoria. He saw nothing on the first sweep, then he made a second, slower sweep, but still saw nothing.

He was about to climb down when a second shot rang out from beyond the trees. He had been looking down when he heard it, and he snapped his head up, his eyes probing the green forest toward the mountain. Still he couldn't see anything, but he thought he knew where the shot had come from.

Quickly O'Reilly slid down the tree, dropped the last ten feet to the ground, and pulled on his tunic and hat. Slipping the field glasses back into a saddle wallet, he pulled himself back up onto his horse and rode off.

He found the trail Corporal Rogers and Constable Bailey had used. It was nothing more than a natural break through the forest of pines, but bending low over his saddle he could pick up here and there a hoofprint in the soft, needle-covered ground. Urging his horse into a canter he rode on. It took him an hour to get through the pines, and when he broke through on the far side the country opened into a rich, lush, green meadow dominated by a long, low ridge running west to east as far as the eye could see, although O'Reilly knew it gave out on the western side of the mountain.

When he topped the ridge he looked down on a panorama of alpine grandeur—a sloping grassy plain, a long line of spruce and poplar, a jade-colored jewel of a lake over beyond the trees, then pine forests sweeping thickly up the side of the mountain. Up on top of the mountain he could see fresh snow that must have fallen during the night. Although the days were warm, the evenings were cool, and in his bedroll last night O'Reilly had felt the creeping hand of approaching winter. Winter was still a long way off, but some of the leaves on the poplar and birch were beginning to show the gold of autumn. It was already August and fall was only a month away.

O'Reilly reined his horse down the slope. He was halfway to the plain when he spotted two small squares of scarlet lying under a grass-topped overhang. When he reached it he found two scarlet tunics, neatly folded together with two bedrolls. Below the overhang was a gravel-filled hollow in which were the remains of a short camp. Dusty and George had taken off their tunics here and ridden on in their shirt-sleeves to make themselves less conspicuous.

Anxiety gnawing at his innards, O'Reilly urged his horse on. He passed from the plain into the line of spruce and poplar. By the time he got through to the other side the northern sun was directly overhead. And then he saw movement. Whipping his field glasses up to his eyes he could see the yellow stripe on a pair of dark blue breeches. Sharpening the focus he could see a khaki-issue police shirt and above it the black-whiskered face of Dusty Rogers. O'Reilly breathed a sigh of relief, for the arm moved. The next instant there was a rifle shot and he saw sparks fly off a rock behind which Dusty was lying. Quickly Dusty moved further down behind the rock, and O'Reilly knew he wasn't lying there wounded. Then he saw Dusty roll over and peer around the far side of the rock, a side that couldn't be seen from over toward the mountain, the direction from where the rifle shot had come. Swinging the glasses in that direction, O'Reilly saw George Bailey hunkered down behind a fallen tree, rifle across his knees, eyes on both Dusty's position and over toward the mountain. In a dip behind George, was hobbled his horse.

O'Reilly could see what had happened. Dusty and George had split up and tried to outflank Mad Old Mike, but the wily old man had guessed their intentions and pinned Dusty down. George was all right . . . he could move out, but if he tried to get closer to Mike's position, Mike would quickly pin him down as well.

Next, O'Reilly swung his glasses over toward the mountain and studied the lower face for two minutes without seeing anything other than rock and trees.

Then he saw a puff of smoke from a pine-covered ledge and the next instant he heard the whip-crack of a bullet passing over his head, a second or two later followed by the roll of the Winchester. Little wonder Old Mike had spotted him in his bright red tunic.

It didn't take O'Reilly more than a few seconds to realize what he had to do. Replacing his field glasses in the saddle wallet again, he legged the dark bay into a trot and rode straight toward the mountain, his naked eye trying to pick out the pine-covered ledge he had seen so clearly through the field glasses.

He rode on past Dusty's rock, skirting it by a good twenty yards.

"Hugh!" he heard Dusty exclaim. "What the hell . . . ?"

"You and George stay low, Dusty," O'Reilly called back. "Don't fire under any circumstances. I'll handle this."

"*Hugh!* That crazy old bastard'll kill you!"

"Just do as I say, Dusty," O'Reilly called back, and he legged his horse into a canter.

Then there was another shot from the mountain and another bullet snapped over O'Reilly's head. This one came closer than the first. O'Reilly's stomach muscles tightened and he shivered for a second or two as a cold chill momentarily took hold of his body when he realized the next one would be closer yet. He hoped Old Mike's hands were still as steady as they used to be.

The next one did come closer, closer enough to nick O'Reilly's hat brim. But this time O'Reilly's naked eye spotted the ledge, and he veered the dark bay slightly to the left, making directly for it.

Watching intently from behind his tree trunk, George Bailey muttered. "He's trying the same damn thing Sergeant Colebrook pulled at Kinistino back in '95. Only thing, Colebrook got himself killed doing it!"

A hundred yards of open grass stood between O'Reilly and the edge of the pines that swept up the side of the mountain, and he could see the ledge plainly now, eighty or ninety feet up.

Suddenly the hidden Winchester exploded again, and this time the bullet took O'Reilly's hat with it, sending it spinning through the air. Bareheaded, O'Reilly reined to and stood in the stirrups, waving up at the ledge.

"Mike! Sergeant Mike Hannan!" he shouted. "It's O'Reilly . . . remember? O'Reilly, of the Flying Patrol . . . down at Standoff."

Silence was the only answer. O'Reilly sat back down in his saddle and legged his horse forward. Then the Winchester barked again, and a spurt of dirt flew up from the ground a foot in front of the dark bay. The horse whinnied and started to prance.

O'Reilly shouted again. "Don't shoot, Mike! I've come to talk to you."

Shortening his reins, O'Reilly legged the horse forward again. The animal balked, so he jabbed it lightly with his spurs. They'd gotten another fifteen yards closer when the side of the mountain erupted as three rifle shots fired in quick succession kicked up three spurts of dirt in front of the horse. Nostrils flaring, the dark bay reared up on its hind legs, its

127

forelegs raking at the air in front of it. Savagely, O'Reilly fought it down under control.

This time O'Reilly's flashing dark eyes glared up at the ledge. "God damn it, Sergeant! Quit that firing. You're scaring hell out of my horse!"

A long, raspy laugh sounded from up on the ledge, then a figure in buckskin and moccasins slowly stepped out from the pines. He held a Winchester into his shoulder, the barrel pointing down at the redcoat.

They stared at each other for a moment, neither speaking. Then the man in buckskin jerked his rifle barrel upward, signaling O'Reilly to come closer. O'Reilly flicked his reins and the dark bay pranced nervously toward the pines. When horse and rider were no more than twenty yards away, the rifleman held up his palm and O'Reilly pulled on his reins. Winchester again pointed at the Mountie, the old man in buckskin clambered down from the ledge.

From his saddle, O'Reilly studied the old man. A flowing mass of red hair topped a sun-and-wind-reddened face, the forehead dappled with a network of freckles, and a shaggy red beard liberally flecked with white covered a heavy square jaw.

Yes . . . it was the same Mike Hannan. Looking much older now, but the long hair and shaggy beard failing to mask that hard-bitten face that O'Reilly remembered from those days down on the southern prairies ten years ago.

The old man scrambled down the last dozen feet, almost losing his balance and sliding the rest of the way on his rump. A muttered string of curses and oaths rattled from his throat, and O'Reilly grinned with the recollection of good memories of a decade ago.

The old man scowled at O'Reilly's grin. "You ain't lost any of that cheekiness, you black young Haligonian, even if that moustache has growed bigger. And you ain't growed any smarter. You could've got yourself killed riding into rifle fire like that."

The voice was as O'Reilly remembered Mike's voice, although it had lost much of its cadence, substantiating the belief that he had been living alone for a long time.

"I knew you wouldn't shoot a man wearing scarlet, Sarge," O'Reilly replied.

For more than a minute the old man didn't answer. He just stood there, Winchester in the crook of his arm, looking at O'Reilly through bright blue eyes, although the eyes had lost a lot of their brightness over the years. Finally the old man spoke again. "How'd you know it was me?"

"The shooting. You weren't trying to kill anyone, just scaring them off. No one else in the Territories could come that close without hitting someone. You were the best shot in the old outfit, Sarge . . . in all the Dominion for that matter."

The old man grunted, but the beard didn't hide the pleased expression the compliment brought to his face. Mike had never been susceptible to flattery, but genuine praise had always pleased him.

"I used to try and pound it through your thick young skull," the old man said, the words coming slowly as though they were being dragged back from the depths of time, "that to a policeman things ain't

129

always the way they seemed. I couldn't have done too good a job."

O'Reilly grinned down at him from his saddle. "There were a couple of other things. Remember one day when we were out looking for whiskey peddlers down near the Montana border? We could see Chief Mountain clear as a bell. It was topped with snow and looked beautiful up against the blue sky. You said that when you retired you were going to look for a mountain like that and live all alone on it. You used to say the Northwest was getting too civilized, what with all the cattle ranches springing up all over the place, and the railroad. I remembered that over at Fort Determination when reports started coming in about this rifleman around Mount Queen Victoria who used to shoot to scare away intruders. A couple of Indians camped with you once and you told them your name was Mike. Some people started calling you Mad Old Mike because they thought living alone had made you a bit strange. I talked to those Indians and they described you, especially your red hair. Right away I thought about you, remembering what you used to say about a mountain."

"I ain't the only red-headed Mike in the Territories."

"There was something else, something that cinched it," said O'Reilly, suddenly reaching into his breeches pocket, just in front of his revolver holster.

Quick as a flash, Old Mike dropped to his knee and snapped the Winchester up to his shoulder, the barrel pointed at O'Reilly's heart.

"Hold it, Mike!" O'Reilly shouted, pulling his

hand quickly away. But the horse, startled by the sudden movement of the old man in buckskin, shied away.

The next instant two shots exploded into the air, almost deafening O'Reilly. His horse reared, and O'Reilly fell from the saddle, remembering nothing else.

Chapter 11

O'Reilly woke to a sickening headache. There was blackness all around, except for a bright light off to his left . . . a heat-giving light.

Then he heard the crackling of a campfire . . . and voices. Slowly . . . painfully . . . he lifted his head.

"Steady there, Hugh," said a familiar voice, and there was movement over by the fire. Then a pair of yellow-striped blue breeches sat down beside him.

Supporting himself on an elbow, O'Reilly raised a hand to his head, feeling for a tender spot at the back. "What . . . what the hell happened?"

"Well, for one thing, your horse threw you and you hit your head on a rock," George Bailey answered.

"How are you, young O'Reilly?" another familiar voice sounded from beyond the fire, and there was movement of buckskin.

George Bailey jumped up and shouted. "You stay right where you are, you crazy old son of a bitch! If it hadn't been for you, he'd be just fine!"

O'Reilly struggled to a sitting position. "I remember now . . . I heard a shot . . ."

"You heard two shots, Hugh," Dusty Rogers's voice drawled quietly. "The old man was about to shoot you when George shot the rifle out of his hands. It's a good thing we decided to disobey your orders. You'd be lying dead on that ground right now, otherwise."

O'Reilly looked half-accusingly across the fire, where he could just make out old Mike's buckskin-clad figure in the shadows.

The old man sat broodingly, looking thoroughly miserable. "I didn't want to shoot you, O'Reilly . . . honest I didn't. I don't know what the hell happened . . . you was goin' for your gun . . . I guess I just reacted snap-like."

"Like hell!" George Bailey retorted hotly. "The sergeant wouldn't have gone for a gun, you mad old bastard! He gave us orders not to shoot."

O'Reilly shook his head, his head aching with the pain of the movement. "No . . . no, he's right, George. He must've thought I was reaching for my revolver. I was reaching into my breeches pocket." O'Reilly thrust his hand into his pocket and withdrew a small round shiny object. "This is what I was reaching for. Pass it to him, George."

George took the shiny yellow object and held it toward the light from the campfire to get a better look at it. "It's a brass button . . . a Mounted Police button . . . one of the old ones." George handed the button to the old man.

"That's right, George. I found it over by Surprise Lake when I was returning off that last long patrol. I never mentioned it when I got back, but someone opened up on me. I didn't realize it was Mike, because those Indians reported he was killed in an avalanche. But when I got around to the north side of the lake I found where he'd been firing from. He was long gone, but the button was there, all bright and polished. If it had been there long, even just a few days, it would have been dull and tarnished. That's when I knew Mike was still alive. I guess I should've realized it from the shooting."

"So that was you that day," Mike said.

"Yes, but why did you fire at me? You knew what shooting at a redcoat would mean. You must have realized one of us would come in after you, sooner or later."

"I figgered you were comin' after me then. I'd scared off some prospector a half moon before that."

"That would have been Jake Raff."

"Whoever he was, he was prospectin.' I could tell by his outfit. He was all set to come right in close, so I decided to warn him off before he got past that lake. It had been right peaceful up here until then. When I saw you comin' a half moon later, I thought you were comin' in to get me, so I reckoned I'd give you a couple of warnin' shots. All I wanted was to be left alone."

A puzzled expression took hold of George Bailey's face. "I don't get that brass button."

134

"That was one of the first buttons issued in the old outfit, wasn't it, Mike?" O'Reilly said.

Old Mike leaned forward on his haunches, looking into the fire as his memory trailed back to years long gone. "Just about. The first Mounted Police into the great North-West, as it was called back in those days, wore buttons that came from the Toronto Military School. When Colonel Macleod was lookin' for a badge for the outfit, he picked a buffalo head. So when they made the new badge back in Canada—that's what we used to call the East back then—they made buttons with the buffalo head on 'em and shipped 'em out. This button—" Mike held the button against the light of the fire—"was among the first issued to old B Troop at Fort Walsh. It was Inspector Cavannagh who gave it to me. It came off his tunic."

Mike started to cackle. "He came down to Standoff one day to inspect. That was before you were there, young O'Reilly. We'd been pretty busy all that summer, what with chasing Indian horse thieves and whiskey peddlers, and we'd hardly had time to even put on our scarlet tunics let along polish the brass buttons. So when he pulled this surprise inspection, he didn't like the color of my brass. I guess the old outfit hasn't changed much in that respect . . . you had to have your brass polished at all times, regardless of whether you wearin' it or not. So I gave him some damn fool story about my brass just plumb refusin' to stay polished even though I'd polished it just the day before, which of course I hadn't. Well, that was sure the wrong thing to say to Mr. Cavannaugh.

"He didn't say too much, as it happened. But the next time he came down he handed me a full set of buttons. He told me they came off one of his scarlet tunics when he was an NCO. He told me he'd always managed to keep 'em polished, even in the hectic days when Sitting Bull's Sioux were camped around the Cypress Hills. He told me to sew 'em on my tunic and said I'd have no trouble polishin' 'em and keeping 'em polished. Then before he left he warned me that the next time he came down to inspect, they'd better be damned good and shiny. And, believe me, they was. Out of respect for him, if for no other reason. When I left the old outfit years later, I didn't have the heart to turn that brass in, so I cut 'em off and kept 'em. And I've polished 'em every day since, even up here. I got the others in my gear. I knew I'd lost this one, but I didn't know where."

Standing up in front of the fire, George Bailey scratched the back of his head as he looked from O'Reilly to old Mike and back again. "I'm damned confused! You mean this old man used to be in the outfit . . . the *old* outfit?"

O'Reilly looked up and nodded. "That's right, George. Sergeant Mike Hannan, used to be in charge of the Flying Patrol out of Standoff. It was my first posting after I got out of the depot at Regina, apart from a brief spell at Fort MacLeod."

"Well . . . I'll be damned!" George paused, confusion still on his face. "But I still don't get it. What the hell's he been doing holed up on a mountain shooting

136

at everyone?"

Looking across the fire at Mike, O'Reilly said, "You better tell him, Mike. I'm not sure I know the answer to that . . . not all of it."

The old man stared into the fire again. "Well . . . I just got tired of seein' people, I guess. It was back in '77 when I joined the outfit and was sent to Fort Walsh, which was headquarters in them days. I only stayed at Walsh a little while, then got transferred to Fort Macleod, and from there to places like Fort Calgary, Blackfoot Crossing, Pincher Creek, the Blood Indian Reserve, and Standoff. There wasn't much in the way of people in them parts, just the Indians and us . . . and the Montana whiskey peddlers we used to chase. It was a good life and I liked it like that. Plenty of action and things never got dull. But after a while cattle ranches started dottin' the southwestern prairies, then the railroad come through, and after it the settlers. Pretty soon there weren't so much room to move around in. Down at Standoff you could see the mountains, all pretty and glitterin' with snow, off in the distance to the west, and I thought to myself it would be nice to be up on one of 'em, out of everyone's way. So, one day when I got busted to the ranks and kicked out for hittin' some jackass officer, I figgered I'd had enough of people, and I got together a saddle horse and a pack horse and struck out for the mountains. Followed the foothills to Rocky Mountain House, worked for the Hudson's Bay Company there a spell to learn somethin' 'bout trappin', then hit out along the valleys northwest until I saw this mountain here behind us, liked it, and decided to stay. That's about all there is to it."

George was losing his initial hostility to the older man. In fact, hearing that Mike had been broken to the ranks made him a man after George's heart. "But why were you shooting at anyone who came near here?"

Mike shrugged buckskin-clad shoulders. "I dunno . . . I jus' wanted to be left alone. Especially when some engineers started pokin' 'round a few summers back. I could see someone strikin' gold or something like that and then half the damned world would've turned up. I didn't want that, so I drove 'em off with a few shots. It worked so well they never come back, so I reckoned I'd try it again. And that's how it happened. Except for some other engineers that came over a couple of moons back. I sneaked up on 'em at night and took their horses and gear. But I guess you heard all about that."

"Engineers . . . no," O'Reilly replied. "A government survey party a week ago . . . yes. They came in to the post to complain, and that's why we're here now. But no engineers reported anything to us. I didn't know there were any engineers interested in this part of the mountains."

Mike frowned. "Well, they was interested enough to get together a new outfit, 'cause they come back. They were lookin' for silver, which would've meant the same to the mountain as if they'd been lookin' for gold and found it. Anyway, the next time I put bullet holes

138

in their hats." He laughed. "They sure didn't come back after that."

"Silver?" O'Reilly's eyebrows drew together in a tight frown. As a Mounted Policeman he was required to know what was going on in his detachment area, and he was beginning to feel a sense of annoyance with himself. "How do you know they were looking for silver, Mike?"

"I heard 'em talkin' about it. I sneaked up on 'em when they was camped. That's when I run off their outfit." He laughed again. "Run their horses off right under the noses of their Indian handlers. Just like the good old days down at Standoff."

Dusty Rogers spoke up. "Those strangers we saw in the Northern Lights earlier in the summer, Hugh . . . they must've been the ones."

"They were coal-mining men, Dusty," O'Reilly replied. "I saw them with Lasher."

The slim American shrugged. "They were the only strangers we've seen around, sure the only ones who'd fill the bill."

"Hmmm . . ." O'Reilly murmured, not convinced.

"Say," George said to Mike, "if they found silver here, you could've become rich."

"I ain't interested in becomin' rich. If I'd wanted that I could've gone to the Yukon when they found gold there. All I wanted was to be left alone." Mike shifted his glance across the fire to O'Reilly. "You couldn't just say you wasn't able to find me, could you, young O'Reilly?"

Slowly O'Reilly shook his head. "Sorry, Mike. I'd

like to, but I can't . . . not any more."

"What'll happen to me, then?"

George pointed his finger to his head and made fast circular movements. "You aren't . . . you're not . . . you know what I mean?"

Mike looked back at George. "Cuckoo? I don't reckon so. Some people might say I am, but I ain't . . . no more than anyone else." He looked back at O'Reilly. "What if I escape?"

O'Reilly met his gaze. "I want your word on that, Mike."

"You mean . . . if I give my word, you won't be handcuffin' me, or puttin' on no leg irons?"

"Your word was always good."

The old man nodded. "You got it."

The next morning, when they were preparing to return to Fort Determination, O'Reilly had a quick word with George Bailey out of old Mike's hearing.

"Thanks for what you did yesterday, George. That was fine shooting. I didn't know you were that good."

Cinching his horse's saddle girth, George snorted. "Good—*hell*! That was a fluke shot. I saw him about to shoot you. The rest was chance reaction."

Standing beside his horse's nearside, O'Reilly held his Winchester and reins in his left hand, reached over to the rear of his California with his right, and thrust a spurred boot into his stirrup. Hopping on his remaining foot as the big dark bay moved around a little, O'Reilly glanced across the animal's back at

George. "That's the same sort of reaction that wins medals in war. You're a good man to have on detachment, George." Then he swung up into the saddle, lifted his Winchester, and slid it barrel-down into the bucket. Gathering his reins he looked around at Mike and Dusty. "All right . . . let's move out."

Chapter 12

At least Inspector Kerr waited until he and O'Reilly were alone before tearing a strip off him. Corporal Rogers and Constable Bailey had gone over to the barracks, old Mike was locked up in the guardroom, and Constable Baxter had left to tell off a constable for provost duty.

"I gave you a distinct order not to go after that lunatic. As you saw fit to willfully disobey that order, I find I have no alternative but to place you under arrest pending the disposition of charges I intend bringing against you."

O'Reilly stood speechless, staring at the blue-uniformed officer sitting primly behind the desk—until the big Nova Scotian's anger shot up to boiling point. "Is that open or close?" he snapped back.

"Open," the inspector replied. "You will continue to perform all your regular duties, but you will not leave the confines of the post under any circumstances unless I specifically instruct so in writing."

"Does that include meals?" O'Reilly's tone was bordering insubordination.

"Yes," Inspector Kerr replied icily. "Is there any reason why it shouldn't?"

"It's the practice here for all members of the detachment to eat down at Mrs. Merrill's dining room."

A smirk crept across the officer's face. "You yourself broke that practice, Sergeant. Since my arrival at this post, you have been preparing your own meals in the barracks mess. I fail to see any reason why you should not continue to do so."

O'Reilly's eyes flashed with barely suppressed fury. *"You son of a bitch!"*

The smirk instantly left the inspector's face. "That will be enough, Sergeant! One more word and I'll have you placed under *close* arrest and your duties turned over to Corporal Rogers. As it is, that remark you just made will see another charge of insubordination brought against you."

It was all O'Reilly could do to restrain himself from leaping across the desk and driving his fist into the officer's face. But he knew that would finish eleven years of generally exemplary service. That's what had happened to old Mike Hannan . . . he'd struck an officer and had been reduced to constable and discharged from the Force after eighteen years' service—just two years short of a twenty-year pension.

The two men glared across the desk at one another, eyes locked, each trying to stare the other down. Finally the inspector dropped his eyes, picked up his cap, gloves, and crop from the desk, and stood up. Jamming his cap on his head, he stalked across the office to the doorway. He was just about to step out into the hallway when he suddenly turned.

"You will parade the detachment in full review order tomorrow morning at ten. There will be an inspection, followed by mounted and dismounted drill. That routine will be repeated for the next ten days. There is a definite need for a tightening of discipline at this post."

O'Reilly listened to the officer's boots and the light tinkle of spurs as he walked along the hallway to the veranda. A moment later O'Reilly saw the blue uniform pass the window and head down toward the settlement. Probably going to the hotel, the sergeant guessed.

"You son of a bitch!" O'Reilly muttered.

"O'Reilly." The voice came from the guardroom.

When O'Reilly reached the guardroom at the other end of the hallway, old Mike Hannan's face was pressed against the bars. "If he'd put you under close arrest," the older man said, "you'd be in here with me."

"You heard all that?"

"Sure as hell did. My hearin's real good. That officer sounds like one mean son of a bitch. Don't seem to me like he knows what he's doin', either. You'd have more to do with your time at a place like this than paradin' and drillin' every day. I don't appreciate him callin' me a lunatic, either. The first time he sticks his head in this guardroom, I'm goin' to tell him so."

Looking at Mike through the bars, with the guardroom window throwing light on the red-bearded face, white hairs lacing the red, O'Reilly had the opportunity to see the face close up for the first time in ten years, and he realized that *old* Mike wasn't so old after all—he couldn't have been more than fifty-five, yet O'Reilly was shocked how much he had aged, how much his dismissal from the Mounted Police and the subsequent hardships and mental strain of living alone had taken out of him. O'Reilly's old sergeant had always been a rough diamond, frequently contemptuous of discipline, but he had been a good NCO who had always worked hard and loyally for the Force, and had never failed to treat the men under him fairly, even though he had often ridden the hell out of them. He'd been a hard taskmaster, but O'Reilly had never forgotten that it had been Sergeant Mike Hannan who had made him into one of the famous Scarlet Riders. The training depot at Regina had cast him into the mold, but it had been Sergeant Mike Hannan who had knocked off the rough edges.

At that moment, O'Reilly felt terribly sorry for Mike Hannan, and resolved to talk to Tom Barr, the local justice of the peace, about giving him a light sentence.

"No, Mike," O'Reilly said, shaking his head. "Don't tell him anything like that."

The next morning Inspector Kerr conducted his review-order inspection of Fort Determination Detachment, following it with an hour of mounted drill under Sergeant O'Reilly and an hour of foot and arms drill, which he gave himself. O'Reilly reluctantly acknowledged that the inspector knew foot drill and had a drill instructor's eye for spotting mistakes and a sergeant major's tongue for correcting them.

The same procedure followed the next day, and the next, and the day after, until the men were thoroughly fed up with inspections, parades, and drills well before the tenth day.

"What the hell is this, anyhow?" they grumbled among themselves in their barracks. "If I'd wanted to spend all my time doing drill, I'd have joined the fucking militia!"

"The trouble is that brass-studded martinet thinks he's still in the ruddy army."

"Yeah . . . we're supposed to be Mounted Policemen, not bloody toy soldiers."

In their room next to the constables' barrack room, Hugh O'Reilly and Dusty Rogers couldn't help hearing these comments as they pulled off their long, sweat-stained Strathconas and breeches and replaced them with brown duck fatigues and stable boots. Never one to complain, even Dusty couldn't help but feel that as Mounted Policemen they were being put to the wrong use.

"Drills and dress parades are all very well at Regina and the divisional posts, Hugh, but up here I reckon once a month, like you were doing all along, should be enough."

"I know, Dusty. I'll have a word with him tomorrow."

Tapping the top of the desk with his riding crop, Inspector Kerr leaned back in the chair and gazed disinterestedly out the window as O'Reilly stood explaining his concern that the succession of daily drills and inspections were cutting into the detachment's regular police duties.

"It's already mid-August, sir, and we have three or four lengthy patrols that should be made before the weather starts turning cool. There's the regular north patrol to link up with a patrol that comes toward the mountains from Peace River Crossing, and another that we send south along the valleys to link up with Banff Detachment's north patrol. Then there's the summer patrol we make southeast to Rocky Mountain House to make contact with a west patrol from Red Deer Detachment. And there are two more we normally do in late summer, one west to the Continental Divide, the other east to the McLeod and Saskatchewan rivers. We can usually expect a snowfall by mid-September, so we should be getting these patrols out with no more delay. In fact, the north and south patrols should have left several days ago."

He had barely finished when the smirk crept across the officer's face, and O'Reilly knew he had wasted his time. The inspector swung the chair around to directly face the big sergeant.

"You never give up trying to thwart me. Even with three orderly-room charges hanging over your head, you persist in defying me and trying to force your will onto me."

Suddenly the inspector's chair cracked forward and

the officer jumped to his feet, slamming his riding crop down so hard on the desktop that the inkwell bounced. "Well, you're not going to get away with it, Sergeant!" he shouted. "You and this detachment will do exactly as I say! Do you understand?"

O'Reilly stood glaring back at him for several seconds before he suddenly swung around and stormed out of the office, leaving the inspector standing behind the desk, his mouth starting to work furiously but nothing coming from it. O'Reilly was out of the log building when the inspector managed to master his voice. "I didn't dismiss you, Sergeant!" he shouted after O'Reilly's retreating back.

"Go to hell!" O'Reilly shouted back and kept on walking.

In the guardroom, Mike Hannan stood listening at his cell door. All he could do was shake his head and mutter, "That's sure some son of a bitch you've got for an officer, O'Reilly lad."

Refflon Lasher had been doing a lot of thinking since the day Inspector Kerr told him that he would not be able to order the removal of Thunder Hawk's Indians from the Valley of the Snake. It had become patently clear to him that he would have to do something to force the inspector's hand. Time was running short . . . he wanted to be mining silver by next year. He wished he had taken a more direct hand months ago, and he would have if he hadn't somehow been afraid of O'Reilly. But now O'Reilly was effectively out of the way, and Lasher felt free to act. If what he planned worked as he wanted to—and it had damned well better work—Inspector Kerr would soon order those Indians moved after all.

"You wanted to see me, Mr. Lasher?" Vince Strathman's voice called from Lasher's office door.

"Yes, Vince. Come on in. Is everything set for next Saturday night?"

The tall mine superintendent stepped inside Lasher's office. "Sure . . . but isn't a Saturday night a bit risky for something like this? That's when the Mounties patrol—"

An exasperated sigh emitted from Lasher's mouth. "Vince, just leave the brainwork to me, will you? I wouldn't stage something like this under the noses of the Mounties. I've got all that covered. Now, you got the word out to the Indians that they're welcome to buy whatever they want from our company store at prices half what the Hudson's Bay are selling for over at Determination?"

"Yeah, but do you reckon Thunder Hawk'll let 'em come into Coal City after that last trouble when Zeke Benders killed that Johnny Blue Sky?"

"He can't stop 'em. This isn't the old Sitting Bull days, you know. Indian chiefs today don't have power like they used to. Some will do what Thunder Hawk says, others won't. We've been going out of our way to be nice to them lately. All we need is half a dozen. You let 'em know there'd be some free hootch?"

Strathman nodded.

"Then, they'll come," Strathman said confidently. "There's damned few Indians who can resist the smell of a bottle of hootch, especially when it's free."

Strathman's brows beetled together. "What if O'Reilly comes nosing around?"

A self-satisfied grin spread across Lasher's face. "We can forget about O'Reilly. He's in Dutch right up to that stupid-looking moustache. The inspector's got him confined to the barracks—which is a damned good place to keep him. It's just a matter of time, Vince, before he's right out of this part of the Territories, maybe out of the Mounties altogether."

Taking a cigar out of his coat pocket, Refflon Lasher leaned back in his chair and swung his booted feet up onto the desk top. "I told O'Reilly I'd get even with him, and that's just what I've done. Only thing is . . . I'm not through with him yet."

Chapter 13

The red, white, and blue of the Union Jack waved serenely over the North-West Mounted Police barracks as a gentle wind sighed through the mountain passes, brushing Fort Determination in its passage. The barracks bore an unmistakable military stamp, and although not as large as the divisional posts at places such as Fort Saskatchewan, Calgary, and Fort Macleod, were nonetheless laid out in the traditional form of a square.

Hugh O'Reilly loved this place, he realized as he strolled along the gravel path that was neatly bordered by the small, whitewashed rocks decorating almost every Mounted Police post in the North-West, from Regina to Dawson City and from Writing-on-Stone to Fort Chipewyan. The four log buildings and pole fence that gave the square its shape, and the parade ground within it, the thick green stands of pine and spruce beyond sweeping up the side of Mount Mac-Donald, the glacial-green ribbon of the Palliser down the slope past the settlement, the clear pine-scented mountain air . . . he loved it all with a passionate intensity. It was his kind of country.

At least, it *had* been—until Inspector Kerr's arrival.

He could hardly believe the change in his life this past month. Until Inspector Kerr had stepped off the *Northern Voyager*, this detachment had been completely his, his to lead and administer as he had seen fit, with no more than a minimum of direction from G Division headquarters at Fort Saskatchewan, two hundred and fifty miles eastward down the Palliser and Saskatchewan rivers—provided of course that he had done so according to those most holy of scriptures, *Regulations and Orders of the North-West Mounted Police.*

It was a big responsibility for a sergeant, especially a young sergeant. Not only did his detachment enforce all Dominion and territorial laws throughout forty thousand square miles of mountains, valleys, and forests, they maintained a guardroom and escorted prisoners to the jails and penitentiary, and lunatics to the asylum, as well as performed the duties of a dozen different government departments, from collecting Crown timber fees for the Department of the Interior to processing mail for the Post Office Department, from conducting census for the Department of the Secretary of State to supervising the storage of explosives at the Pacific & Western Mining Company's mines for the Department of Mines and Resources. O'Reilly could remember his delight, upon returning from the war in South Africa, when he was promoted to sergeant with only nine years' service and sent to take charge at Fort Determination, the largest sergeant's post in the Force. With a good military record and a decoration for gallantry in the field, he had hoped that when Fort Determination was raised to a sub-district headquarters, as he knew it eventually must, he would have been in line for the new command.

He would not have minded so much if Regina had sent an experienced officer who had worked his way up through the ranks, but he resented the appointment of an outsider. O'Reilly had served for more than eleven years over much of the Territories and the Yukon, and he had gained valuable practical knowledge, but this man had nothing to offer the Force other than a few years as an army officer. And if Wolsley Wellington Kerr had spent most of his time in South Africa on Lord Roberts's staff he would hardly have even seen action.

It was bad enough that Inspector Wolsley Wellington Kerr, with no more than a year's service in the Force, had been sent to Fort Determination to command the post and investigate a series of grossly exaggerated complaints against Sergeant Hugh O'Reilly, DCM, who had more than eleven years' service, but to add to O'Reilly's indignation the inspector had placed him under arrest for three disciplinary offenses and threatened to relieve him of his duties.

O'Reilly reached the pole fence just north of the detachment building, passed through the gate, and stopped. This was as far as he could go. Any further and he would be off the confines of the post, so he turned around and looked back the way he had come . . . back toward the barracks over to the left and the stables to the right. Down at the far end stood the stores building, where George Bailey, when drunk or melancholy, used to sit on an upturned box and sound *boots and saddles, the charge,* and all the other trumpet calls as he relived a wild and carefree youth. Since Inspector Kerr's arrival, George hadn't done that.

It was quiet on the post this day, a situation not solely attributable to the fact that it was Sunday. Inspector Kerr was gone. He had taken Baxter, his orderly, and ridden over to Coal City at Refflon Lasher's invitation to tour the mine. O'Reilly idly wondered what mischief Lasher was scheming this time. Whatever it was, it would hardly occupy his time anymore. It was a relief to have the inspector gone, if only for the day. His absence eased the tension that had been much too prevalent since his arrival.

Dusty Rogers was also gone, and George too, as well as Harry Somers. Dusty had taken the McLeod River patrol, while George had ridden to the north and Somers south to Rocky Mountain House. Another constable had just left the day before on the *Indian Princess* for Fort Saskatchewan with Mike Hannan. Tom Barr, sitting as the justice of the peace, had considered it in Mike's interest to sentence him to six months in the North-West Mounted Police guardroom there, where he could be observed by the Force surgeon to make sure he wasn't "a little bit strange in the head," as Tom had put it. That left two constables in barracks to handle whatever else might arise. It would be twenty days before Dusty returned, whereas George and Somers would be gone for five or six weeks.

Still gazing across the grass parade ground, his eyes

traveling beyond the fence to the deep greens of the pine and spruce, then swinging over to take in the growing gold on the birch and poplar trees down toward the Palliser's bank, O'Reilly pulled his pipe out of his pocket and thumbed tobacco into the bowl.

The orderly-room charges against him had been sent with the constable escorting Mike Hannan to Fort Saskatchewan. It would take six days for them to reach the OC's desk. Major Cavannagh would then decide whether to order him down to G Division headquarters to stand trial, or to himself journey up to Fort Determination to preside. O'Reilly guessed he would come up to Fort Determination.

Well, O'Reilly reflected as he struck a match and held the flame over the bowl until the tobacco caught and its pungent aroma mixed with the scent of pine as he puffed clouds of blue smoke into the gentle breeze, this finished him for commissioned rank. He would never qualify now. Commission—*hell*! he wouldn't even hang onto his stripes. He'd be reduced to corporal, perhaps even to constable, and transferred to another post. At that thought bitterness welled up inside him. All the work he'd put into this detachment, into all his police service for that matter, and to have it all swept away by a pompous, dictatorial son of a bitch of a politically appointed tin soldier the ink on whose commission was barely dry.

Of course, O'Reilly realized, he shouldn't have let his temper get out of hand, although he was convinced he had been right in going out after Mike Hannan because Mike otherwise wouldn't have allowed himself to be brought in. It was the way O'Reilly had gone out in defiance of the inspector's

155

order that wouldn't sit well. Granted the inspector had been off the post, he had not been far away and O'Reilly could have taken the time to seek him out and report the new circumstances, requesting further instructions. But he'd been too damned mad to do that, too consumed by jealousy. Yes, *jealousy*—damn it all! That's what it had been.

There was no doubt in O'Reilly's mind what Major Cavannagh would do about the charges, regardless of mitigating circumstances. He was a good officer, the major, but he was Mounted Police to the core. The Force's commissioned hierarchy always supported its own. In any conflict between a commissioned officer and an NCO or constable, the officer was always right. That was the way the Force's disciplinary process worked. It was the only way it could, in a corps such as the North-West Mounted Police, with six hundred men scattered across a million square miles.

He needn't be facing these disciplinary charges if it hadn't been for his resentment over the inspector courting Catherine. His jealousy! But why? What difference should it have made to him if the inspector courted her? Hugh O'Reilly wasn't in love with Catherine. He hadn't time for women. He was too much a part of the Force, and it was too much a part of him. His love was the Mounted Police, his first and only love. Duty . . . service . . . patrols . . . adventure . . . new challenges. When he left these mountains he wanted to go down north to the new frontier, down the Mackenzie, beyond the Arctic Circle. Sergeant Frank Fitzgerald, O'Reilly's fellow Haligonian, had already left Fort McPherson on his way to the Arctic Ocean.

156

Maybe Fitzgerald could use a good ex-sergeant. After his orderly-room trial, O'Reilly would request a transfer to the far north. Perhaps with more hard work and exceptional service he could get back up to sergeant. Perhaps even sergeant major. A commission was definitely out, but sergeant major . . . a good rank. No, there was no time for a woman in Hugh O'Reilly's life.

For a moment he felt better as his spirits rose to meet the challenges his mind projected in front of him. Great Slave Lake . . . Fort Resolution . . . Great Bear Lake . . . the far reaches of the Mackenzie . . . the Arctic Ocean. With no tin soldier like Wolsley Wellington Kerr riding him, he could work his way back up to senior NCO. The Force rewarded those who served it well.

However, for only a moment did he feel better . . . until the bitterness rose within him again and his resentment toward Inspector Kerr welled over. Yes . . . he had defied the inspector and disobeyed an order, and had then been insubordinate and insolent as well. But the inspector was an arrogant, dictatorial misfit who wasn't qualified to command the post. He was no good for it or the men of the detachment. The Force was just as much as fault for having sent him.

"Oh—to hell with it!"

As O'Reilly angrily and desperately blurted out those few words, he didn't hear the soft footfalls behind him, nor did he smell the scent of perfume, because the pungent aroma of his pipe tobacco blocked all that out. So he almost jumped out of his skin when he heard the feminine voice behind him.

"May I intrude on your soliloquy, Sergeant?"

O'Reilly whirled around, the pipe dropping from

his mouth, just managing to catch it before it fell to the ground, knocking blackened ash onto his shirt and down his brown duck fatigue trousers.

"Why . . . er . . . Cath . . . er, Mrs. Merrill . . ." he stammered, his face reddening under its deep tan.

She smiled sweetly. "I do apologize for coming up behind you like that. I thought you would hear me and I was surprised when you didn't. You must have been very deep in thought."

With the back of his hand O'Reilly brushed the ashes from his shirt and trousers. "Yes . . . well, I was, actually."

"Were you admiring the scenery?" she asked, gazing around at the mountains thrust giantlike against the blue sky, then at the flecks of gold down along the river. "It is beautiful at this time of the year. Everything is so peaceful. I love late summer and early autumn. It's my favorite time of the year . . . until the leaves fall. Of course, it's not so pretty out here at it is back home in the Ottawa Valley. The maples, you know. They're so colorful, when their leaves turn scarlet. It's a pity, don't you think, that there are no maples out here? But then if there were, it would be beautiful beyond imagination with the mountains. Perhaps it's Nature's way that no place on earth should have so much beauty."

His eyes fully on her as she talked, O'Reilly felt his stomach twisting into knots. A pale blue hat failed to keep the warm August sun from highlighting the golden red hair piled in coils on top of her head, while a frilly, high-necked white blouse, pale blue gloves, and long matching skirt completed a picture of womanly delight. In fact, she looked damned ravishing, and O'Reilly swallowed hard.

"Yes, I know what you mean about maples. We have them in the Maritimes, too."

"I know. I visited New Brunswick and Prince Edward Island after I was married. Carl took me there on our honeymoon. Have you ever been to Charlottetown?"

It hurt O'Reilly to hear her talk about her life with her late husband . . . their honeymoon. Surprising, for it was the first time he'd felt like that. Not that he'd heard her talk about her married life much before, but now, with her womanly figure and startingly attractive face before him, he found it painful to think of her with any other man. This new feeling stirred him, yet it also confused him.

"No." He was about to tell her that there hadn't been much money around when he was growing up. Those were the years of the great Depression and he'd gone to work in a grocery store when he was only thirteen and he'd stayed there until he went to sea at sixteen. From then until he joined the Mounted Police at twenty-two, he'd been no further west than a dozen miles beyond Halifax, other than aboard ship. But he wasn't in any mood to tell her the story of his life.

"What a pity," she said. "It's a delightful place. Every Canadian should visit the home of Confederation if he has the opportunity." Suddenly she smiled again. "You were a naughty boy, Hugh O'Reilly. You were so close, yet you didn't visit it. What sort of Canadian are you?"

"I suppose Inspector Kerr has been there." He couldn't resist that.

The smile left her face. "I'm afraid I don't quite

know what you mean by that."

He looked away. "It doesn't matter."

Neither of them spoke after that . . . at least, not for what seemed an age, as O'Reilly looked over at the peak of Mount Queen Victoria and Catherine dropped her eyes to the ground. It was Catherine who spoke first.

"You haven't been down to the dining room in a long time."

"I'm under arrest," O'Reilly replied simply, still looking over at the mountain. He hadn't meant to tell her that, either. But she probably knew.

Catherine frowned. "Arrested? What does that mean? I know what it means for you to arrest a criminal, but for you to be under arrest . . . ?"

"I'm not allowed to leave the post, for one thing. Hasn't *he* told you?"

"*He?*"

"Inspector Kerr."

Catherine looked up at O'Reilly until he turned his eyes from the mountain and looked back at her. "Oh," she said. "I see. Well, Wolsley—"

"*Wolsley!*" O'Reilly interrupted sharply, his dark eyes flashing. "That's nice! Wolsley!"

Her green eyes sparkled and a most delightful smile lit up her face. "Sergeant O'Reilly! I do believe you're jealous."

"*Jealous?*" O'Reilly exploded.

The smile remained on Catherine's face. "Yes, and I must say I'm pleased."

O'Reilly felt himself melting, but he quickly looked away again, steeling himself against her.

There was another period of silence, during which

160

Catherine stood scrutinizing the big man standing no more than four feet from her. She noticed, in the strong sunlight, how incredibly black was his hair, which he wore brushed back at the sides, while a loose wave allowed a natural part to fall into place on the left side, and an unruly lock tumbled forward over his brow. She observed how deeply tanned he was and her eyes lingered, not for the first time, on the straightness of his nose and the firm line of his mouth. It was the wide, upswept moustache that gave him that rugged, devil-may-care appearance. The moustache suited the spur-jangling swagger he affected when in uniform. That swagger, though, was not really so much an affectation of Hugh O'Reilly as it was a characteristic of the trained cavalrymen of a proud and famous corps, for she had seen it in the other Mounties.

This was not the first time Catherine Merrill had studied Hugh O'Reilly, but it was the first time she was able to see him in the full light of day, stripped of the scarlet tunic, yellow-striped blue breeches, and stiff-brimmed Stetson hat that gave him the stern, official identity of the law-and-order-maintaining Mountie. She had seen him without his hat many times before, but always indoors under artificial light. Now she could see him as Hugh O'Reilly, the man, not as Sergeant O'Reilly, DCM, of the North-West Mounted Police.

It was Catherine who broke the silence again. "I knew you were confined to barracks, but it wasn't Inspector Kerr who told me. It was Tom Barr. He didn't say you were under arrest, though."

O'Reilly turned his head to face her. "Did he tell you why?"

Catherine looked back at him. She liked his handsome face, which was not the face of a lady's man, nor really the face of a soldier or a fighting man; it was more the face of a sensitive man. Then she looked into the dark, flashing eyes, seeking to penetrate the depths of his soul, and she realized that those eyes had seen much, that the soul had come to grips with life, but that there was now turmoil there. And her heart reached out to him . . . and her hand suddenly reached up and touched his cheek.

The next instant she withdrew her hand, whirled around, and hurried, almost ran, away, back toward the settlement.

Hugh O'Reilly stood watching her go, the coolness of her hand still on his face, and he lifted his own hand to the spot on his cheek where her hand had momentarily touched, as if reluctant to lose it.

Chapter 14

It was Saturday night and Coal City was wide open.
The miners had been paid, both bootleg and permit
liquor flowed freely, and the honky-tonk dance hall
and the rest of Main Street shook with revelry and
excitement.

Sitting in his office, his booted feet up on his roll-
top desk, Refflon Lasher lighted a cigar. "Indians in
town tonight, Vince?"

Vince Strathman, leaning against the door, nodded.
"Sure are, Mr. Lasher."

Lasher grinned. "So Thunder Hawk doesn't have
as much clout with 'em as he likes to think. How are
they? Drunk?"

This time Strathman grinned too. "They're on the
way. The boys are bein' real nice to 'em."

"Good. Everything's going to plan."

"Are you sure the Mounties won't be sendin' a
patrol over tonight, Mr. Lasher?"

"No worries about that, Vince. I told the inspector last Sunday when he was over here that there was no more trouble on Friday and Saturday nights and that we don't need any more patrols. As it happened, he was just as glad because he's short-handed over at Fort Determination right now. He's only got O'Reilly and two men."

Strathman frowned. "I sure hope O'Reilly doesn't take it into his head to come pokin' his nose into things anyhow. He's got a damned bad habit of doin' that."

Scowling, Lasher swung his feet off the desk and hit the floor with a bang. "He's still confined to barracks. With Inspector Kerr over at Determination, we don't have to worry about O'Reilly. Come on, let's go uptown. It'll soon be time to get things moving."

Snatching his hat, Lasher led the way out of the office, and he and Strathman made their way up the crooked main street toward the center of Coal City. The closer they got to the dance hall the louder the noise became. Passing the company store, Lasher glanced in and noted with satisfaction the presence of a dozen Indians, more than half of them drunk. A few doors up the street at the dance hall, half a dozen more stood just inside the door watching half-drunk miners stomping across the rough board floor with gaudily painted dance-hall girls.

After watching for a few minutes, Lasher motioned Strathman to follow him and they stepped back outside. The streets were dark, except for the splashes of light thrown onto the ground from the buildings.

"Yeah . . . I think the time's getting just about right, Vince. Let's go and find us a sacrificial lamb."

They walked back down the street toward the company store, the tinny music and yelling and shouting diminishing behind them. They paused outside the store while Lasher peered in through the window. Fisher, the storekeeper, was behind the counter packing coffee, tobacco, tea, and blankets, as well as a variety of other commodities, into boxes, which he passed across to the Indians on the other side.

Looking over Lasher's shoulder, Strathman cackled. "Get a load of the look on Fisher's face. You'd think he's payin' for them supplies himself."

Lasher grunted. "Well, he's not. I am. But it's a small price for what we're going to get out of it. Here come some of those Indians now."

The door opened and several drunken Indians staggered out into the street, and a minute later were swallowed up by the darkness as they made their way toward the town's outskirts. Not long behind them reeled two or three more, laughing and talking, holding their boxes of trade goods in front of them. They continued coming out in twos or threes for the next few minutes, some so drunk they had to be helped by their only-slightly-less-inebriated companions. Lasher and Strathman stood back in the shadows watching. When there were only two Indians remaining in the store, Lasher turned to Strathman.

"All right, Vince. You know what to do."

Strathman reached down the leg of his trousers and pulled out a hard wood club. Then he slunk back into the shadows while Lasher stepped into the store.

"All right, Fisher," Lasher said to the storekeeper. "Time to close up."

A relieved expression lit up Fisher's somber face.

"Not before time, Mr. Lasher. We must've lost a couple of hundred dollars tonight, us bein' so damn generous to these damn redsk—er . . . these people tonight."

"That's all right, Fisher," Lasher replied, smiling beatifically at the two drunken, grinning Indians. "It's all in a good cause." Stepping over between the two Indians he put an arm around each of their shoulders and steered them to the door. "But the party's coming to a close, fellas. Time to be heading back to the reservation, or whatever you call it over your way. You've got yourselves a box of goodies and a nice bellyful of booze. Now you've got to be heading home."

As he herded them out the door, Lasher glanced back over his shoulder. "Lock up behind me, Fisher, but don't lock the back door. I'll return a little later to go over the books."

Guiding the two drunken Indians along the front of the building, Lasher chatted patronizingly to them. "It's sure been nice to have you fellas in Coal City. After all, there's no good reason why the whites and red men shouldn't get along together, eh? We're all sharing this great country together."

The two drunken Indians simply grinned, overcome by all the sudden display of the white man's uncharacteristic generosity.

But an instant later, as they came level with a dark alley, Lasher gave the one on his right an unholy shove, sending him careening into pitch-blackness. Before the startled Indian knew what had happened, Strathman's hard club smashed him over the skull and he dropped like a sack of potatoes to the ground.

By then, Lasher's hitherto-friendly arm on the other Indian's shoulder had turned into a vicelike grip around the unfortunate man's throat. He dropped his box of store goods and reached up to grasp at the choking arm, but the grip was too tight.

"Quick, Vince! Let me have that club. No, for crissake! Don't use it. You might hit me. Pass the goddamn thing to me."

In blackness Lasher couldn't find the proffered club. "Where the hell are you?" he snapped. "Quick! Give me the goddamn thing!"

Now the Indian, showing surprising strength for one so drunk, struggled wildly and almost succeeded in wriggling out of Lasher's grip. In frustration Lasher reached under his coat and drew a pistol. With a savage swing he brought it down hard on the Indian's head, the barrel and part of the cylinder crushing in the skull with a sickening crack. Lasher loosened his hold and let the Indian's body slide slowly to the ground.

"God damn it!" Lasher muttered.

"What's the matter, Mr. Lasher?" Strathman whispered.

"I think I might've killed him."

"Mine ain't dead. Mebbe we could get by with just one."

"I suppose, if we have to. But two would be better. Anyway, let's get these bodies moved."

They dragged the two bodies to the end of the alley, then along the ground behind the buildings.

"Christ, this one's heavy," Strathman panted. "We should've got some of the boys to help us."

"I don't want anyone else knowing about this,"

Lasher grunted in reply. "Now shut up and save your energy. We've still got a distance to go."

They dragged the two bodies another hundred yards before turning in to a lean-to behind one of the buildings.

"Lean 'em up against the wall," Lasher said. "Just like they'd sat down to sleep off a drunk."

When that was done Lasher started feeling along the log wall. "Where's that sack—ah, here it is."

There was a clink as he pulled out of a burlap sack two whiskey bottles. He handed one to Strathman. Their eyes had become accustomed to the darkness now and they had no trouble seeing one another. "Pour half of this down that Indian's throat, then dump the rest all over him."

Strathman did as Lasher told him, while Lasher did the same to the other Indian. When they had finished, Lasher stood up. "Now you stay here and watch 'em. Make sure nothing goes wrong. If either one of 'em wakes up, hit 'em unconscious."

Lasher hurried off through the darkness back along behind the buildings until he reached the rear of the company store. He found the back door unlocked. Opening it he went inside. Fisher was bent over his store ledger. Hearing the movement behind him, he looked up.

"Oh . . . Mr. Lasher. Didn't reckon you'd be back so soon. I ain't through with the ledger yet."

"That's all right, Vince. We can check it later. Right now I want you to help me carry some coal oil out back."

"Coal oil?"

Lasher nodded impatiently. "That's right. Don't

168

tell me we haven't got any."

Fisher shook his head. "Oh, no . . . we got lots of it."

"Good. Let's get moving."

They each carried a two-gallon jar of coal oil in each hand out the back door and down along behind the buildings to the lean-to where Lasher had left Strathman with the two unconscious Indians.

"Everything all right, Vince?" Lasher asked in a low voice.

"Yeah, Mr. Lasher. Neither one of 'em has stirred."

"Good." Lasher pulled the cork from one of the jars and poured part of the contents over the Indians' trousers. When he had finished he said, "All right, Vince. Keep an eye on 'em like you were before. I'll be back in fifteen minutes."

Lasher took Fisher by the arm and they returned to the company store. As soon as they were inside, Lasher said, "Now I want a rifle and ammunition."

"What sort?" Fisher asked. "We got—"

"Something an Indian would use," Lasher replied before Fisher could finish. "A Winchester seems the most likely."

Fisher unlocked a cabinet and produced a brand-new Winchester. From a drawer below the cabinet he brought out a box of shells. Handing both to Lasher, Fisher relocked the cabinet while Lasher fed a handful of shells into the rifle's magazine, then stuffed the box into his coat pocket.

"All right," Lasher said when Fisher turned around. "Let's tear this place apart so that it looks like it's been ransacked."

Fisher looked incredulous. *"Ransacked?"*

169

"That's what I said," Lasher replied impatiently. "I want this place to look like Indians broke into it." He picked up an axe and started smashing it into the cabinet Fisher had just locked.

"Jesus!" Fisher protested. "Mr. Lasher—"

"Shut up, Fisher," Lasher snapped at him. "Just do like I said."

Fisher watched as Lasher finished chopping the gun cabinet to splinters; then, as Lasher swept armloads of merchandise from the shelves, scattering cans, packages, and bottles all over the floor, Fisher reluctantly joined in. When the store looked like a shambles, Lasher stopped and looked around, satisfaction written across his face. "That looks just about right."

Fisher's face registered bewilderment. "I don't get it."

Instead of replying, Lasher picked up the rifle, slowly raising the barrel until it pointed at Fisher's chest. The storekeeper's eyes widened like two saucers.

"Hey . . . don't point that rifle at me like that, Mr. Lasher. It makes me feel downright uncomfortable."

Lasher's finger tightened around the trigger. The rifle bucked in his hands and a stab of flame shot out from the muzzle. Fisher was knocked backward by the force of the bullet. Quickly Lasher levered the action and pulled the trigger again . . . a second bullet crashed into the storekeeper's chest before he collapsed to the floor.

"Your trouble, Fisher," Lasher said as he stared down at the fallen body, "was that you knew too much."

Then Lasher turned around and walked out the back door, hurrying through the darkness back behind the buildings to where he had left Strathman to watch the two unconscious Indians. But when he got there Strathman was doubled over groaning. Only one of the Indians was still propped against the log wall.

"What the hell—?" Lasher burst out.

Strathman turned a pain-wracked face up at him. "That Indian you thought you killed . . . I was watchin' him and the other one . . . then I heard a rifle shot. I looked up to see what it was and that Indian suddenly kicked me in the—"

"*Where is he?*"

"I dunno . . . he ran off . . . disappeared into the darkness . . . the goddamned son of a bitch!"

"Christ Almighty!" Lasher exploded. "Can't I trust you to do anything right?" He stood for a moment, then he tossed the Winchester into the lap of the unconscious Indian. After that he picked up one of the coal-oil jars, pulled out the cork, and started sloshing coal oil over the walls of the next building. When he finished he uncorked the second jar and did the same. Then he struck a match and flicked it at the soaked wall. An instant later the wall caught with a sudden *whoosh* and a flash of flame. Seconds later the entire building caught fire. Lasher threw the empty jar down beside the Indian.

While that fire burned, Lasher opened another jar and poured coal oil on the adjacent building, throwing another match at it, with the same result. He repeated the process at a third building, tossing the empty coal-oil jar at the foot of the unconscious Indian, who was just beginning to stir into a drunken stupor.

"All right, Vince . . . let's get out of here!"

With the leaping flames highlighting the pain still on his face, Strathman followed Lasher along the rear of the buildings until they were back behind the company store. Just then they heard someone shouting, "Fire! Fire!" Looking back over their shoulders they could see the darkness growing red as flames enveloped the buildings where they had come from.

"Come on," Lasher said, leading the way into the company store.

"Christ!" Strathman gasped when he saw Fisher's body lying on the floor in a pool of blood. "You didn't tell me—"

Lasher cut him off impatiently. "Shut up! It was that damned Indian who shot him."

"But the shot—"

"Shutup!" Lasher repeated urgently. "Do you want to spoil everything? Fisher knew too much. I had to get rid of him."

Just then they heard the loud clanging of the town's fire bell, followed by more shouts of "Fire! Fire!"

Lasher gripped Strathman by the shoulder. "Don't you see? We can blame all this on drunken Indians— Fisher's murder, the looting of the store, the fire. Half the town'll burn before anyone can put the fire out. By the time I'm finished I'll get things stirred up so bad the Mounties will have to move Thunder Hawk's tribe out of the Snake. They won't have any choice. Then we'll be all set to bring our equipment in and start mining for silver."

A greedy light crept into Strathman's eyes. "Yeah . . . you're right."

Outside the front of the store they could hear the

sounds of men running down the street from the dance hall toward the fire.

"Come on," Lasher said, and he and Strathman burst out the front door. "What's going on?" Lasher shouted at the passing miners.

"Fire, Mr. Lasher," a miner yelled back at him as he ran past. "The town's on fire. We gotta put it out or the whole place'll go up."

"Someone shot Fisher!" Lasher bellowed at the top of his voice. "Murdered him and looted the store."

A couple of running miners stopped and stared at him. "Murdered Fisher?"

"That's right—murdered him in cold blood. Come and look."

Lasher led the men inside. "Jesus!" one exclaimed, glancing around at the mess. "I ain't seen this place look like this since Big Zeke Benders—"

"In here . . . in the back . . ." Lasher said, leading them into the back of the store to where Fisher lay dead on the floor. One of the miners, looking down at the body, made the sign of the cross. The other shrank back in horror.

"Mr. Strathman and I just found him," Lasher said. "We came in to check the books after the day's business and found him lying on the floor in all that blood. And this place a hell of a mess. I'd left him just a short while before, just as some Indians were leaving. Looks like one or two of them sneaked back and did him in. Those holes in his chest . . . damned big. Looks like he was shot with a Winchester."

"Dirty, stinkin' Indians!" one of the miners said.

"Yeah," agreed the other. "That's who it'd be, for sure. None of the miners'd do that."

"You two fellas are witnesses to this," Lasher said.

"Yeah, sure thing, Mr. Lasher."

"All right. Let's put the fire out."

They hurried out the front door and ran down the street toward the fire. A bucket brigade was already forming, but the flames were taking hold quickly.

"Where the hell's the fire engine?" Lasher shouted.

A clanging bell from somewhere down the street answered him, and a horse-drawn fire engine came bouncing around the corner.

"Hey—look!" one of the miners yelled, pointing excitedly between the buildings. "An Injun!"

The Indian who Lasher and Strathman had left lying in the alley staggered out into the street. In his right hand he trailed the Winchester Lasher had tossed into his lap. As he reeled dazedly into the light cast by the burning buildings, Lasher lunged forward.

"He's carrying a Winchester!" he shouted accusingly. "That's the gun that was used to murder Fisher!"

"Fisher?" yelled a miner.

"Yeah," answered one of the miners whom Lasher had led into the store. "Some Indian murdered Fisher in the back of the company store. Used a rifle, a Winchester most likely. It must've been him what done it!"

"That's right," shouted the other miner who'd seen the body. "Let's string him up, the murderin' son of a bitch!"

Lasher snatched the rifle out of the Indian's hand. "Hey," he said, for the benefit of the others, grabbing the Indian by his shirt and dragging him forward. "This Indian stinks of coal oil. I'll bet he stole coal oil

174

from the company store and tried to burn the town down. I heard him arguing with Fisher earlier. One of you boys check around the back. I'll bet you'll find some empty coal-oil jars down there."

Amidst the flames and confusion, several miners ran around behind the buildings, returning a moment later triumphantly holding aloft the empty coal-oil jars. "You were right, Mr. Lasher."

"Just like I said!" Lasher shouted. "It was the goddamned Indians that killed Fisher and looted the company store. Stole this Winchester, too." He held the rifle up in front of him. "Brand-new, see. Then they tried to burn our town down, to boot."

"Yeah! Let's string this son of a bitch up!"

The Indian looked frightened. It was a frightening scene . . . leaping flames, hostile white faces, angry shouts, shaking fists, rough hands dragging and pushing him, the roaring of the fire. From nowhere a rope appeared. Quickly sobering, the Indian cringed.

"No!" a miner shouted above the noise. "The Mounties won't tolerate no lynch law!"

Lasher shot a filthy look at the miner and made a mental note to fire the man when this was over. Turning to Strathman, he said something in the mine boss's ear. Strathman nodded.

"He's right, men," Lasher shouted. "Lock him up for the Mounties. Keep this Winchester for evidence."

Then Vince Strathman shouted. "I got me a good idea, men! Let's go and drive all them damned troublesome Indians right out of the Snake. Let's herd 'em back to the prairies where they belong!"

Caught up in the mob hysteria, the miners shouted in agreement. "Yah! Yah! Ve run dem oot of town.

Let's go to d' Snake!"

"That's right, boys!" Strathman shouted encouragingly. "I'll even let you use company horses and wagons to get there."

"Yeah! Yeah! What are we waitin' for!"

"Hey, you drunken bastards!" one of the fire fighters bellowed. "How about givin' us a hand puttin' out this fire first!"

Simone Laboucan had been unable to sleep. For most of the night, it seemed, drunken Indians clattering past her cabin in their wagons had kept her awake with their singing and chanting as they made their way back to their village up the Snake.

It had puzzled her why the white men who ran the coal mines had welcomed the Indians to their town. It was unlike them. She knew the white men had lured the Indians to town by offering them rotgut hootch. The word had got out. Too bad it hadn't reached the redcoats at Fort Determination. Not that she had any particular love for the redcoats . . . not since that Clyde Baxter had dumped her three months ago. She just hadn't seen him since that last night when he'd brought the other redcoat called Harry, the night there'd been that big fight in Coal City. But she hated the miners, most particularly the bosses like that big pig of a big boss called Lasher, who'd taken her for a common whore and tried to screw her. He would've gotten away with it if it hadn't been for Thunder Hawk. Either that or she would have plunged a knife into him, or shot him when he'd left . . . and then the redcoats would've come and taken her away.

Thunder Hawk wouldn't be pleased with his people for having gone into the white miners' town. He had never liked them going there. But the company store was closer by half than the journey to the Hudson's Bay store at Fort Determination. After that last time, when Johnny Blue Sky was killed in that fight, Thunder Hawk had persuaded his people to go the the Hudson's Bay store at the fort, where prices were better and credit easier. But when the white man offered free hootch, the Indians ignored Thunder Hawk's advice. Or some of them had.

Simone had always liked Thunder Hawk. Even though she wasn't one of his people—her mother had been a Dogrib from the north country, her father a descendant of the French *voyageurs* of the old North-West Company—Thunder Hawk had always kept a brotherly eye on her, keeping her with meat and flour during the long winters, and sending his squaw to look after her when she was sick during one Long Snow. Like the time big boss Lasher forced his way into her place. Thunder Hawk had suddenly turned up, threw the white dog of a big boss out, then just as suddenly left, without waiting to be thanked.

Still unable to get to sleep, Simone lay on her back, her eyes open, staring up at the darkness of the ceiling of her solitary log cabin, wondering whether she should turn over on her side and try to sleep, or whether she should get into her dwindling supply of tea and make herself a cup. She decided on the cup of tea, threw back the bearskin covering, and swung her legs to the floor. The instant her feet hit the floor, her eyes were on the window, looking to the south. And in that instant she saw dozens of bobbing lights sparkling in the night's blackness, like dozens of fireflies in the night air. Fascinated, she stood stock-still for many seconds before it dawned on her that the lights were coming from the trail to Coal City. Quickly throwing on her buckskin clothing, she crossed the cabin and opened the door.

In the distance she heard the muted rumbling of wagons, singing, and a lot of shouting. As she watched, shivering against the chill late summer night, she noticed the lights were getting closer and the rumble of wagons and occasional shouting growing louder. Almost hypnotized, she stood and watched.

Closer . . . closer . . . the rumble of wagons louder . . . shouts, angry shouts. Then, in pain-stabbing terror, she realized they were coming toward her cabin. *They were coming for her!* They were going to drive her from her home. It was that dog of a big boss, Lasher, doing this. He was out to get even with her.

Breaking free of the hypnotic effect of the moving lights, Simone turned around and fled . . . fled for her life, fleet-footed on moccasined feet, fled toward the sanctuary of Thunder Hawk's village.

Thunder Hawk was fully dressed when the mixed-blood woman who lived alone in the cabin by the fork of the trail reached the northern Stoney village at the mouth of the Valley of the Snake. He had worried that something bad would happen if his tribesmen succumbed to the temptation of free food and white man's blaze-belly hootch and went into the black-rock mining town. It was not the white man's way to be generous to the red man. The noise of drunken revelers returning to the village had kept him awake—and dressed, because he hadn't known whether he would have to take a firm hand in suppressing a continuation of revelry—and now a hammering on the door.

Lithe as a mountain lion, Thunder Hawk sprang across the floor and threw open the door. As he did so, Simone fell into the cabin. Hawk quickly helped her up and led her to a chair.

"White men come to get me," she panted as she caught her breath. "Many . . . with burning sticks. I run away . . . but they follow. They coming here now. I frightened."

Thunder Hawk's eyes narrowed. "Why do they do this?"

"I don't know. I do nothing to any of them. Only that big mine boss . . . you know . . . that time . . . "

"That was not enough. There must be something else." Thunder Hawk went into another room to get his wife to look after Simone. Then he took his rifle off the wall and went out the door. It was still dark but dawn wasn't far away. The sky was heavily overcast, not a star showing, and the smell of rain was in the air.

The Indian village sat on a grassy benchland just above the Snake River at the entrance to the Valley of the Snake. Not far away was the trail from Coal City, which passed Simone's cabin over by the fork of the trail. Thunder Hawk loped over the distance to the trail in two or three minutes. He saw the dozens of dots of light against the blackness almost at once. He could hear the rumble of wagons carrying the lights and knew they would reach the village in less than half an hour.

Turning, Thunder Hawk loped back to the village. There were a few lights burning here and there in the teepees, tents, and log cabins that comprised the village. These were the lights of the drunken revelers who had come back from their night in Coal City.

Without wasting time on formalities, Thunder Hawk used his rifle to sweep aside the bearskin coverings that served as doors. In the first cabin he found the occupants lying all over the floor, snoring loudly, whiskey fumes filling the foul air. With a savage gesture of disgust, he let the door covering fall back into place as he stepped back outside.

The next place in which he saw a light was a teepee. Stooping his way through the opening, Thunder Hawk found Mike Mountain Bull sitting cross-legged on a bearskin, with a dirty rag held against a gaping gash across his forehead, dried blood caked down the side of his face. Instantly Thunder Hawk smelled the odor of coal oil above the whiskey fumes. And he remembered earlier in the night seeing a glow of orange-red over in the direction of Coal City.

"What is wrong with you?" Thunder Hawk demanded.

Mike Mountain Bull lifted a pair of bleary, bloodshot eyes. "Someone hit me over the head in the white man's town."

"Why?"

Mike Mountain Bull shrugged.

Thunder Hawk's hand shot out, grabbed him by the collar, and yanked him to his feet. "I told all of you not to go there! Now the whites come here. Many of them. What did you do?"

Mike Mountain Bull's eyes shone with fright. "Nothing! Nothing! Little Beaver and I were leaving the white man's store with food when we were attacked by two white-eyes. One was the white-eyes' digging chief . . . the one they call *Lash-er*—"

"You stink of the flame-water the white-eyes burn in their lamps. Why?"

Thunder Hawk's tone was urgent, and Mike Mountain Bull's next words tumbled quickly from his mouth. "The white men knocked us unconscious and dragged us behind some of their buildings. I woke up when one of them—the chief called Lash-*er*—poured blaze-belly down my throat. Then he poured it all over me. After that he went away. I was afraid to move because the other one watched with a big stick to hit us again if we woke up, so I pretended to be asleep. Then the chief Lash-*er* came back with another man. I think it was the storekeeper. They carried jars and poured some of it over us. It was the flame-water. I was very scared they were going to burn us. Then Lash-*er* and the storekeeper left again, but the other one, a big man with the stick, he stayed watching us, ready to hit us if we moved. Then there was a shot. He looked away for a minute and I kicked him in his bag. When he cried and doubled over, I jumped up and ran away."

"What about Little Beaver?"

"I left him there. I was afraid. I couldn't carry him."

"Where did you go then?"

"Back here. Everyone else was gone. All our people had left."

Thunder Hawk threw Mike Mountain Bull back onto the bearskin and darted out through the opening. He thought again of the orange-red glow he had seen over toward the white man's mining town, and he was sure the coming of the torch-carrying white men had nothing to do with the mixed-blood woman. There was some other reason for it, and the pouring of flame-water over Mike Mountain Bull had something to do with it.

Hurrying to one of the darkened cabins, Thunder Hawk banged on the door, waited until a voice answered from within, replied in rapid Stoney, and darted to the next cabin, then the next and next, where he repeated the process, and again at a tent, two teepees, and another cabin. By then he could clearly hear the rumble of the approaching wagons, interspersed with occasional shouts. And by the time the torch-carrying miners packed into the horse-drawn wagons rounded the bend and entered the valley, Thunder Hawk and a dozen and a half Indians met them.

Vince Strathman, waving a flaming torch, jumped down from the lead wagon. "All right, fellas! We're here. Now let's drive these redskins to hell outta here."

"Yeah!" shouted others, jumping down after him. "Let's burn their goddamn village just like they tried to burn our town!"

"Yah! Yah! Burn d' place down! Let's pay 'em back for vat dey done!"

The miners all spilled over the sides of the wagons and surged toward the Indian village.

"Wait!" shouted Thunder Hawk in a deep, booming voice. A big, fine-looking Indian in deerskin jacket and trousers, with black hair plaited in a long braid running halfway down his back, a brightly beaded headband around his forehead and proud, coppery features. In the flickering light of the hand-held torches, he looked an imposing figure, and with rifle by his side, a formidable one.

But Vince Strathman, taller than Thunder Hawk, was not intimidated by the Indian's powerful build, nor by the rifle at his side. Strathman was the kind of man who would allow himself to be bossed around by a bigger or smarter white man, but never would he allow an Indian to deter him.

"We ain't waitin' for nothin', Hiawatha," Strathman shouted back. "Come on, boys. Let's get at it."

"Why have you come here like this?" Thunder Hawk's booming voice demanded, the Stoney chief standing in their way.

"We're goin' to teach you redskins a lesson for tryin' to burn our town down," Strathman told him. "We're goin' to drive you back to the prairies where you belong."

"None of my people burn town," was Thunder Hawk's answer.

"Ah . . . shut up, Hiawatha. Come on, boys!"

The miners surged forward again. More Indians stepped forward out of the shadows and joined Thunder Hawk and his eighteen braves, but the hundred-odd miners outnumbered them by more than four to one. The blazing torches lit up the darkness, showing the rough, bearded faces of the miners in ugly relief. And every miner not holding a torch carried a pick handle. Of the Indians, only Thunder Hawk had a rifle.

"Stop!" shouted Thunder Hawk, his deep, booming voice rising above the miners' shouts.

"Come on, boys!" urged Strathman. "Burn this goddamn village to the ground!"

"Yeah! Yah! Burn d' village!"

The surge of miners pushed the Indians aside. Thunder Hawk brought up his rifle across his chest and used it to block Strathman's way. Strathman poked his flaming torch at Thunder Hawk's face. Thunder Hawk ducked, then like lightning he whipped his rifle butt up under Strathman's jaw, almost snapping the tall mine boss's head off. Strathman dropped the torch and reeled back, but was instantly swept forward by the miners behind him.

"You redskinned son of a bitch!" Strathman swore, reaching under his coat and pulling a revolver.

Thunder Hawk swung his rifle butt again just as Strathman pulled the trigger. The big Colt bucked in his hand as a stab of red spat from the muzzle, and a rocking explosion punched the air.

At the sound of the gunshot, the Indians turned and fled in all directions. Yelling like fiends the miners chased them with their pick handles and flaming torches.

"Look at 'em go! Hah hah hah! We got the Indians on the run, boys!"

"Yah. Jus' like dose stories of Indian battles in d' old days. Only dis time it's us vat's winning."

Strathman stood, Colt in one hand, his other hand up to his aching jaw. Thunder Hawk darted away.

184

Strathman raised the Colt and snapped a shot at the Indian chief. The bullet went over Thunder Hawk's shoulder. Thunder Hawk tried to get beyond the illumination of the flaming torches. At the same time he reviled the members of his tribe who had succumbed to the temptation to visit the white man's town. It was not that he blamed them for having caused this trouble, because he did not believe they had, no matter what the white men said. But if they were not lying around in a drunken stupor now, they would have been able to help the rest of them in making a more aggressive defense of their village. Throwing a glance over his shoulder as he darted in a zigzagging movement away from the miners, Thunder Hawk saw pick handles arcing down onto fallen braves as the miners poured over them. He was tempted to go back to help them, but he realized he could act more effectively if he could reach a position from where he could command the broad front of the oncoming miners. And then he reviled himself for not having had the wisdom to place braves with rifles at the fringes of the village, out of the way of the blazing torches. The trouble was that he had never expected an attack on his village. The Indian today was beyond that sort of thing, and so should have been the white man.

Shouting and yelling continued, and the torch lights bobbed with the running movement of their bearers. Strathman fired another shot at Thunder Hawk, but the mine boss's face was so painful that he couldn't aim properly. Besides, Thunder Hawk's zigzag movement was making him a hard target. Cursing, Strathman fired a fourth shot, which also missed.

He was about to fire a fifth when he realized he could no longer see the Stoney chief.

Beyond the ring of light, Thunder Hawk reached the base of the valley wall and started scrambling up the rocks.

Chapter 15

Refflon Lasher couldn't resist the temptation to
drive out to the Valley of the Snake to see how his plan
was going. He knew he shouldn't; he had taken pains
to make sure he had been seen around Coal City
during the night, even manning the bucket brigade
and the volunteer fire department's hose. Then, after
they had put out the fire, he had made a big play
about being "all in" and wanting to get to bed. After
that he had slipped out the back door of the building
where he had both his office and living quarters,
hitched his team, and stole out of town.

He wasn't making as good time as he had hoped,
for the night was dark because of the heavy overcast.
The lantern he had fixed to the buckboard cast not
much light, and the horses had to pick their way along
the trail, relying more on instinct than sight. Lasher
wore a slicker, for besides being cool the smell of rain
hung heavy in the air.

Passing the half-breed woman's darkened cabin, Lasher was sorely tempted to stop and go in to do what he had wanted that first time. He had little to fear from Thunder Hawk now, because the Stoney chief would have his hands full at his village. And although the temptation grew as lust and passion rose within him, Lasher flicked his whip and drove the team harder. Mix a woman with business and you could expect trouble.

The reason Lasher was taking the risk of driving out to the Snake was because he didn't have complete confidence in Strathman. Not that he doubted the tall mine boss's loyalty, but there were always things that could go wrong at the last moment, and Strathman wasn't smart enough to make the right decisions if that happened. Anyway, Lasher mused, if it did become known that he had come out to the Snake, he could explain it away by saying that he had learned incensed miners had left town and marched on the Indian village in retaliation for the Indians burning part of Coal City and that he, as a public-spirited and responsible citizen, had driven out to try to stop them. Yes, he grinned to himself . . . that sounded pretty good . . . he liked it. No matter what, he was in the clear. He had made sure of that. Strathman had done all the stirring, all the stirring that showed. It was Strathman who had publicly provided company wagons to carry the mob to the Indian village. If anyone could get into trouble as a ringleader, it was Strathman. Of course, Lasher realized, he would have to get Vince out of it somehow if that happened. Strathman would point a finger at him otherwise. It reinforced what Lasher had always known—have as few partners as possible. That was why he had killed Fisher. He would like to get Meecher out of the way, too . . . although Meecher didn't know anything more than that they were looking for silver. He knew nothing of the less savory aspects of the activities. Only Fisher and Strathman knew. Now Fisher was dead. As for Strathman . . . well, Lasher needed Strathman.

Thunder Hawk climbed the rocks to find a position high enough from where he could open up with his rifle and drive the torch-carrying white men from his village. But when he heard shouts of triumph from behind, he knew he was too late.

The miners had surged too close to the village. A few hurled their flaming torches at the irregular line of cabins and teepees. Most fell short and dropped to the ground, starting small fires in the dry grass, but one reached a teepee. With a loud crackling, it quickly caught hold. Shouting encouragement to one another the miners threw more torches, while others with the same intention held theirs until they were close enough to land on top of the cabins.

Looking down on the scene below, Thunder Hawk saw the miners were just yards from the nearest cabins. By the time he levered a shell into the breech of his rifle and whipped the weapon up to his shoulder, some of the white men were into the village. Quickly he sighted and pulled the trigger. With the echoes of the shot rolling across the valley, Thunder

Hawk levered again and fired a second time.

Amidst the excitement of their own vengeful emotions, the noise of their shouting, and the crackling of the burning teepees, the rampaging miners at first did not comprehend that they were being shot at. It wasn't until Thunder Hawk's third bullet knocked over one of them that they began to realize what was happening. By then two of the torches had landed on top of one cabin, while three more landed on another. Flames leaped into the air and a woman's cries of fear mingled with the enraged shouting of the white men.

Vince Strathman was the first to realize what was happening. Standing well to the rear, he had spotted the muzzle flash from Thunder Hawk's rifle at the first shot. Raising his revolver he pointed at the cliffs and thumbed back the hammer. The long-barreled Colt jumped in his hand, but the continued flashes from up in the rocks told him his bullet hadn't found its mark.

It took just as long for Thunder Hawk to realize someone was shooting at him, taking three shots from Strathman's Colt. Part of the reason was that the range was too great, and Strathman's shots weren't even coming close. Of more concern to Thunder Hawk was the fact that one of the burning cabins was his, in which were his wife and the mixed-blood woman.

Now an urgency took hold of him. He fired off five more shots into the miners below, slid fresh shells into the magazine, and opened up again.

While Thunder Hawk was reloading, Strathman ran toward the rocks to get the Stoney chief in his sights. The sky was beginning to lighten, with long fingers of gray streaking above the lower ranges to the east, and the tall mine boss could at last see where he was going.

In the village the teepee that had first caught fire was now a solid sheet of flames. The roofs of two of the cabins were also burning fiercely. Frightened Indians fled from one, only to be set upon by yelling miners and clubbed to the ground by pick handles. An Indian tried to flee from the second cabin, but the shouting, club-wielding miners beat him back. A miner threw a flaming torch through the doorway of a third cabin. Screams and cries rent the air, mixed with blasphemous curses and brutal laughter. Then, above it all, boomed the noise of rifle shots, one after another, like the continuous roll of thunder.

"Oh, Christ!" screamed a miner, dropping his torch and beating his hands to his chest as his knees buckled beneath him and frothy red blood bubbled from his mouth.

The miner beside him stared down in sobering horror. "Jesus!" he muttered, and made the sign of the cross.

Another miner was more vocal. "*Christ Almighty!*" he shouted, his ears cocked to catch the thunder of the rifle. "Some son of a bitch's shooting at us!"

At that precise moment another miner toppled, as though struck suddenly by an invisible giant hand.

"Holy shit! Let's get the hell outta here."

Panic hit the miners as two more of them fell. They had not bargained for this, thinking their numbers would have easily intimidated the Indians. They weren't aware that it was just one determined Indian with a Winchester repeater who was dropping them one after another. Their lawless rampaging turned to stark fear as another torchbearer uttered a choking cry of pain and stumbled to the ground. Those still holding torches quickly dropped them as they turned and scattered wildly.

Thunder Hawk emptied his rifle a second time. Then, his eyes on his burning cabin, he clambered down the rocks to the ground below and raced toward it. As he ran, Strathman raised his Colt, took very careful aim, sighting just a fraction ahead of the running Indian, and pulled the trigger. Thunder Hawk pitched headlong to the grass.

Refflon Lasher heard the first shot.

"Christ!" he muttered, recognizing the sharp punchlike sound of a pistol. One of the miners must have taken along a revolver. It was unlikely to have been an Indian; as far as Lasher knew, Indians always used rifles. Then, as he sat listening alertly, he heard more pistol shots.

"Damned fools!" he cursed, and whipped his team into greater speed. He didn't want gunplay. He wanted to stir up resentment against the Indians. That was why he had made it look like they had tried to burn Coal City, why he had made it look as though they had broken into the company store and murdered Fisher. He wanted the Indian village burned down in what would appear to be retaliation, and it didn't matter if some of the Indians were beaten up, but he didn't want any of them killed. It was essential for public sympathy to side with the miners, and if an Indian was killed, it could go the other way.

"Faster!" Lasher yelled as he cracked the whip over the horses' backs again. It was reckless to drive them too fast, for it was still dark, despite the faint glimmering of light just beginning to show over the mountains to the east, but he felt more confident in the horses' ability to find their way over the trail than he had earlier, and right now he had a feeling that he'd better get to the Indian village fast.

Then he heard rifle shots. Unmistakably rifle shots. The Indians must be returning the firing he heard a short while before. Grinning, he eased off with the whip and sat back from the edge of the buckboard seat. Now, if the Indians shot a few miners, that was a different thing. In fact, that would suit Refflon Lasher's cause admirably. It would strengthen his argument that the Indians were troublemakers whose presence in the mountains was interfering with the country's coal mining. Then the police would have to move them. With Uncle Wilbur's behind-the-scenes prodding, the government would be compelled to cooperate. After all, coal was important to the country's fledgling industry, and Ottawa, alert to the need to broaden the North-West's economic base, would place the value of the coal-mining industry far above the welfare of a small band of Indians.

It took Lasher only a few minutes to reach the opening to the Snake, and as soon as his buckboard swung around the side of the mountain he could see the orange flames bright against the dark backdrop of the early morning. Miners were running toward the wagons, followed by the few rifle shots from the burning village.

Deciding he had better play the role of the public-spirited citizen trying to put a stop to the rampaging, Lasher drove into the midst of them.

"What the hell's going on here?" he shouted in well-feigned indignation. While a couple of miners babbled what had happened, Lasher's eyes searched for his mine superintendent. "Where's Mr. Strathman?"

The miners didn't know, but when he asked the same question of another miner, the man pointed toward the rocks at the base of the valley wall. Then Lasher saw the tall figure of his mine boss. "All right, you men," Lasher shouted. "Get back to town right away."

Lasher drove his team over to where Vince Strathman was walking toward the prostrate form of a buckskin-clad Indian lying face-down on the ground. Strathman just reached it when Lasher braked the buckboard to the grass-skidding stop beside him.

Surprised to see Lasher out at the Indian village, Strathman grinned foolishly and waved his Colt at the prostrate Indian.

"Know who that is, Mr. Lasher? That's Thunder Hawk."

Lasher knew he shouldn't have trusted Strathman to do the job without bungling. He'd done the very thing Lasher had not wanted—he'd shot an Indian. However, the mention of Thunder Hawk's hated name overcame Lasher's anger. "Is he dead?"

194

Digging his boot under Thunder Hawk's ribs, Strathman rolled him over on his back. Blood covered the Indian's dusky forehead. "Looks pretty dead to me, but just to make sure . . ." Strathman cocked the Colt and pointed it down at Thunder Hawk.

But suddenly a bullet smashed into Strathman's shoulder, spinning him to the ground. The big Colt exploded, the bullet ripping harmlessly into the grass. Startled, Lasher dropped to a knee, his eyes probing the shadows over toward the Indian village. Just then the rifle crashed again and a bullet cracked overhead. Beside him, Strathman moaned as he nursed his shattered shoulder.

"Think you can move, Vince?" Lasher asked urgently.

"I reckon so," Strathman gasped.

"Then, let's get out of here. We've done what we wanted. The yellow-legs will have to move these Indians out of the Snake now. Once they're gone, we can move in and start mining for silver. Come on, I'll help you."

Lasher got his arms around Strathman's ribs from behind and lifted. Strathman groaned in pain, but Lasher pulled him to his feet. Together they staggered to the buckboard just as the dull gray clouds above opened up, dropping their build-up of rain that had been threatening most of the night. With heavy drops splashing onto the brim of his hat, Lasher pushed Strathman up onto the buckboard and climbed up himself. Settling Strathman onto the seat, Lasher grasped the traces and whipped the team into movement.

Rain washing the blood from his aching forehead, Thunder Hawk lifted his head and through pain-wracked eyes watched the buckboard disappear into the downpour. He struggled to his feet just as Mike Mountain Bull, rifle in hand, came running toward him.

Chapter 16

Pelted by driving rain, Thunder Hawk stood among the blackened ruins of his roofless cabin and stared down dazedly at the charred remains of his wife and the mixed-blood woman. A thoroughly miserable Mike Mountain Bull stood a little way behind him, shifting his weight uncomfortably from one foot to the other.

His head a dull ache from the gash along his temple where Strathman's bullet had grazed it, Thunder Hawk stood there a long time . . . silent . . . unmoving . . . only the rise and fall of his chest as he breathed betraying what otherwise might have been a wet, dripping, bronze statue. Then suddenly he lifted his eyes to the gray sky and let forth a great, long, ear-splitting howl that startled Mike Mountain Bull so badly that he almost jumped out of his moccasins.

Presently he searched through the ruins until he found an undamaged Hudson's Bay blanket, wrapped it carefully around his wife's corpse, and lifted it gently up in his arms. He turned around and stepped past Mike Mountain Bull, went through what had been the door, and walked toward the mountains.

Mike watched him until he could no longer see him in the rain.

When Thunder Hawk returned much later, Mike Mountain Bull was gone.

Thunder Hawk wasted no time. Soaking wet, he picked up his Winchester and made his way to the meadow where the band kept their horses. Selecting a long-legged sorrel that was sheltering among the birch trees, he slipped on a rawhide rein, threw on a blanket, and jumped up onto the animal's back.

If Thunder Hawk hadn't known the way to where he was going, the water-filled ruts made by the wheels of the miners' wagons would have shown him quite plainly. But Thunder Hawk didn't see the ruts—all he could see were his wife's face, the flames of his burning cabin, and two hated white men.

The rain had not abated when he passed the mixed-blood woman's cabin, and it was still raining just as heavily when he nosed the sorrel away from the trail and galloped it up the side of a mountain. He left the animal under a rock overhang and scrambled up crumbling rock walls until he was a hundred feet above the flat below, where he could see the dirty gray and black layout of the mining town beneath him. Almost half of it had burned and, despite the rain, the smell of smoke hung heavily.

Thunder Hawk didn't feel the cold and wet chilling him to the bone, nor did he feel hunger gnawing at his insides. He was too consumed by one thought— *revenge*!

When he reached a short plateau, covered by stunted pine and matted grass, he loped along until he found the mine directly below. Here he wiped the rain off his Winchester with a handful of pine needles and settled down to wait.

For a long time he watched. Then, not satisfied, he climbed down the shale-like rock until he was no more than fifty feet above the mine and watched further. The steady rain kept the miners indoors, but whenever he saw any movement below he tensed and lifted his rifle, squinting down the sights, only to lower the weapon again when he realized the person in his sights wasn't either of the two white men he sought.

Thunder Hawk intended killing the two mine leaders. He was well aware that it was against the law for man to kill man—what the redcoats called *murder* and that the penalty was hanging. Bitterly, Thunder Hawk reflected that law seemed only to apply to Indians. What happened to the white man who killed John Blue Sky? The white man's law said he was guilty of killing John Blue Sky, but they gave it another name and sent him to the big jail at the Stony Mountain. They had not hanged him. What would the law do about the killing of Thunder Hawk's wife, caused as much by the hands of those two white men as if they had struck her down directly? The white man's law would say it could not be proven. Well, they would answer to the law of Thunder Hawk! The law of the Great Spirit! The good law the Indians had lived by before the white-eyes came and made the Indian change his laws for those of the whites.

When he didn't see either Lasher or Strathman around the mine, Thunder Hawk left the shale-covered slope and made his way around to the mine company's offices. He had never spent much time in Coal City, regarding it as an evil place where his people were mistreated. He preferred to live the old Indian way and was as self-sufficient as possible, but whenever he needed white men's supplies such as bullets or perhaps a new rifle, he had traveled the extra distance to Fort Determination rather than the much shorter distance to the mining town. However, on the rare occasions that he had come to the mining town, his natural Indian's curiosity had made him observant enough to have seen that the big miner chief, Lash-*er*, was more likely to be at the mining company office, while his headman, Strathman, the white man who had led the miners to the Stoney village, spent much of his time at the mine. Yet, Thunder Hawk knew they were often together.

Finding a position from which he could see both doors to the mining company offices, Thunder Hawk settled down to watch and wait once more. The position into which he settled was a grassy bench about twenty-five feet above the offices, high enough to see the roofs of the squalid, gray and black town. The rain continued without letup and Thunder Hawk found shelter under a lone pine. Not that he needed shelter; quite the contrary, for shelter could lull him into a mental numbness as he watched, and he might then miss his quarry. He preferred to be uncomfortable and wet—and his senses as alert as those of a mountain lion. But he wanted to keep his Winchester dry.

As he waited, Thunder Hawk had ample opportunity to think. He needed to think, he had to prepare himself for the journey that would soon come, the journey that would take him beyond the Shining Mountains into the next world, where he would be reunited with his wife and the ancestral Stoney people of the past. In the next world, the Happy Hunting Ground, a better life awaited, where all the Great Spirit's creatures lived in perfect harmony, as they had before the coming of the white man. But before he departed on that journey he must first kill a white chief, for then he would cross over the Shining Mountains as a greater warrior. The bigger the chief he killed, the greater a warrior he would become. *Wapamathe!* The big chief Lash-*er* of the Diggers of the Black Stone had a thousand men, which made him a big chief. Besides, he had made war on the Stoney people, he and the tall one who was his headman, and they had killed Thunder Hawk's wife. They deserved to die!

The white man was wrong when he said the Stoneys did not belong in the mountains, that they should be back on the prairies, for it was Mother Earth who had called the Stoney people to the mountains in the first place. Life had been good to the northern Stoneys in the Valley of the Snake until the white men had come digging for the black rock. The Valley of the Snake had given the Stoneys everything, as Mother Earth had promised—lush green meadows for their horses; tall straight spruce trees for the bark teepees they lived in during the hot mountain summers, and logs for the houses they built for the cold winters; pure mountain water to keep them healthy and strong in both body and mind; special herbs and medicines to make them well when they fell sick; and moose, elk, deer, wild sheep, and goats for them to eat and from which to make their clothing.

It was the white man who—!

Thunder Hawk tensed! The door to Lash-*er's* building opened and a man stepped out. Pulling the Winchester into his shoulder, Thunder Hawk peered down the barrel. The man was wearing a long yellow coat, the kind white men wore to keep the rain off them, and he had a hat on his head, the wide brim covering his face so that Thunder Hawk could not see his features, but he was very tall and he carried one arm strangely, as a man would with a bullet in his shoulder. The Stoney chief knew he had to be Strathman, not Lash-*er*. He eased his grip on the Winchester, letting the barrel drop. It was Lash-*er* he wanted to kill first. Then he could kill this one. If he shot this one first, he might not get the opportunity to kill Lash-*er*, and he wanted Lash-*er*. He wanted them both, but he wanted Lash-*er* first. Lash-*er* was the cunning one, like the coyote.

Watching as the tall man in the long yellow coat walked along the street in the driving rain, Thunder Hawk waited until he disappeared among some dingy buildings that had not been touched by the fire. Then he gripped his Winchester, rose to his feet, and in a series of fast, low, crouchlike runs, made his way down the side of the mountain until he was on the flat. There he paused, looked around quickly, and darted toward the coal company's offices. He reached the side of the building next to a window and flattened his back against the wall. Not hearing any noise from within, he risked a quick look through the window. Almost immediately he saw Lasher, his back to the window, kneeling down beside a big iron safe. Thunder Hawk moved swiftly to the end of the building, turned the corner, and made for the door. He was about to open it when a shout stopped him.

"Hey, Indian! You with the rifle. Hold it right there!"

Whipping his head around, Thunder Hawk saw riding out of the rain toward him two men in long black waterproof slickers and dripping, wide-brimmed Stetsons.

"What're you doing sneaking around that building? You're Thunder Hawk, aren't you? We want to talk to you about—hey! Hold it!"

Thunder Hawk darted to the far corner of the building and disappeared around the corner. The two Mounties spurred their horses after him. Thunder Hawk tore along the side of the building and raced over behind the stables. Then he paused—there was no place to go. The company's offices were separate from the rest of the town. The nearest buildings were seventy yards away, while the protective cover of a few stunted trees alongside the foot of the mountains was over a hundred. The police would have him before he could cover a quarter of the distance. They would lock him up for shooting those white miners. And then they would hang him! He would never cross the Shining Mountains to the Happy Hunting Grounds that way.

Thunder Hawk would not allow the yellow-legs to take him!

The two Mounties had split up and Thunder Hawk could hear the noises of their horses' hoofs splashing over the waterlogged ground as they came around the stables from either side. One, he could hear, was closer than the other. The Indian gripped his Winchester and tensed.

The Mountie swung wide. He had expected to see the Indian darting toward the trees, and when he didn't he guessed he was waiting around the rear of the stables, and had swung wide so as not to be caught off guard. But he hadn't expected the Indian to act with such speed.

A blur of buckskin hurtled toward horse and rider. It startled the horse, and as the animal veered and momentarily diverted the constable's attention, Thunder Hawk struck them both, his outstretched arms holding his Winchester out in front of him like a staff, slamming the constable clean out of the saddle.

A shout from behind him told Thunder Hawk the other Mountie had rounded the stables from the other side. Like a flash the Indian grabbled the first horse's reins with one hand, whirled around, and with his free hand pointed his rifle and fired over the ears of the oncoming second horse. Moving so fast the eye could hardly keep up, Thunder Hawk levered his Winchester twice and fired two more shots over the second horse's ears. The frightened animal broke its gallop and reared up on its hind legs, its front legs pawing the rain in front of it. A fourth shot from the rifle, now almost in the horse's face, sent it bolting headlong into the town, the rider shouting a string of oaths as he tried to stop it.

The shooting had startled the horse Thunder Hawk held, and he jerked hard on its reins to keep it from bolting also. The unsaddled Mountie, the back of his rain slicker covered in slimy coal-dust-coated gravel, had just struggled to his feet. Thunder Hawk whirled and struck him full in the chest with a hard, moccasined foot that sent him sprawling with a splashlike

204

slap onto the sloppy black ground again. The next instant the Stoney chief threw himself up into the saddle and kicked the horse into a full-length gallop away from the coal-mining town. The Mountie struggled to his feet a second time, his hand clawing at the front buttons of his burdensome slicker, trying to reach the revolver holstered underneath. By the time he got it out, his horse and Thunder Hawk had disappeared into the enveloping rain.

Chapter 17

By Monday the skies over the eastern ranges of the Rocky Mountains were a brilliant blue, and everywhere there was that smell of freshness that follows a good rain. A covering of fresh snow lay on the mountaintops, dazzlingly white on the red rock slopes of Mount Queen Victoria and Mount MacDonald.

All of Fort Determination's small population knew of the events that had taken place at Coal City and the Valley of the Snake on Saturday night and Sunday.

"Those damn miners should leave the Indians alone," was Tom Barr's unequivocal comment over Monday morning's breakfast at the Northern Lights.

"Leave them alone!" retorted Mr. Grant, the bank manager. "After they tried to burn down Black Town?"

"Pshaw!" Tom Barr grunted. "Probably some drunken miner knocked over his own coal-oil lamp."

"And Thunder Hawk shooting those miners!

That's manslaughter, you know."

"Of course I know! I'm a justice of the peace, aren't I? Anyway, what would you expect him to do? Light their bloody torches for them?"

Up at the North-West Mounted Police post, Sergeant O'Reilly would have sympathized with Tom Barr's comments, but he knew it wasn't as simple as that. He had on the desk in front of him a handwritten statement a constable had taken from Vince Strathman swearing that he had seen Thunder Hawk shoot down four unarmed men, and the constable's report that he had observed Thunder Hawk armed with a rifle sneaking around the offices of the Pacific & Western Coal Company at Coal City, that Thunder Hawk had assaulted a North-West Mounted Police constable, fired at another, and stole a police horse.

Actually, the whole damned thing made O'Reilly fume. A murder had been committed at Coal City, as well as arson and an alleged break-in. Then a mob of vengeance-seeking miners had marched on the Stoney village at the entrance to the Valley of the Snake and burned half of it down. These were serious crimes that warranted the attention of an experienced investigator. Instead there were two green constables stumbling around Coal City like two lambs in a wolves' den listening to Vince Strathman and Lasher's miners telling them what were just as likely a string of lies; two green constables who not only let a suspected murderer slip through their hands but allowed him to steal one of their horses after he assaulted one of them and stampeded the other's mount with him still on it, galloping all the way along Coal City's main street, much to the amusement of some drunken miners who hadn't had enough sense to get in out of the rain. And here was he, Sergeant Hugh O'Reilly, an experienced NCO, confined to the post by the orders of an incompetent officer who didn't have the seasoning to command a police post.

It took another two days of investigations for the rest of the story to come out. The death of Thunder Hawk's wife and Simone Laboucan in the burning cabin, and the brutal beating of several Indians by the miners. The police recovered their horse, but Thunder Hawk had disappeared and the investigating constables encountered a wall of silence in the Stoney village. Which hardly surprised O'Reilly, seeing that the barracks guardroom contained Little Beaver, the Stoney suspected of murdering Fisher.

"I suppose you yellow-legs will be laying charges against Thunder Hawk," Tom Barr said to O'Reilly when he came up to the guardroom to remand Little Beaver on a charge of murder.

"Yes," O'Reilly replied.

"What'll the charges be?"

"Murder."

Tom Barr's watery blue eyes looked at the Mountie for a long moment. "Murder, eh?"

O'Reilly didn't answer.

"That's a bit rough, isn't it, Hughie . . . under the circumstances?"

Pulling his pipe out of his breeches pocket, O'Reilly started filling it from a worn tobacco pouch. "A man intentionally kills another man, that's murder—unless he's got a hell of a good reason."

"A hell of a good reason!" Tom Barr exploded. "Good God, Hughie! What the hell do you think he had? A gang of lawless, torch-carrying ruffians goes marching on his village in the middle of the night and tries to burn it down! In his moccasins, I'd have done the same thing. It's Strathman and those damn miners you should be laying charges against, not Thunder Hawk. What about murder charges against whoever set his cabin alight?"

"When we find enough evidence, we'll do that."

"Evidence—*hell*! Based on the evidence, I won't be accepting any murder charges against Thunder Hawk. You'll have to find yourself another JP. For that matter, I'm not very happy about this Indian you've got in your guardroom now. All you've got is that rifle that was found beside him."

"A brand-new Winchester exactly the same as the ones the company store was selling. And it was found in his hands, Tom, not beside him. He was carrying it."

"Pshw! So says Lasher, Strathman, and a handful of their mine workers. I wouldn't believe that lot no matter how many oaths they took. Murder isn't the trade of those Stoneys, and neither is stealing. I don't believe any Indian broke into the company store. More likely it was some miner with a grudge against the company, and when Fisher caught him at it, he killed him. There's some bad characters among them miners, Hughie. It's all too easy to blame things on a drunk Indian. That's what they tried with Johnny Blue Sky's death at the hands of Big Zeke Benders."

O'Reilly struck a match and held it to his pipe. Clouds of blue smoke rolled toward the ceiling. When he had the pipe burning to his satisfaction, he dropped the blackened match stick into a tin ashtray.

"We have to lay charges against Thunder Hawk, Tom. I don't have the power to decide his guilt or innocence. No policeman does. Neither do you. But I know this—no court in the country would convict him of murder, under the circumstances. The Crown wouldn't even ask for a reduction to manslaughter. He'd walk out of court a free man. Call it a formality, if you like. But he has to be charged to be cleared. That's the law."

Tom Barr snorted. "Try and explain that to him beforehand. All he'll understand is he's locked up with the threat of a rope around his neck."

"Well, what would you suggest?" asked O'Reilly, a note of exasperation creeping into his voice.

The Hudson's Bay man fixed his watery blue eyes on O'Reilly again. "You won't appreciate me tellin' you how to do your job, Hughie. You never do, and maybe I shouldn't do it, but I will tell you this. If you handle this the wrong way, you'll have another Almighty Voice affair on your hands."

After Tom Barr left, O'Reilly realized the trader was right. Nevertheless, Thunder Hawk had to be brought before a court of justice. There was no question about that, otherwise he would spend the rest of his days as a fugitive-at-large dodging the police, or would be killed in a bloody clash of arms with the forces of law and order as had happened to Almighty Voice six years earlier. Thunder Hawk deserved better than that.

It had become Inspector Kerr's habit to take a horse out for a ride every morning—in an effort to improve his horsemanship, O'Reilly presumed—and when he returned to the post at eleven o'clock that

210

morning, O'Reilly had laid on his desk the reports on the Coal City and Snake Valley affairs, as the inspector had instructed. It therefore came as no surprise to O'Reilly when Inspector Kerr called him into his office that afternoon, after he had had time to read them.

"Draw up charges against Thunder Hawk, Sergeant. Then obtain a warrant for his arrest."

O'Reilly stood in front of the desk, waiting for the officer to continue. When he didn't, O'Reilly remained. Inspector Kerr wrote a few lines on the bottom of the last page of the report, put down his pen and looked up.

"Well, Sergeant?"

"The warrant to arrest Thunder Hawk . . . ?"

"What about it? I'll send Constables Green and Mardling to execute it."

"Thunder Hawk is no ordinary Indian. He's a Stoney warrior. Green and Mardling don't have the experience to bring him in."

"Then, Corporal Rogers can execute it when he returns off patrol."

"That won't be for another two weeks. Thunder Hawk could be anywhere by then."

Inspector Kerr leaned back in his chair and regarded O'Reilly coldly. An amused smirk crept across the officer's face. "Are you inferring that I should lift your arrest so you can go over to the Valley of the Snake and apprehend him?"

O'Reilly shook his head. "No, I'm not inferring that. Under open arrest I can be detailed for normal police duties as you see fit. But Thunder Hawk should be brought in right away. If we waste time he might be forced into a life of crime. In his grief over the death of his wife at the hands of white men, he could be tempted to seek revenge. I think that's why he was sneaking around the coal company's offices when Green and Mardling saw him on Sunday. He knows very well that Strathman led those miners—"

Inspector Kerr interrupted. "There's no evidence that Mr. Strathman led the miners out to the Valley of the Snake. I presume that's what you were going to say, that he did."

"There's no doubt in my mind that Strathman led them, put up to it by Lasher. And Thunder Hawk will see it that way. He may not connect Lasher—"

"Preposterous!" Inspector Kerr interrupted again. "Absolutely preposterous!"

"Our responsibility is to prevent the commission of an offense," O'Reilly argued without raising his voice, "as much as it is to detect crime and bring the perpetrators to justice. If Thunder Hawk guns down Strathman or any of the miners now, he'll be guilty of murder and will hang. As things stand at present, he has a valid excuse for what he's done and he'll be acquitted. We must prevent him from doing anything foolish or from trying to take the law into his own hands—and we must do it right away."

The smirk hadn't quite left the inspector's face. "A noble speech, Sergeant. Quite eloquent for an NCO. However, despite the fact that I have not been in the Mounted Police as long as you, I am sufficiently knowledgeable on the role and function of a police force. I am not prepared to vary my philosophy on the duties and responsibilities of sergeants on detachment, and certainly not for the sake of some Indian who chooses not to abide by the laws of the British Crown. You attempted to vary it once, when you went after that lunatic on the other side of the mountain across the river. I won't allow you to vary it again."

O'Reilly's temper climbed. The inspector's superior manner irritated him, and he was becoming less and less inclined to accord him the deference and respect his rank entitled him to. "Why don't you want me off the post, Inspector? Not even to go down to the Northern Lights to eat. Is there something personal in all this? Are you afraid I might cut your time with Mrs. Merrill?"

Inspector Kerr straightened in his chair and his hands slammed down hard on the desk. The smirk completely vanished and his face turned white with rage. "Hold your tongue, Sergeant!" he shouted, glaring up at O'Reilly. "I've had just about enough of you!"

O'Reilly leaned forward over the desk and stared down hard at the blue-uniformed officer. "No, Inspector, it's *I* who've had enough! I've had enough of your dictatorial attitude and the way you've been running this post. You came here and told me about my shortcomings, but I don't think you're any improvement, and you've certainly knocked morale to rock-bottom. There's more to discipline than salutes and inspections. Discipline needs respect before it can work properly. The men jump for you because they're disciplined and they know they're expected to, but they don't respect you, and in a crunch that's what counts—as far as I'm concerned, *this* is the crunch! Now I'm going to saddle up and bring Thunder Hawk in, because if I don't no one else will, and this can't wait until Corporal Rogers gets back."

Leaning back off the desk, O'Reilly turned to leave, but Inspector Kerr jumped to his feet and stabbed the air with his forefinger. "I will not permit you to leave this post, Sergeant!"

O'Reilly glared at him. "Who's going to stop me? You? Baxter?"

The big sergeant turned his back on the inspector and stormed out of the office. As he strided angrily along the hallway and out of the building, Inspector Kerr's words trailed him. "If you leave this post I'll charge you with desertion!"

O'Reilly marched along the white-rock-bordered pathway to the barracks. Inside he threw his Stetson onto his bed and prepared for his ride to the Valley of the Snake, and wherever else he might have to go in pursuit of Thunder Hawk. First of all he pulled his dunnage bag from under his bed and withdrew two blankets, which he rolled into a long sausage shape inside a waterproof canvas groundsheet. He strapped this tightly so it would fit snugly behind the saddle. Then he packed shaving gear, spare clothing, and a pair of field glasses into one of his saddle wallets. Glancing briefly at his blue pea jacket hanging on a wall hook behind his bed, he thought about that fresh snow that had fallen on the mountain slopes during Sunday's rain. It was September now and you could never tell whether an early blizzard would strike the high country. Against that, he considered the extra weight the cold-weather coat would add to the load his horse would be carrying. He didn't expect to be gone more than eight or nine days, but . . . Reaching out, he took it from its hanger and quickly folded it into his other saddle wallet. Next he exchanged his scarlet tunic for a brown duck patrol jacket and buckled on his sidearms. Finally he jammed his Stetson on his head and left the barracks building, carrying bedroll and saddle wallets as well as Winchester and bandolier.

From the barracks building O'Reilly went to the stores building at the far end of the grass parade ground, where he broke out rations for ten days, filling whatever space he had left in his saddle wallets. Then he marched over to the stables and saddled his horse. He was just about to lead the dark bay out when Constable Baxter appeared in the doorway. Baxter wore sidearms, something he hadn't ordinarily been doing since his appointment as the inspector's orderly.

O'Reilly threw a threatening look at the constable. "What do you want, Baxter?"

Baxter fidgeted nervously with his belt buckle. "Inspector Kerr ordered me to . . . er . . ."

"To put me under close arrest?"O'Reilly finished for him.

Baxter nodded. "If you try to leave the post."

O'Reilly's big black moustache bristled straight out. "Well, you go back and tell that tin soldier to read the blue bible again. If he wants me under arrest, he better try doing it himself. Now get the hell out of my way!"

Baxter quickly stepped aside. O'Reilly led his horse from the stables and swung up into the saddle. Gathering his reins, he rode out of the fenced parade ground and beyond the bounds of the police post. Trotting down toward the settlement he glimpsed out of the corner of his eye Inspector Kerr's blue uniform in the doorway of the detachment building, but he wouldn't give the officer the satisfaction of seeing him look over. O'Reilly simply ignored him and rode on.

Outside the Hudson's Bay store, O'Reilly reined to and dismounted. He found Tom Barr inside behind his counter. Surprise covered the white-haired trader's face when he looked up from his books to see O'Reilly, not only off the post, but dressed in full service order.

"What the b'Jesus—"

O'Reilly didn't let him finish. "Where do you think Thunder Hawk is likely to be, Tom?"

Tom Barr eyed the Mountie levelly. "Probably the Bear's Teeth ranges. You goin' to bring him in?"

"I have to. It's the only way. It'll be best for him."

The trader nodded slowly. "I guess you're right. I'm glad it's you and not one of them green young constables, but I'm surprised that inspector of yours is lettin' you go."

"He's not," O'Reilly replied matter-of-factly. "This is my idea. He threatened to charge me with desertion."

Tom Barr sucked in his breath. "Desertion? That's a hell of a threat."

"It's not a threat. He means it. Anyway, I don't want to waste time talking about him. If I can't find Thunder Hawk in the Bear's Teeth, where's he likely to go?"

Scratching the back of his head, Tom Barr looked at the floor. "The Shining Mountains, I guess."

"The Shining Mountains? I've never heard of them."

"When the sun sets behind the mountains, just as

it's goin' down. West of wherever a Stoney happens to be. They reckon that's the way to the Happy Hunting Grounds. But you'd be out of the Territories then and into British Columbia. The Continental Divide's only an arrow's flight from the Bear's Teeth. You yellow-legs don't have jurisdiction in British Columbia."

"Then, I'll have to catch him before he gets that far. Thanks, Tom."

O'Reilly turned and went back outside. Thrusting his foot into a stirrup he paused for a moment, looking across his saddle at the Northern Lights Hotel across the street, wondering whether he should go over and say good-bye to Catherine Merrill. He decided against it, swung himself up into the saddle, and was just about to ride off when she appeared at the door and called his name.

O'Reilly wheeled and walked his horse across the street. "Afternoon, ma'am," he said, touching his Stetson brim in salute.

As Catherine stepped out of the doorway, her womanly beauty drove a painful longing through O'Reilly as the warm afternoon sun beamed down, highlighting the rich red of her long, neatly coiled hair, which was swept up from her forehead and neck as always. She moved with a ladylike grace, and her green eyes shone as the suggestion of a smile lit up her face.

"Good afternoon, Sergeant. I haven't seen you since . . ." She left the rest unsaid.

"I know, ma'am. I'm still under arrest, although it's closer to desertion now."

She frowned. "I don't understand."

"It doesn't matter," O'Reilly replied, steeling himself against her charm. "I have to go now."

"Where are you going? Tom Barr said you might go after Thunder Hawk."

"That's right."

Concern leaped into Catherine's eyes. "He might kill you. Tom said he won't allow himself to be taken."

O'Reilly's face showed no emotion. "I've been shot at before—by marksmen as good as Thunder Hawk."

"When will you be back . . . if . . ."

"I don't know. However long it takes to find him."

"Do you think he really shot those miners?"

"There's not much doubt about that, ma'am. The point is, he had the right to, under the circumstances. He was protecting his village and his people. But he has to be brought before the courts to answer to charges. There, once the circumstances are given to a jury, he's bound to be acquitted. He has to be brought before the courts to be cleared, though. That's the judicial system."

Hope sprang onto her face. "Then, wouldn't it be simpler for him to give himself up? There's no need for him to resist."

"Thunder Hawk won't see it like that. Indians don't like losing their freedom to sit in jail, not even for a short while. There's been two or three of them who died in the Manitoba Penitentiary at Stoney Mountain. They died of tuberculosis, which they had when they went in there, but the Indians think the government killed them, or that the place is infested with evil spirits. Stories like that spread wide via the moccasin telegraph."

Eager to be off, O'Reilly's dark bay tossed its head and stamped a hoof. As he leaned forward in his saddle to pat the animal on the neck, O'Reilly glanced up the street. From the North-West Mounted Police post he saw Inspector Kerr, cap on his head and riding crop in his hand, marching down toward them. Anticipating trouble, O'Reilly watched for several seconds, until Catherine followed the direction of his stare.

Impulsively O'Reilly turned to look at Catherine again, questions in his dark eyes. "What do you see in him?" he found himself asking before he realized it.

Her green eyes widened in surprise. "See in him? Inspector Kerr?"

Pain on his face, O'Reilly nodded. "Yes."

Understanding at last, Catherine smiled, almost laughed. O'Reilly's instant reaction was one of hurt, for he thought she was laughing at him. Then he realized she was not.

"Oh, Hugh O'Reilly!" Catherine laughed sweetly, tears forming in her eyes. "So that's it."

"That's what?" O'Reilly asked urgently, the inspector drawing nearer.

"You think Inspector Kerr means something to me? You really do."

"Well, doesn't he? I mean . . . he's been visiting you almost every day."

"That doesn't mean I'm interested in him. I'm not, and I never have been."

"But you've been receiving him," O'Reilly blurted quickly.

"I've had no reason not to. He's been positively charming and so gallant, but that's not to say I'm fond of him."

"But—"

"You don't understand women, do you, Hugh?"

He like her calling him *Hugh*. It was like music in his ears. He wanted to hear her call him that again.

"When a man showers compliments on a woman," Catherine said gently, "as Inspector Kerr has, with such charm and polished manners, it goes to a woman's head, I suppose. I've not had that since the days when Carl was courting me. It was rather nice to have had it again." She paused, dropping her eyes to the ground. "I would have been much happier if it had been you showering me so, Hugh."

"You would?"

Her eyes met his and she smiled. "Of course."

Suddenly O'Reilly didn't want to go chasing Thunder Hawk. He would rather have stayed talking to Catherine. He didn't want to leave here ever again, not leave this very spot.

But he had to, for Inspector Kerr was now so close that O'Reilly could hear the *thud thud* of his riding boots on the soft ground, the light tinkle of his spurs, the creak of his Sam Browne leather.

"Catherine," O'Reilly said, calling her by her Christian name for the first time, and the same feeling passed through Catherine at the sound of her name on Hugh's lips. "I have to go now, but I'll be back. Will you wait for me?"

She smiled. "Of course I will, Hugh. I've been waiting for you these past two years. I can wait a little longer. But please be careful. Come back to me safely."

He wanted to jump down out of the saddle and sweep her up into his arms. But then a sharp voice barked out.

"Sergeant! I'm giving you one more chance to come to your senses. Return to the post immediately and I will forget this latest instance of disobedience. Defy me and I will press charges to the utmost, including desertion—and you know the statutory penalty for that. If you ride out of Fort Determination, I promise I'll see you go to prison!"

Chapter 18

Right in the middle of a thick stand of pine and spruce on a grassy plateau just below the highest peak of the Bear's Teeth, Thunder Hawk had erected his teepee. He had chosen this spot well, for the teepee couldn't be seen unless one stumbled onto it. In true Stoney warrior manner, Thunder Hawk had made sure no one would get near him without him becoming aware of it. He did not expect visitors, but he would not be caught off-guard.

From no more than a quarter of a mile away he could look down on the Valley of the Snake far below and see the silver ribbon of the river winding its way southeastward, looking very much like the long reptile after which it was named. Only one trail led up from the valley, and it had taken him the best part of the day to climb up it. Therefore, if anyone were to come looking for him, he would see them coming long before they would see him. He did not expect anyone to come seeking him. Not even the police, who wanted to lock him up. They would come to the village, but not up to the Bear's Teeth, for who of the Stoney people would tell them where to look? More likely one of his own people might follow him. Mike Mountain Bull, for instance, who was anxious to make amends. But at this time Thunder Hawk had neither the desire nor the patience to care about soothing Mike Mountain Bull's conscience. He would forgive when he was ready, but at the moment he sought solitude.

Thunder Hawk had come to the Bear's Teeth to pray to the Great Spirit for wisdom and guidance, for this was his vision quest. He had set up his teepee in the form of a sacred lodge, except that he had had to use spruce instead of willow for its frame, denying it the rounded top that distinguished a sacred lodge. He had peeled the bark off the spruce trees and laid it over the teepee's tanned skins, then had overlaid that with spruce boughs. Once that was done, Thunder Hawk had spent an entire day gathering the most perfectly round rocks he could find for the sacred fire he would light the next day, his fourth in his mountain solitude. Already he had fasted for three days and two nights. Tomorrow he would be ready to pray to *Waka Taga*.

The mountains were sacred to the Stoneys, for the great solid masses of rock stood firm and immovable. Thunder Hawk strived to purify his thoughts so they would be as firm as the mountains. When he prayed, *Waka Taga* would reveal to him a vision, showing the way to the Shining Mountains. Once he arrived there, Thunder Hawk would meet his tribal ancestors and rejoin his beloved wife.

So it was, on the fourth day, after three days and three nights of fasting, Thunder Hawk rubbed together two wood sticks to provide the spark that would light the sacred fire. Once the fire was burning he added sweet grass and cedar needles, then laid over the flames four boughs, each pointing to one of the four corners of the universe. Next he produced from a richly decorated skin bag a long, carved pipe. Putting the stem into his mouth he pulled a burning twig from the fire and held it over the pipe's bowl while he puffed until clouds of smoke rewarded his efforts.

As smoke from the sacred fire rose to the blue sky, Thunder Hawk pointed the ceremonial pipe first in the direction from where the sun had risen that morning, then to the south, then to where the sun would touch the snow-topped mountains at the end of the day, and finally he pointed the stem to the north.

After that he prayed.

Down along the Snake River far below, Sergeant O'Reilly sat his saddle and studied through field glasses the long, thin column of smoke rising from Thunder Hawk's sacred fire.

Finding the trail, O'Reilly rode up toward the Bear's Teeth, but the sun sank behind the western ranges before he was more than halfway to Thunder Hawk's grassy plateau, forcing him to camp for the night.

Thunder Hawk did not see the Mountie's approach, for he had prayed all day.

At first light O'Reilly resumed his ascent to Thunder Hawk's plateau. The same time, Thunder Hawk left his sacred lodge to climb the highest peak of the Bear's Teeth. If *Waka Taga* answered his prayers, up there would be revealed to him the vision he sought.

The September sun was directly overhead when O'Reilly reached the plateau. It took him an hour to find Thunder Hawk's sacred lodge, after his dark bay planted a hoof down firmly on a dry twig that snapped with a loud, pistol-like crack that alerted O'Reilly to the fact that it had been put there for that purpose. When he knelt down beside the fireplace and felt the rocks, he knew Thunder Hawk had left hours before.

O'Reilly tracked Thunder Hawk through the trees until he emerged on the other side, where he swept the plateau ahead through his glasses, seeing nothing but wind-blown grass and beyond it the Bear's Teeth.

Thunder Hawk had already reached the foot of the long, jagged piece of rock that looked like a giant grizzly bear's tooth thrust up to the sky. It was the highest of six such peaks, collectively known as the Bear's Teeth. Leaving his sorrel hobbled, he took only his decorated skin bag, which he slung over his shoulder, and started climbing. He reached the snow-covered top an hour before sunset and stood in his soaked moccasins, gazing in wonder at the sea of white-mantled peaks of the endless mountain ranges to the west, slowly hueing to pink and then rose—a glistening, shining rose as the sun dipped to begin its spectacular slide behind them.

Several miles away O'Reilly sat his saddle once more peering through glasses at the country ahead, looking for campfire smoke. Having no reason to think Thunder Hawk would climb up the rock, O'Reilly didn't scan the tallest of the Bear's Teeth. For several minutes, though, he held his binoculars on the mountains to the west, shining pink as the sun started to go down behind them, fascinated by their incredible grandeur and majesty.

Up on the peak, Thunder Hawk saw not only the Shining Mountains. He saw the vision he sought from *Waka Taga*, but disappointingly the vision did not reveal to him the way to the Shining Mountains. Instead it showed Lasher, Strathman, and a horde of white men desecrating the Stoney's sacred tribal lands in a scrambling search for shining, silver rocks.

And just before the sun went down behind the Bear's Teeth, it caught the lenses of O'Reilly's field glasses. Thunder Hawk spotted that brief flash of reflected light.

Chapter 19

Thunder Hawk spent a long, cold night on the rocky tooth. He had dallied too long up there in the first place, so intensely had the sight of the beauty of the Shining Mountains gripped him. Even the stabbing urgency of the remembered image of reflected sunlight off a white man's looking-glass hadn't been enough to compel him to tackle the entire descent in darkness. He had gone a good way down, until a wet moccasin slipped on a wind-smoothed rock and almost sent him hurtling to his death. Fortunately he found a recess under a craggy overhang that at least kept the wind off him. Only his Indian's ability to push the physical world away while he concentrated on an inner life of tribal and ancestral imagery enabled him to stoically endure the sub-zero night.

The moment the newly rising sun's light sent streaks of crimson across the eastern sky, Thunder Hawk painfully massaged the real world into his cold-stiffened limbs and muscles before attempting the final descent. The shadows on the plateau below were too deep for him to see whether the owner of the white man's looking-glass was down there at the base of the tooth waiting for him. That the white man was a policeman, Thunder Hawk had no doubt. A policeman had come to take him away and lock him up in jail. And then hang him!

A white man's rope was not the way to the Shining Mountains. A rope around Thunder Hawk's neck would imprison his spirit inside him forever, and it would lie within his dead, rotting body in a box buried beneath a man's height of stone and dirt.

Thunder Hawk was determined that no rope would ever circle his neck!

O'Reilly broke camp at dawn, after taking the time to eat a quick breakfast. Anxious to catch up to the Stoney chief, he wouldn't have camped at all but for the fact that he couldn't track the Indian in the dark. It was, therefore, a disappointment to reach the spot where Thunder Hawk's sorrel had grazed during the night and find both horse and rider gone. Even so, the Mountie drew heart from the realization that his man was little more than an hour ahead. With certainty, he would have him in custody by nightfall, perhaps even by midday.

If O'Reilly had known Thunder Hawk's run-down condition, weakened by five days and nights of fasting and praying, and a night of exposure in below-zero temperatures, he would have been even more convinced that he would have his man within hours. However, he was dealing with a Stoney warrior in the best traditions of the *Wapamathe*.

Legging the dark bay into a canter, O'Reilly followed Thunder Hawk's track across the grassy plateau, leaving the high, snow-covered rocky tooth behind. After four miles the plateau dipped as the mountain slanted to its western slope, and O'Reilly impatiently quickened his horse's pace. Then two miles further on he had to rein the dark bay back to a walk as the grassy plateau gave way to a wide stretch of gray rock and broken ledges.

"God damn it!" he cursed, eyes narrowing as they searched the rock for the sorrel's track, knowing he wouldn't find any because the Indian horse was unshod. Seeing the danger of his quarry slipping away, O'Reilly legged the dark bay on again. He had no choice but to continue in the same direction he had been going, hoping that the rocky surface underfoot would give way to soft ground again. But a mile further on, it had not done so, and O'Reilly reined to and glassed the terrain in front of him. All he could see was more rock and the mountain slope gradually dropping away. Over to his left were heavy drifts of snow, deposited on the windward side of the mountain during the storm several days ago. He could feel the chill of it as the wind whistled over him with gusts that nearly blew his hat off his head. At least he knew Thunder Hawk hadn't gone that way.

Putting the field glasses back into his saddle wallet, O'Reilly rode on once more. The further he rode the steeper became the rate of descent until finally he found himself at the edge of a rocky ledge overlooking the western side of the mountain, where the slope dropped sharply. Below, he could see green sweeps of pine and spruce lining the mountain's sides, with light brown patches here and there where rockslides had slashed all the timber in their path as they hurtled their way to the valley below. In the valley he could see a silver-blue ribbon of river, and beyond it the beautiful jade jewel of an alpine lake. Further on was a break in the mountain ranges, and he knew he was looking at the Continental Divide, which marked the end of Mounted Police jurisdiction. On the other side lay British Columbia.

But Thunder Hawk had dropped from sight. Had he fallen off the ledge? O'Reilly swung down from his saddle and stepped over as close to the edge of the rocky ledge as he dared. All he could see were rock and trees below. He walked along the edge of the ledge, first in one direction, then the other, his eyes searching for any sign of fresh breakage or frantic scuffing . . . anything to indicate a fall. However, he saw no such thing.

Puzzled, O'Reilly reached into his saddle wallet and pulled out his field glasses again. Holding them to his eyes he carefully glassed the slopes below, failing to see how anything, especially a man on a horse, could negotiate them. But Thunder Hawk had vanished! Yet there was no way he could have done so without falling over the edge. There was just the rocky ledge— then nothing! Not until the point-topped pine trees at least two hundred feet below. At that moment a prickly feeling crawled over O'Reilly. Could Thunder Hawk have somehow gotten around behind him? Quickly the Mountie spun around, looking all about. Nothing! Nothing except himself, his horse, and the howling wind. It was eerie.

O'Reilly was about to climb back up into his saddle

when his naked eye caught a flicker of movement down along the tree line below. Whipping up the glasses he tried to find the spot, creeping them in an ever-widening, circular movement . . . *There it was!* A blur of tawny brown. An animal—or an Indian? Slowly O'Reilly twisted the focus wheel . . . the image blurred, then sharpened. There it was again—a movement of yellow this time . . . yes, a sorrel horse with a buckskin-clad Indian on its back. Thunder Hawk! But how the hell could he have gotten down there?

Impatiently O'Reilly backtrailed the glasses along behind Thunder Hawk, trying to find the way the Stoney had taken to get down there. There it was . . . an almost-imperceptible path angling away from the rocky ledge at about twenty-five degrees leading from a fold in the side of the mountain where two sections of rock formed an inverted corner. Thunder Hawk must have known it was there. He had ridden directly for it.

Springing back up into the saddle, O'Reilly reined the dark bay along the ledge toward the commencement of the trail Thunder Hawk had taken. It took him several minutes to reach it, and once he swung over the ledge and guided his horse downward he realized the trail was none too wide. The drop to the valley below almost made his head swim. It had its effect on the bay too, for the horse whinnied nervously and picked its way uneasily. Shortening his reins, O'Reilly legged it on.

Half a mile down the trail narrowed alarmingly, where it became less than two feet wide. Freshly turned rock showed O'Reilly that part of it had crumbled with the passage of Thunder Hawk's sorrel.

How much more of it would be like that?

O'Reilly climbed down from the saddle and edged carefully past the dark bay until his spurred boots were on the narrowed portion of the trail. As he took another step forward and put down his weight, small rocks rolled away from underneath him, tumbling all the way down the steep cliff-face. He stepped back quickly.

For a moment he stood studying the trail ahead. The narrow portion wasn't long . . . seven or eight feet, then it widened again. If he could get past that . . .

Without further delay, O'Reilly moved back to his horse. Grasping the reins immediately below the bit with his right hand and stroking the bay's neck with his left, he talked reassuringly to the animal as he carefully walked it backward along the mountain trail for some thirty feet. Then he pulled himself back up into the saddle, shortened his reins, and jabbed the bay's side with his spurs.

"Come on, boy—walk—trot—*canterrr*! Quickly!"

The bay started off at a brisk trot and then, in response to its rider's leg and rein movement, stretched into a canter. *"Up!"* O'Reilly shouted and the horse gathered itself, bunched its muscles, and arced into the air, soaring over the narrow portion of the trail and landing firmly on the wider ground on the far side.

"Good boy," O'Reilly smiled, leaning forward and patting the horse's neck affectionately. "Good boy, indeed. Come on, now. The rest of the way should be easy."

It took all morning to reach the valley below, and

then O'Reilly paused only long enough to eat a hasty lunch and rest his horse briefly. Following that he resumed the pursuit. He couldn't afford to let Thunder Hawk lengthen the distance between them any further. The British Columbia border was only twenty miles away and he had to catch Thunder Hawk before then.

There was only one trail along the valley and it led westward. The silver-blue river he had seen from up on the Bear's Teeth bounded it on one side, and a treed mountain slope on the other. The ground was soft and the Mountie had no trouble following Thunder Hawk's track. O'Reilly could track with the best of white men, and as well as many Indians, which wasn't a bad feat for a man who had grown up in Halifax with the smell of salt air in his nostrils. While riding with Sergeant Mike Hannan's Flying Patrol down in the Fort MacLeod country, O'Reilly had befriended a wild young Blood buck named Porcupine Quill, who had taught him to track. Chasing Cree war parties and white cattle-rustlers had given him the opportunity to develop his newfound skill, and again years later when fighting Boer commandos on the South African veldt.

From time to time O'Reilly swept the trail ahead with his field glasses, searching for Thunder Hawk. But the valley angled around from northwest to west, with the tree line closely paralleling the trail, and he couldn't narrow the distance enough to line up the Stoney chief in his glasses. The sorrel was a good horse with lots of endurance. It also carried less weight—no saddle, no wallets, no field service gear. O'Reilly regretted having taken the extra weight of his pea jacket, ammunition bandolier, and even so much rations . . . although when he caught Thunder Hawk and took him back, he'd have to feed two mouths.

Even after the sun went down, O'Reilly pushed on, anxious to overtake Thunder Hawk before he reached the Continental Divide. A full moon rode the milky black sky and O'Reilly could see the trail well enough, but by midnight he had to stop. The dark bay was tiring.

Reluctantly O'Reilly reined to and dismounted. As he took the saddle off his horse, he resolved to sleep only briefly and to be back on Thunder Hawk's trail before first light in the morning.

Thunder Hawk woke with a start!

The sun was already too high, even though it was not yet above the treetops. Drained by fatigue following five days without food, his cold, cramped night on the peak of the Bear's Teeth, and a painful, chest-rasping cough, he had slept too long.

However, it was not the sun that had woke him. It was something else. Then he realized what it was. He heard—no, *felt*, a drumming in the ground. Rolling quickly from a bed he'd made of pine boughs, he darted through knee-high grass to the trail and pressed his ear to the ground. He couldn't hear it— the noise of the rushing river was too loud—but he could feel the vibration of drumming hoofs coming along the trail. The policeman! He was coming.

Springing to his feet, Thunder Hawk ran back to his pine-bough bed and quickly pulled it deeper into the trees to make sure it couldn't be seen from the trail. Then he snatched the sorrel's rawhide headrope and led the horse back into the trees thirty yards from a solitary, lopsided pine standing apart from the other trees. He was just in time, for a moment later yellow-striped blue breeches, brass-buttoned brown jacket, and Stetson hat cantered into view around the bend.

Dropping flat onto his belly among the underbrush at the edge of the trees, Thunder Hawk propped his left elbow on the ground in front of him and slid forward his rifle. He cocked the action and squinted down the barrel until he had the Mountie's chest in his sights. Then he curled his finger around the trigger.

At this range he couldn't miss.

All he had to do was squeeze . . . then ride off to the sanctuary of the mountains across the Divide. No one would know he had killed a policeman. There was no one else around within thirty miles; apart from his own people in their village along the Snake, there was no one within sixty miles. No one would know.

As the policeman cantered past the solitary pine with the lopsided branches, Thunder Hawk's finger tightened around the trigger.

O'Reilly pushed the dark bay hard. He kept expecting to sight his quarry around the next bend. And at each bend of the trail as it curved gradually around the side of the mountain he was disappointed. And increasingly mystified. He should have overtaken Thunder Hawk by now. Or at least narrowed the gap substantially. The Indian couldn't have ridden all night. Even an Indian like Thunder Hawk had to rest. Even the sorrel's stamina would have to give out if ridden nonstop like this.

O'Reilly was tempted to climb the side of the mountain to see what he could of the trail ahead. Thunder Hawk had to be somewhere around the next bend, not far ahead. But the Mountie dared not take the time.

If it weren't for the fact that he could see the sorrel's track plainly along the ground in front of him, O'Reilly would have wondered whether Thunder Hawk hadn't pulled off the trail and gone in a different direction. However, there was nowhere else to go—just the river on one side and the tree-covered slope on the other, which led nowhere but up the side of the mountain.

O'Reilly's attention was only momentarily drawn to the lopsided pine, with half its branches on one side missing. He wouldn't have noticed it if it hadn't been standing out by itself. He guessed that a brown or black bear had ripped off the missing branches in a fit of temper. Once it passed from his line of vision, it was gone from his mind.

It passed through O'Reilly's mind, too, that he and Thunder Hawk were the only humans around. Fort Determination would be some seventy trail miles away, although probably only thirty as the eagle flew. The trail he followed had been made by animals— mostly elk herds—not horses or humans. The further toward the Continental Divide the trail led, the further from habitation he and Thunder Hawk would be.

Thunder Hawk did not exert that final pound or

two of pressure that would have sent a .45 caliber bullet smashing into O'Reilly's chest. And even though the Indian swung the rifle around and kept it trained on the Mountie as his horse carried him by, Thunder Hawk still did not fire.

Instead, as soon as the Mountie disappeared around the next bend, Thunder Hawk was on his feet once more, unroped the rawhide muzzle around the sorrel's nose, and threw himself onto the animal's back. Urging it deeper into the trees, he went up the mountain slope at a near gallop. He had spotted something as he rode by last night, something that O'Reilly hadn't seen because of his preoccupation with keeping his eyes glued on Thunder Hawk's trail. Now he desperately hoped it would offer salvation. At least for the moment. If not, he might have to resort to his rifle yet.

The sorrel raced up through the trees, and after climbing hard for a hundred yards reached a ledge that had just barely been noticeable from the trail below. Thunder Hawk sprang down off the horse for a moment to give the animal a chance to get its breath while he quickly looked around to see where the ledge went. It ran the same direction as the trail. There was no point in following it back along the direction he had been riding, so he had no choice but to take it toward the Divide, hoping that both the ledge and the trees screening it from the trail below would hold out far enough for him to get past the Mountie without being seen.

Suddenly O'Reilly reined the dark bay to stop. He

had lost Thunder Hawk's track!

Swinging the bay around, he stared hard at the ground. After a moment he legged the horse back along the trail, a growing scowl twisting his rugged good looks.

Then he found it . . . the grass flattened a little here, and again there. The track was so faint he had to lean well over the side of his saddle to follow it. It led over to the pine trees and along beside them, paralleling the way he had just come. And the trail was old, several hours old. Thunder Hawk had pulled into the trees somewhere.

He located Thunder Hawk's pine-bough bed, saw the flattened grass where the Indian had lain with pointed rifle. Now excitement gripped the Mountie, for he knew Thunder Hawk was only minutes away. Eagerly he picked his way through the trees, following the sorrel's trail up the slope until he came to the ledge above. With a quick jab of his spurs, O'Reilly sent the dark bay thundering in pursuit.

Half a mile ahead, Thunder Hawk's plucky sorrel pounded along the ledge. He knew the policeman would not be far behind. He thought he might have to shoot the yellow-stripe yet. He thought of just how he would do this when his sorrel suddenly snorted and reared.

Thunder Hawk quickly saw what had frightened his horse. A grizzly sow was standing over the carcass of a mountain goat, and beside her were two cubs. She let out a bellow and stood up on her hind legs.

But she didn't charge.

Thunder Hawk sat the sorrel's back and watched the bear. She stared back at him through bright, buttonlike eyes. She was a good forty yards up the slope above the ledge, but Thunder Hawk knew he couldn't get past her. With a powerful downhill charge she would be onto him before he could make half the distance.

It was Stoney tribal lore that *Waka Taga*'s chosen people could talk to the animals of the forests and the birds of the sky as well as to the rocks and rivers. The animals and birds could tell the Stoneys of hidden truths, of approaching danger, and could help them. For they were all the Creator's creatures who lived together in harmony.

The greatest Stoney warriors could turn themselves into animals to fight their foes or elude their enemies. If Thunder Hawk could, he would turn himself into the hawk after which he was named, and fly away from the pursuing yellow-stripe. However, *Waka Taga* had not yet given him such power. Therefore, Thunder Hawk asked the mother grizzly to help him.

Mother Grizzly remained standing on her hind feet and looked at the Indian as he talked to her. When he had finished, she let out a bellow, dropped to her four paws, and turned back to the goat carcass.

Thunder Hawk rode by below.

O'Reilly galloped the dark bay as fast as he dared along the ledge. But when he saw the grizzly up on the slope, he jerked the horse back onto its haunches.

He had to move fast, for the grizzly saw him, reared on her hind legs, and let out a frightening bellow. The next instant she charged down at him like a shell from a twelve-pounder field gun.

Reining hard right, O'Reilly legged his horse furiously down off the ledge into the trees, choosing the slightly less dangerous alternative of pelting madly downhill through thick timber to remaining and being mauled to death by a ferocious grizzly.

Miraculously horse and rider reached the trail on the valley below without injury. O'Reilly was about to gallop the bay along the trail, to head Thunder Hawk off as the Indian came down from the ledge further on, when the grizzly, to the accompaniment of breaking timber and roaring bellows, smashed through the trees twenty yards in front of him and stood on her hind legs, blocking his way.

The bay pranced nervously and reared, forelegs pawing the air in front. O'Reilly fought to control him, at the same time keeping a wary eye on the grizzly. The bay danced sideways, tossing its head and swishing its tail, moving away from the grizzly. The grizzly roared and stood astride the trail, but made no effort to charge again. With some thirty yards separating them from the bellowing sow, O'Reilly was able to bring the bay under full control, although the horse stood snorting and blowing, and O'Reilly could feel it trembling between his legs.

Minutes passed. The bear still made no move, although she dropped to all fours and watched horse and rider. O'Reilly eyed the ferocious beast, noting the hump on her back rippling under the coat of shining black-brown fur. He couldn't get past her, he couldn't veer over toward the river and make a dash to get by. At the speed at which she could hurtle across the ground, he'd never make it, even if he could urge the bay to attempt it. Yet he had to get along the trail. He had to get on after Thunder Hawk. He had almost caught him until this.

An instant before the grizzly had charged him up on the ledge, O'Reilly had glimpsed the two cubs. As near as he could tell they were about six months old. Now, with the bear making no attempt to come after him, he reasoned she must have been chasing him away from her cubs and the food. As if to reinforce this reasoning, the grizzly started snapping her jaws at him, as though warning him to keep his distance. So, he reckoned, she should return up the slope to the cubs once she became satisfied he wasn't going after them or their food. As long as he remained where he was, the grizzly should soon amble away.

But the grizzly didn't move. She stayed watching him, snapping her jaws almost constantly.

Only too well aware that Thunder Hawk was getting away, O'Reilly fretted impatiently. He was tempted to pull his .45-75 Winchester from the saddle bucket behind his right leg and kill the grizzly, but if he did the cubs would be left motherless and would have a hard time surviving the winter, if they would survive it at all. Besides, he didn't want to kill the animal. It had as much right to be there as he did. He knew he couldn't scare it off with a couple of shots over its head. The grizzly would interpret that as aggression and would probably charge instantly.

So O'Reilly waited—impatiently waited.

It seemed a long time before the grizzly finally turned and ambled back toward the pines. Before entering them and making her way back up the slope, she turned her head and looked at the Mountie, snapping her jaws once more. Then she disappeared into the trees. O'Reilly waited a few moments in case she was lurking in the timber watching to see what he would do.

When he deemed it safe to go ahead, O'Reilly clucked with his teeth and legged the dark bay forward. But the scent of the grizzly was still there, and O'Reilly had to leg the horse again, more firmly this time. Reluctantly the bay stepped forward, snorting and blowing, tossing its head, nostrils flared, eyes on the pines where it had seen the grizzly disappear.

The bay's nervousness made O'Reilly edgy too, and he cautiously eyed the trees as well, half-expecting the sow to come charging out again. As he edged the bay forward, he wondered whether grizzlies stalked man, the way he had been told polar bears did.

Then a bellow from up on the ledge told him the grizzly had rejoined her cubs.

"Come on, boy," he said to the dark bay. "It's all right now. Let's move."

As the Mountie's confidence flowed down through his seat and knees and the touch of the reins, the bay picked up its hoofs and broke into a canter. Soon they were well along the trail and O'Reilly found the place where Thunder Hawk had ridden down from the ridge and returned to the trail.

The dark bay settled into a smooth canter and the miles passed. By the time the sun was directly overhead, O'Reilly was riding alongside the jade-colored lake he had seen from up on the Bear's Teeth. Mountain walls towered on either side. Just beyond was Iroquois Pass, which cut through the high-spined range running down from the northwest . . . the Continental Divide. He would reach it before nightfall.

Suddenly disappointment pressed down heavily on O'Reilly as he realized that Thunder Hawk had made good his escape.

Chapter 20

O'Reilly didn't stop at the Continental Divide.

He knew he had reached it because of Hector Glacier, high up on the east side of Mount Campbell, snow-crusted and sparkling under the sun as though millions of jewels had been sprinkled over it. Its melting water fed the Palliser, which flowed eastward down the mountains before swinging around to the north to join the Peace and Mackenzie, eventually sweeping out into the Arctic Ocean. Runoff from the other side of the glacier trickled down the western side of the mountain to the Fraser and so on to the Pacific.

Without even breaking the dark bay's gait, O'Reilly rode on through Iroquois Pass into British Columbia. By nightfall he was a dozen miles beyond North-West Mounted Police jurisdiction.

At first light next morning he was back in the saddle following Thunder Hawk's trail, wondering whether the Indian would ease the punishing pace he had set for both of them. Did Thunder Hawk know he had crossed the border out of the North-West

Territories? Why not? O'Reilly asked himself, remembering those carefree early days down south in the Fort Macleod country when he and old Sergeant Mike Hannan's Flying Patrol chased horse-raiding Crow and Gros Ventre war parties back across the international boundary. They had sure as hell known where the medicine line lay.

As he rode westward along a wide valley, O'Reilly swung off to a height of land, where he took out his binoculars and glassed the country ahead. The autumn colors presented a sea of gold stretching ahead as far as he could see, running up the lower slopes of the surrounding mountains. The animal trail that Thunder Hawk had been following veered around to the south a few miles further on. O'Reilly reckoned it probably led to a valley system running down the main ranges all the way to the Canadian Pacific transcontinental rail line to Vancouver. But no sight of Thunder Hawk.

Returning to the trail, O'Reilly followed it westward again, his eyes glued to the ground so as not to miss Thunder Hawk's track should the Indian branch off somewhere. There was no telling what he would do now. Ahead the valley widened more, and with that sea of poplar and birch, there were plenty of places to hide.

When O'Reilly reached the place where the animal trail swung south, he could see where Thunder Hawk's sorrel had left it.

"He's staying west," O'Reilly said to the bay. "Heading for the Shining Mountains, like Tom Barr said."

The smell of fall was in the air, dry and warm, the

afternoon sun beaming down from a blue sky, hardly a cloud in view. That could change quickly, though, O'Reilly mused as he eased himself forward in his creaking California stock saddle and gazed up at the sky. You could never tell what was drifting in over the mountains.

Suddenly a rifle shot shattered the mountain stillness!

O'Reilly sat bolt-upright. Unless there were someone else roaming around these lonely ranges—which was highly unlikely—that had been Thunder Hawk's rifle. He grinned beneath his bushy black moustache. No bullet had come in his direction, so Thunder Hawk must have shot a deer or an elk for food. He must be feeling pretty confident that he was safe from pursuit now.

Trotting the dark bay over to the shade of a forest of gold-leafed poplar, O'Reilly swung down from his saddle and undid the cinches. Then he sat on the grass with his back against the California and idly watched his horse graze.

For two hours he sat, until he saw what he had been waiting for . . . just the suggestion of a thin column of smoke rising from over among poplar and birch trees about two miles away. Climbing to his feet, he unhurriedly slapped the California back on the bay, tightened the cinches, and mounted up. Then he reined the horse toward the smoke.

O'Reilly took his time getting to Thunder Hawk's fire, making a wide detour to approach from the south rather than the east. Thunder Hawk was cooking the meat he had shot when O'Reilly rode into the clearing.

Thunder Hawk heard the stamping of a horse hoof too late. Whipping his head around he found himself looking up at a big .45 Enfield held rock-steady in the hand of a black-moustached man wearing a Mounted Police uniform.

"In the name of the King, I arrest you for murder, Thunder Hawk," said O'Reilly, stepping down from his saddle and taking a pair of handcuffs from a saddle wallet before walking across the clearing toward the Indian.

O'Reilly was about to clamp the handcuffs around Thunder Hawk's wrists when a voice snapped out from behind him.

"Hold it right there, soldier!"

O'Reilly froze, revolver in one hand, handcuffs in the other. He was about to turn his head when the voice rapped again.

"No! Just keep lookin' straight ahead. Right . . . now just put that pistol back in the holster where it belongs. That's right, soldier. Now get your hand away from it. Yeah . . . that's good. Now drop them handcuffs. All right . . . you can turn around."

Turning, O'Reilly saw a dozen yards away a bearded man in green mackinaw, whipcord breeches, and a battered hat. The man stood beside a big brown horse and pointed a rifle at O'Reilly.

"Who the hell are you?" O'Reilly demanded.

Ignoring O'Reilly's question, the bearded man motioned to Thunder Hawk. "You're free to go, Indian. Go on, git . . . while you got the chance."

His face expressionless, Thunder Hawk looked from the one white man to the other.

O'Reilly's black moustache bristled as he glared at

the bearded man. "You're interfering with the course of justice! This Indian's wanted for murder."

The bearded man spat a stream of brown tobacco juice onto the grass. "You ain't got no authority here in the province of British Columbia, soldier."

"Who are you to be telling me that?" O'Reilly snapped back at him.

Grinning as he walked slowly forward, the bearded man pulled aside his mackinaw jacket to reveal a shiny round badge pinned to his shirt underneath. "British Columbia Provincial Police."

With a final glance at the two white men, Thunder Hawk picked up his rifle and blanket and broke into a run toward the edge of the clearing. For a moment the bearded man took his eyes off O'Reilly to watch the Indian's retreating back. But O'Reilly, seeing his prisoner about to escape into the trees, snatched his revolver from its holster and snapped off a shot above Thunder Hawk's head.

"Stop where you are, Thunder Hawk!" O'Reilly shouted.

Jerked from his momentary lapse, the bearded man jumped forward and smashed his rifle barrel across O'Reilly's wrist. The big Enfield dropped from the Mountie's hand, dangling at the end of the white lanyard around his neck.

"Like I said, soldier," the bearded man rasped. "You ain't got no authority here in British Columbia."

Clapping his left hand around his stinging wrist, O'Reilly glowered at him. "Haven't you heard of fresh pursuit?"

The bearded man scowled. "The way I see it, I

could arrest you for attempted murder."

"Try it!" O'Reilly barked back. Then he yanked his revolver up by its lanyard, rammed it into his holster, and stooped to pick up his handcuffs. Turning back to his horse, he thrust a spurred boot into the stirrup and swung himself up into the saddle.

The bearded provincial policeman stared hard at O'Reilly. "You Mounted Police think you're pretty damned good, but as far as I'm concerned you're just a bunch of upstart soldiers that make up your own laws. Us provincials are *real* policemen. We don't need no brass buttons and shiny boots to do our policin'. We were enforcin' the law fourteen years before you Scarlet Riders even got started, and we'll still be enforcin' it after you're disbanded."

O'Reilly sat his saddle, looking down at the bearded man. When the provincial finished, O'Reilly spoke to him in tightly restrained words. "I've heard you provincial police do a good job, but you're the first one I've met. I hope the rest of your force don't have the same petty jealousies you have."

Pulling on his reins, Sergeant O'Reilly wheeled his horse and rode after Thunder Hawk.

Thunder Hawk had gained half a mile, but instead of continuing west he had struck north from the clearing, heading toward a long pine-tree-covered ridge marking the northern side of the valley and separating it from the mountain range that walled it in. Watching through field glasses, O'Reilly glimpsed the Indian riding between interspersing stands of golden birch and poplar. Guessing he would veer west once he got close to the ridge, O'Reilly gambled, and angled northwest to cut him off.

As he galloped the dark bay across the grassy valley, O'Reilly grinned with satisfaction. He had guessed correctly . . . Thunder Hawk swung west. The dark bay galloped on. Soon only a quarter of a mile separated the Mountie from the man he was after. Urging his horse to give its best, O'Reilly leaned forward low in the saddle. The thrill of the chase gripped him! At last he almost had Thunder Hawk. This time he would make sure the provincial policeman didn't interfere.

After galloping for more than a quarter of a mile, O'Reilly suddenly realized something was wrong. Thunder Hawk had dropped from sight. Jerking the bay to its haunches, O'Reilly whipped up his glasses and studied the stretch of birch-dotted valley between where he was and where he had last seen the Indian. Neither Thunder Hawk nor the sorrel were anywhere in sight.

"Christ!" O'Reilly swore.

Wheeling the bay around, O'Reilly galloped back to where he had last seen Thunder Hawk. When he got there he saw where the Indian had swung back in the opposite direction, not only regaining lost ground but making some up. Following the sorrel's track as it stayed close to the base of the ridge, O'Reilly wished he had tried to enlist the aid of the provincial policeman. Together they could have boxed Thunder Hawk in.

"At least he's heading in the right direction," O'Reilly half-said to his horse. "Maybe we can chase him back into the Territories."

The sorrel's track continued east, hugging the base of the ridge, but after four or five miles the ridge dropped away and the hoofprints edged over to the foot of the mountain, following it around as the mountain pulled in to the northeast. Hope again surged through O'Reilly as the bay pounded in pursuit. The way he figured it, the Indian would have been smarter to have left the mountain wall and struck out along the broad valley floor, using the clumps of poplar for cover. By following the line of the mountain he would run into a dead end. The Mountie was sure there was no break along the valley's north wall. He had purposely looked for one when he'd ridden in. The handcuffs would be around Thunder Hawk's wrists before sundown.

Rounding the curve, O'Reilly found what he expected—an indentation in the valley wall like the bottom of a raindrop. And there was Thunder Hawk—O'Reilly could see him through the glasses—streaking across the grass to the bottom of the raindrop. A wide grin stretched the Mountie's big black moustache for the second time since his encounter with the provincial policeman.

O'Reilly slowed the bay's pace. No sense running him until he blowed. Thunder Hawk couldn't escape now. He had boxed himself in.

O'Reilly was only halfway across the raindrop when the grin left his face. "That crazy damn Indian! He's trying to ride up the side of the mountain."

Riding closer to the mountain, O'Reilly could see it as all broken shale and sharp, bare rock. Besides, the slope was too steep.

"He'll never make it," the Mountie told himself.

When he reached the foot of the mountain, O'Reilly reined to and sat his saddle, watching Thunder Hawk and the sorrel scramble up the slope. He waited for Thunder Hawk to realize the futility of continuing his desperate struggle for freedom . . . waited for him to give up, turn around and ride back down.

Amazingly, as O'Reilly watched, the Indian got higher and higher. O'Reilly realized he had underestimated the sorrel's agility and endurance. But he still won't make it—he *can't* make it. He's not even halfway up.

Cupping his hands around his mouth, O'Reilly yelled at Thunder Hawk to come down, adding that he couldn't get away. When the Indian kept going, the Mountie pulled his Winchester from its bucket and fired two shots in the the shale above him. Still Thunder Hawk and the sorrel kept climbing.

As O'Reilly watched, the yellow pony and its buckskin rider reached the halfway point, marked by a rocky overhang running partway around the mountain's side. Almost breathlessly, O'Reilly continued watching Thunder Hawk go even higher. And the higher Thunder Hawk got, the lower O'Reilly's spirits dropped. Thunder Hawk might get away after all.

Yet it seemed impossible.

Now the Stoney chief dismounted and started leading the pony, pulling it up the steep, rocky slope. His jaw muscles twitching, O'Reilly restlessly trotted his horse backward and forward along the foot of the mountain, his neck aching from constantly looking upward. Small pieces of rock and shale tumbled down the slope, dislodged by Thunder Hawk's passage. O'Reilly reined the bay aside to avoid them.

Once, O'Reilly tried to ride up the shale slope in pursuit of the Stoney, but it was useless. Even when he dismounted and stubbornly tried to follow Thunder Hawk's example by pulling the dark bay up by the reins, it was no use. Iron shoes slipped on the shale. Angered and frustrated, O'Reilly led his horse down again.

When O'Reilly looked up next, Thunder Hawk had almost reached the top of the slope. The only way he could stop him now was to shoot him.

Chapter 21

O'Reilly could not return to Fort Determination without Thunder Hawk. The reasons were painfully obvious to him, but there was another, one deeply ingrained arising from eleven and a half years service with the Scarlet Riders—the Force did not acknowledge failure. He *had* to bring Thunder Hawk in.

It took him seven days of riding, climbing, probing, and exploring to get in around the mountains to the other side of the slope over which Thunder Hawk had escaped. He found the Indian had reached the top of a lateral moraine—a long ridge left over from the Ice Age—which acted as a bridge between two mountains, and had dropped down into a valley and gone north.

Before plunging off in pursuit, O'Reilly shot an elk to supplement his nearly-depleted rations, and cooked himself fresh meat. He had no sooner done this than a violent sleet storm struck the mountains and the valley, dumping snow on the peaks and stripping the poplar and birch on the lower slopes and along the valley floor of their golden foliage, leaving the yellow leaves wet and soggy on the ground.

The storm kept a fumingly impatient O'Reilly in a wet, miserable camp for two days. When he was finally able to ride out, he found the storm had obliterated Thunder Hawk's trail, so he followed the valley, for there was no way else to go. Twice he found the remains of campfires. He knew they had been made by Thunder Hawk because of the way stones had been used for the fire, with nothing else disturbed except where he had lashed together the tops of some spruce trees to provide a shelter. Thunder Hawk had shot another elk, for he had smoked the meat in one of the camps. That would have cost him a couple of days, O'Reilly reckoned.

Before O'Reilly got very far along the valley, a snowstorm swept in. It only lasted a day, but it brought lower temperatures, and he was thankful that he had carried his cold-weather pea jacket after all.

O'Reilly knew he was traveling north, with a swing north-northeast with the line of the valley, and up on the sides of the mountains, spilling over their upper slopes, he saw from time to time glaciers. Then heavy cloud rolled in, not only hiding the mountaintops and lower slopes but seeming to press so low that all O'Reilly had to do was reach up and touch them. His world turned black and white—white on the ground, white-gray cloud above, and black pine and spruce looming grotesquely through the gray cloud all around him. The only real colors were the yellow stripes down the sides of his dark blue breeches, the dull tarnish of his once-bright brass buttons, and the brown of his leather. Even the dark bay coloring of his horse as he looked down from his saddle seemed black in the eerie, ghostlike world surrounding him. White frosty clouds blew from the mouths of horse and rider. It was almost as though they were no longer on earth, as though they were alone on some mysterious, uninhabited planet somewhere. Just the two of them. O'Reilly had to fight down the impulse to shout out to see if anyone else was in this world. He couldn't hear the sounds of animals or birds, not even the trickle of water down from the glaciers. He was used to loneliness, and he even enjoyed solitude, but this was almost frightening, certainly depressing.

O'Reilly rode through this unreal world for two days, not knowing where he was going, just following the line of the trees.

When the clouds finally broke and the sun commenced shining feebly through, showing patches of pale blue here and there, O'Reilly felt as though he had returned to earth. But there was something else, too . . . something he couldn't quite understand until the clouds dissipated and he could see a glacier over his left shoulder, and water cascading down the mountainside until it reached the valley floor to form the headwaters of a river, flowing past him to the north. He must have recrossed the Continental Divide! He was sure of it the next day, when the river— still only a stream—swerved around to the northeast. He was back in the North-West Territories, back in Mounted Police jurisdiction. At least he would have unrestricted authority to arrest Thunder Hawk.

Where was Thunder Hawk?

O'Reilly wasn't even sure he was still on the Indian's trail. Sixteen days had passed since he'd seen him disappear over the top of that shale slope, and four since he had found pine boughs marking his last resting place. O'Reilly had kept on because there hadn't seemed any other place to go. One thing he did know—Thunder Hawk was not looking for the Shining Mountains.

After two more days, when the stream he had been riding alongside had widened and deepened into a river, O'Reilly's tenacious determination was rewarded by the sight of an Indian village. The instant he spotted the village's horse herd, he saw the sorrel among them.

Several Indians met the Mountie at the outskirts of the village. Sullen dark eyes stared up at him from squat, flat faces. These were faces he hadn't seen before. They were not the long, lean faces of the Blood warriors he had encountered during his early service in the Force, nor the more oval, high-cheekboned faces of the Sioux-related Stoneys. They were more like the Indians he had seen in the Yukon. From the height of his saddle, he looked around for further sign of Thunder Hawk.

"Where is the owner of that yellow horse?" O'Reilly asked them, pointing at the sorrel.

The flat faces staring up at him were completely unresponsive, and no one answered.

"The man who owns that yellow horse," O'Reilly repeated slowly. "A Stoney . . . where is he?"

Still no one answered.

"Doesn't anyone here speak English?"

"Yes . . . I do."

The voice came from behind him. Turning in his saddle, O'Reilly saw a tall, thin white man with sallow complexion, long black stringy hair, and a flowing, black beard flecked with gray, standing on a rock. His long, black priest's raiment was worn almost threadbare, and the once-white liner of his high collar was gray and frayed. He stepped down off the rock, walked a few paces toward the Mountie, and stopped.

For a moment O'Reilly sat in his saddle staring down at the priest. Finally he said, "You're with these Indians, Father?"

Smiling slightly, the priest tilted his head to one side. "Yes. I am Father Marchand, of the Oblate Order," he replied in heavily-French-accented English.

O'Reilly pointed to the sorrel again. "The man who rode that horse, Father . . . I have come to arrest him for murder. Where is he?"

"Gone," the priest replied simply.

"Where? When?"

"I am not sure I should tell you t'at."

O'Reilly reined his horse around until he faced the priest fully. "Why not?"

"Because I am not convinced it would be in the best interests of . . . 'ow you say it—justice?"

"He's wanted for murder, Father." There was a touch of ragged anger in O'Reilly's voice.

The priest closed his eyes as though he was tired and nodded his head. "I know. 'e told me about it." Opening his eyes, he looked up sadly at O'Reilly. "T'at is the problem. 'e was protecting 'is people and 'is village. I t'ink it is the evil men who started everyt'ing t'at should be put in jail."

O'Reilly nodded impatiently. "I'll do whatever I can about that when I get back to Fort Determination, Father, but I have to take him with me."

258

The priest's sad brown eyes looked up at O'Reilly imploringly. " 'e desperately wants to go back to 'elp 'is people. At first, when 'is wife was killed, 'e wanted to join 'is Maker, but I told 'im it was not time to do t'at, t'at only God can tell 'im when it is time. So now 'e wants to go back to 'elp 'is people because t'ose evil white men want to drive t'em from t'eir 'ome so t'ey can mine for silver. But 'e is afraid t'at if 'e goes back, 'e will be t'rown into prison and 'ung."

Pulling at the end of his moustache, O'Reilly said half to himself, "Silver! So that's what Lasher's been up to! Yes . . . it all ties in." Then he addressed himself to the priest. "Does he have any proof of this Father?"

The priest slowly shook his head. "Not what your courts would call proof. 'e knows in 'is 'eart t'at it is true. But 'e did 'ear t'em talking."

O'Reilly leaned forward eagerly in his saddle. "I might be able to help him, Father. I might be able to put the leader of those men behind bars. But I must find Thunder Hawk and hear what he has to say. It's important."

Father Marchand said nothing for a moment, until he looked down toward the river. " 'e went down 'ere."

Reining the dark bay around so that he could look down the river, O'Reilly stood in his stirrups and stared. Just beyond the village he saw half a dozen canoes pulled up on the gravel shore. "How long ago?"

"Just before you arrived. 'e saw you coming."

"Damnation!" O'Reilly exploded at the realization of how close he had been. He quickly added, "Sorry,

259

Father. But I must go after him right away. Will these people let me have a canoe?"

The priest nodded. "First you should rest. 'e rested 'ere several days. 'e needed to. 'e is sick wit' bad cough."

O'Reilly shook his head and swung down from the saddle. "I don't have time, Father. I'd be greatly obliged if you'd look after my horse until I come back. I'll see you're reimbursed."

"You need not worry. I will look after your 'orse."

Ten minutes later O'Reilly pushed a birch-bark canoe out into the water, jumped in, and started paddling. The current quickly took him down the river between grassy banks lined with spruce and pine. All around him the snow-capped mountains walled him in. Overhead the sky was a cloud-puffed blue, a blue suggestive of cold. The water ahead was turquoise, but around the canoe it swirled white and pale green-gray.

With any luck he hoped to overtake Thunder Hawk before nightfall. There wasn't any particular reason why he should have been able to do so, except confidence in himself, and he settled well down in the canoe's stern and paddled, paddled with all the strength of his muscled arms. If Thunder Hawk was sick, even though he'd rested for several days, O'Reilly reasoned he had an advantage. Although he hadn't rested, he was superbly fit, apart from his trail diet of perhaps too much meat.

As it happened, he did not overtake Thunder Hawk by sundown, and once darkness fell he impatiently nosed the canoe to shore. He couldn't afford to travel at night, for he needed daylight to watch for any sign of the Stoney pulling into shore.

Before sunup next morning O'Reilly was ready to go again, waiting with unrestrained patience for the first pink streaks of dawn. When dawn did break it was gray, not pink, and black-tinged cloud, low and thick, threatened a storm. O'Reilly watched the sky anxiously as he shot down the river. The current was stronger now, and it carried the frail, birch-bark canoe with startling speed, while O'Reilly helped it along with great swinging thrusts of the paddle. One thing, he thought, when I catch Thunder Hawk it'll be a hard pull back upriver against the current, even with the two of them paddling.

However, as he paddled without sighting Thunder Hawk, even on the long, straight stretches of river, O'Reilly's aspirations of apprehending the Indian began to fade. At the same time his admiration for the Stoney's ability to keep ahead of him grew. Maybe the Almighty was on Thunder Hawk's side. On four occasions O'Reilly had almost caught him, and there was the time he had gotten away from Green and Mardling. Maybe the course of man's justice wasn't so right after all, O'Reilly mused, but it's the best we've got, and no country I know of has anything better.

Shooting down the river, O'Reilly constantly scanned the banks for signs of a canoe having been pulled up, and once he had to lose valuable minutes while he veered to shore for a closer look at what had appeared to have been canoe marks but in reality had been made by a piece of driftwood rammed against the riverbank by the current. Another time he climbed a tall pine standing up on a ridge and glassed the river miles ahead. He thought he caught a glimpse of the tail-end of a canoe disappearing around a high cliff along the river, but he couldn't be sure he actually saw it or whether his imagination was playing tricks.

For two more days he traveled at an ever-increasing speed down the river, coursing generally northeast. Then a fierce snowstorm blew down with unbridled fury from the north, forcing him to shore, where he had to build a big fire just to keep from freezing in quickly dipping temperatures. There was plenty of windfall timber around and he was able to make himself reasonably comfortable, but the storm lasted three days, and the enforced idleness was made bearable solely by the realization that Thunder Hawk was in a similar predicament.

When he was able to move his canoe back into the river, O'Reilly had to first break his way through ice that had formed along the edges, and the entire countryside was white, from the mountaintops all the way down to the riverbanks. The river itself was a cold gray, just like the sky above.

After another day of travel O'Reilly struck whitewater rapids, and only experience he'd gained from handling canoes in the Yukon during the gold rush saved his life. Once he reached calmer water, he paddled to shore and searched for sign of Thunder Hawk, looking for any indication that Thunder Hawk had met with disaster. But he found no such thing, and he marveled at the Indian's skill.

The next stretch of rapids, a dozen miles downriver, looked worse as O'Reilly sat low in the stern, peering anxiously over the pointed prow. He could feel the current clutching at the frail canoe, pulling and pushing it faster toward the swirling white water that he could see and hear roaring ahead, attempting to smash it pitilessly against sharp, jagged rocks rearing their terrifying heads high to split the water rushing by on either side. The current was trying to hurtle him out of control to certain destruction. Using every ounce of strength in him, O'Reilly drove his dripping paddle into the mad, boiling water and fought his way over to the bank just in time. Jumping out of the canoe, he pulled it up onto the snow-covered bank, where he rested briefly. Then he hefted his saddle wallets, bedroll, and rifle, and crunched over the wet snow for two miles until he had passed the rapids. After that he returned to the canoe, lifted it onto his shoulders, and turned around to retrace his steps to where he had left his rifle and gear. The only consolation in all this was that moccasin tracks showed him where Thunder Hawk had also portaged.

Back in the river below the rapids, paddling once more, O'Reilly became aware of a difference in the scenery—there were no more mountains towering above him, only hills. The further he paddled the smaller the hills became, until finally the country flattened out altogether. Even so, everywhere he looked the landscape and trees were white, with ice once again forming at the river's edges.

In camp at the end of a hard day's paddling, O'Reilly ate the last of his meat before turning in. In the black of night he woke to pain-wracking stomach cramps that broke out sweat all over him, despite temperatures well below freezing. He stumbled from his bedroll, doubled over with diarrhea. When he returned he collapsed, drawing only enough strength to throw another branch onto his fire and draw his blankets over himself.

For three days he lay sick in camp. More snow fell, but finally he was able to summon enough energy to kill a porcupine and eat it. Then, unshaven and filthy, he doggedly pushed his canoe out through new ice and paddled down the river once more.

The weather had turned much colder, and hunched shivering and miserable in the stern of the canoe, O'Reilly was beginning to despair of ever catching Thunder Hawk. With the passage of more days, and with skies remaining leaden, he grew sick, hungry, and nearly exhausted, and all he wanted was to find a trapper's or missionary's cabin where he could rest in a warm bed and eat properly cooked food. He was now able to recognize the country through which he was traveling—he had reached the land of the Peace. If only he could get to the Mounted Police post at Peace River Crossing, he could rest there until he was well enough to return to Fort Determination, where he would turn himself in. Hell! He didn't even have to go to all that trouble. He could simply turn himself over to the NCO in charge at the Crossing.

Then something happened to change O'Reilly's plans. He saw a canoe pulled up onto the snow-covered beach off to his left. He had almost missed it in his sick, near-exhausted state. In fact, he could have missed it a dozen times over these last few days. But now excitement surged through him once more, giving him an energy he hadn't known for days.

Swinging his paddle over to his left, he steered the canoe to the icy shore. Jumping out, he crashed through the ice, thoroughly soaking his feet, and pulled the canoe behind him. He stepped over to the other canoe. There was nothing in it, but it bore the same painted symbols on its prow as O'Reilly's, and there were moccasin prints leading away from it.

The tracks led toward a grove of pine trees. Taking his rifle, O'Reilly followed them. They took him through and beyond the pines and continued on across a white expanse. They led on for as far as he could see . . . onward across the snow-covered vastness.

O'Reilly followed.

By nightfall O'Reilly saw a yellow patch of light in the distance. The moccasin tracks led toward it. As he got closer, he could see the light from a cabin window. Gripping his Winchester he hurried forward. Thunder Hawk could be inside that cabin at this very moment. Then the brisk night air was rent by the howling of dogs, and with it went his chances of taking the Indian by surprise. Muttering an oath, O'Reilly lurched forward as fast as his weakened legs would carry him. He had to get to that cabin before Thunder Hawk could escape. The blood pounded across his temple as his stiff, wet boots hammered into the snow. Once . . . twice, the boots slipped on the snow and he sprawled full-length, only to stagger to his feet and stumble forward again. The square of yellow grew larger . . . the blood in his temples pounded faster, harder . . . pounded from his heart and lungs . . . his chest ached and his legs felt like lead, but he picked them up one after the other and drove them down again hard into the snow. The dogs' howling gave way to frenzied barking.

Another patch of light loomed ahead of him . . . the dark figure of a man appeared in it. O'Reilly slipped and fell again. He was just picking himself up when he felt a strong grip under his arms and he found himself being half-carried, half-dragged toward the light.

"I'll be damned—a Mountie!" a man's voice exclaimed as O'Reilly felt the warmth of the inside of a cabin flow over him. The man lowered him into a crude, homemade chair.

"That Indian," O'Reilly gasped, looking up into a gray-bearded face. "The one who made . . . those moccasin tracks . . . Where is he?"

"Gone," the gray-bearded trapper replied, yelling at the dogs penned up behind the cabin to keep quiet, then slamming shut the door. "He staggered in here jus' like you. Hungry and in damn bad shape. I fed him, and he jus' lit out. Gave him an old parka before he left. Wouldna' lasted long in this weather if I hadn't."

"How . . . long ago?" O'Reilly's chest heaved with the effort of asking.

"Not long before you got here . . . jus' before dark. Couple hours, mebbe. Not much more."

O'Reilly struggled to stand, swayed on his feet, then reached out for a table to suport himself. "Got to get . . . got to get after him." He lurched toward the door. The trapper grabbed him by the shoulders and pushed him back onto the chair.

"Whoa, there. You ain't in no shape to be goin' anywhere, least of all chasin' him. Not that he was in any better shape than you."

Shaking his head, O'Reilly gripped the trapper's

wrists and removed them from his shoulders. "I've got
to go after him. . . . right away. Been chasing him for
a month."

"You need food and rest. You're in a hell of a
shape."

O'Reilly was back on his feet and moving unstead-
y toward the door. "Got to go right away. If I don't
. . catch him now, I'll never get this . . . close to him
again."

"You must want him pretty bad. What's he done?"

O'Reilly's hand was on the door. "Murder."

"Murder, huh? Well, you don't have to worry none,
cause he won't be gettin' far. He's in worse shape
than you. You can rest up and go after him in the
mornin'. You'll probably find him dead somewheres
along the trail, anyways."

Leaning heavily against the cabin's chinked log
walls, his hand still on the door, O'Reilly looked at the
trapper through glazed eyes. "I can't let that happen
to him. Could I borrow your dogs? I'll make better
progress with them. I'll need them to bring him
back."

The trapper nodded. "I guess so. You'll need better
clothin', too. It's gettin' plumb colder out there by the
hour. I'll lend you a parka and fur cap." The trapper's
eyes glanced down at the Mountie's soaked
strathconas. "Them boots ain't no good for travelin'
over snow. I'll lend you a pair of Eskimo mukluks.
But first you better move your arse back over to that
table and I'll fix you up some hot rabbit stew. Then
you can go chase your Indian."

* * *

The pale northern lights danced across the blue-black sky as Sergeant O'Reilly—yellow-striped blue breeches, Eskimo mukluks replacing spurred boots, feet spread twenty inches apart and strapped into long narrow snowshoes with turned-up fronts, brown fur parka with hood pulled over his head, dog whip held in front of him in hands thrust into fur-lined mitts, breath coming out of his black-whiskered mouth in frost clouds—stood in front of his dog team, looking down at the body of Thunder Hawk sprawled face-down in the snow at his feet.

Chapter 22

For ninety miles Sergeant O'Reilly mushed the dog team, carrying a nearly-dead Thunder Hawk heavily swaddled in furs on the sled. It was a race against time, for only prompt medical treatment would save the Indian's life.

Upon finding Thunder Hawk sprawled face-down in the snow, O'Reilly had built a huge fire in an attempt to raise his body heat. Then he had loaded him aboard the sled, struck out for the Smoky, and followed it to Peace River Crossing, where he turned him over to the missionary hospital before reporting in to the Mounted Police post.

For two days Hugh O'Reilly remained in barracks resting, eating, having a bath and shaving. The NCO in charge, Sergeant Seymour, gave no indication of knowing anything about O'Reilly having been listed as a deserter, nor about the disciplinary charges against him. But then, O'Reilly hadn't expected him to know. Not yet. News took time to reach the more-remote North-West Mounted Police outposts.

On the third day, O'Reilly visited the hospital, where the doctor told him Thunder Hawk's condition was still critical and that he could not be disturbed. O'Reilly returned to the barracks and fretted, impatiently pacing the floor like a caged lion, until Sergeant Seymour told him to stop before he wore down the bloody floorboards.

While he waited, O'Reilly worried that a courier from Edmonton would bring word of his desertion, with orders that he be arrested on sight and escorted to the Fort Saskatchewan guardroom. He was resigned to winding up there eventually, and in some ways he thought it would be simpler to just report his status to Sergeant Seymour and let him take him there now, rather than go back to Fort Determination to face Inspector Kerr's irritating smirk. O'Reilly preferred to front Major Cavannagh as soon as possible and get the thing over with. But he wasn't finished with this matter yet. If at all possible, he was going to put Refflon Lasher behind bars.

Another five days passed before Thunder Hawk was well enough for O'Reilly to talk with him. His condition had been complicated by pnuemonia and the doctor had only barely saved his life. At first Thunder Hawk would not speak, but when the doctor told him that O'Reilly, on the verge of collapse, had brought him to the hospital and made the saving of his life possible, Thunder Hawk changed his mind, and on the sixth day they had a long talk. When he got back to the barracks, O'Reilly sat at the table and wrote several pages of paper. On the seventh day he returned to the hospital with the local justice of the peace and took a sworn declaration from Thunder Hawk. O'Reilly gave one copy to Sergeant Seymour and folded the original into his pocket.

O'Reilly had it plainly in his mind what he was going to do. All he needed was cold, clear weather. While he waited he took short dog-team trips to condition himself and the dogs for the long, hard journey that awaited them. He couldn't take Thunder Hawk, for the Indian would not be fit to travel for weeks. Instead, O'Reilly arranged with Sergeant Seymour to stage Thunder Hawk on the easier journey to Fort Saskatchewan when he was well enough, with rests at Lesser Slave Lake Post and Athabasca Landing. If necessary they could wait until spring and make the trip by paddle steamer. From Fort Saskatchewan, river steamer would take him on to Fort Determination.

Sergeant O'Reilly waited impatiently. At first the weather turned mild, making travel impossible. Then it snowed, and after that it turned cold, then colder, with the temperature dropping to twenty below.

When he finally struck out for Fort Determination, the sky was brilliantly blue, with fresh snow covering everything, draping spruce and pine trees with a mantle of glittering white. At first the snow was deep and the going hard as he mushed along the banks of the Smoky, his sled heavy with the weight of food for himself and the dogs. Far, far off to the southwest were the mountains, *his* mountains—or what had been his mountains until Inspector Kerr's arrival at Fort Determination. The further he progressed the lighter became the snow on the ground and, with the passing of more days the lower the temperature dropped. Satisfied that it was now cold enough for the river to have completely frozen over, O'Reilly dropped down over the snow-covered bank and traveled along the ice. Each night he was back up on the banks camped in the shelter of spruce and pine beside a blazing fire.

Days later he reached the foothills and commenced the long climb. The going became harder, even though partly offset by the reduced weight of the sled now that he and the dogs had eaten part of the food they carried.

As he mushed deeper into the mountains, O'Reilly thought about little other than putting Refflon Lasher behind bars. Occasionally his thoughts wandered to Catherine, but mostly he thought about Lasher. Of what awaited him at Fort Determination after it was all over, he thought not at all. Not just yet.

His mind dwelled on his conversation with Thunder Hawk, and one night after supper he lay in his sleeping bag by the light of his campfire rereading the Stoney's sworn declaration. Thunder Hawk's vision, although interesting, was of no value as evidence, and for that reason O'Reilly hadn't written it into the declaration. But the Stoney's account of the brief conversation he had heard between Lasher and Strathman when they stood over him, thinking him dead, was decidedly valuable. So was what Mike Mountain Bull had told Thunder Hawk about what he saw and heard down the alley behind Coal City's main street the night of the fire. And the rifle shot he had heard, coinciding with Lasher's brief disappearance, was almost undoubtedly the shot that had killed

Fisher. At first O'Reilly couldn't think of a reason why Lasher would have killed his own store clerk. However, the more he thought about it, the more plausible it seemed, and by the time he turned over to go to sleep, he was practically convinced it had been part of Lasher's overall plan to stir up enough resentment against the Indians that would lead to them being driven out of the valley one way or another. Proving it was another matter, of course, but Strathman would know about it. Once Lasher was in custody, Strathman could be questioned. If enough pressure was brought on him, he would talk. He was the weak link.

By following the Smoky, O'Reilly found his way back into familiar mountain country. He had made good time for the most part, sometimes thirty miles in a day, other times as little as fifteen when the weather turned bad. Fortunately the weather had generally remained clear and cold, and even going uphill he had averaged better than twenty miles a day.

Leaving the Smoky, O'Reilly followed another river system until he reached the upper Valley of the Snake, then dropped down to its lower end, arriving at the Stoney village the day before Christmas. Finding Mike Mountain Bull, O'Reilly questioned him about the night of the Coal City fire. The Stoney repeated exactly what he had told Thunder Hawk. Under careful cross-examination he clung to his story, until O'Reilly was not only satisfied it was true but that it would stand up under cross-examination in a court of law.

Early next morning, O'Reilly left the Indian village. Mushing across very familiar country, thoughts of Fort Determination flooded in on him . . . of Inspector Kerr, and what awaited him—almost certainly a term of imprisonment in either the guardroom at Fort Saskatchewan or Regina, followed by dismissal from the Force. A once-promising career ruined. And of Catherine . . . what could he offer her?

Pushing these thoughts from his mind, O'Reilly shouted his dogs to greater speed as he ran tirelessly behind the sled, steering it toward Coal City.

It was just before midday when he reached the coal-mining community. Even under its covering of snow, the place managed to look dirty and gray. If anything, the snow seemed to emphasize the drabness of the place.

He pulled the team to a stop outside the mining company office and anchored the sled before kicking off his snowshoes and barging inside. To his surprise the place was full of mine company employees, all standing around with glasses or tin mugs in their hands, laughing and talking. In the middle of them stood Refflon Lasher and Vince Strathman. At that moment it dawned upon O'Reilly that it was Christmas Day.

If O'Reilly was surprised to find Lasher—whom he had expected to find alone—surrounded by his cronies and employees, Lasher was doubly surprised at the sudden throwing-open of his office door and seeing framed in the entranceway a big-black-moustached man wearing yellow-striped blue breeches and a fur parka.

All eyes turned on the big Mountie, and there was

utter silence. It took Lasher several seconds before he could speak. "What the hell are you doing here, O'Reilly? Your inspector said you'd deserted."

"He was wrong," O'Reilly replied grimly.

"Anyway . . . what the hell do you want? This is a private party and you're not invited."

"I'm arresting you, Lasher, in the name of the King."

Lasher looked incredulous. "Arresting *me*! On what charge?"

"Take your pick—murder, manslaughter, arson, conspiracy."

Lasher uttered a weak laugh. "You're crazy. Wherever you've been hiding out must've turned your mind."

"Don't you believe it, Lasher. Now throw on some trail clothes. You're coming to Determination."

This time Lasher's voice had more force to it. "You're a deserter. You don't have authority to arrest me."

O'Reilly stepped forward. "I'm in no mood to argue, Lasher!"

Lasher looked around wildly, seeking some avenue of escape, but the Mountie blocked the door. He shouted at Strathman and his cronies. "Get him, boys! He's nothing but a dirty deserter. You know how he feels about us. Get him and we'll take *him* to Fort Determination. They'll thank us for bringing him in."

The miners looked hard at O'Reilly, but confronted by that determined face with its flashing dark eyes and fierce black moustache tinged with white frost, they hesitated.

"Go on, boys," Lasher urged. "Get him!"

It was Vince Strathman who made the first move. Encumbered by the awkwardness of his bulky parka, O'Reilly wasn't able to move fast enough, and Strathman's lunge caught him off-guard. Seeing the Mountie knocked against the wall by their mine superintendent, the miners surged forward. Somehow O'Reilly managed to throw Strathman back into them, following up with a savage kick to the stomach that doubled the mine boss over in pain. In a blur of movement, O'Reilly whipped off his parka and threw it aside, just in time to meet the miners' renewed rush. Hardened by a month of strenuous travel, muscles tempered to the toughness of steel, lean and fighting fit, Sergeant O'Reilly tore into them with a furious anger born of months of frustration and bitterness. He drove his fist into a bearded face, sending its owner sprawling onto a table. He struck out with a fierce kick at another, landing him on the point of his chin and somersaulting him backward. He aimed a vicious chop at the head of a third man who was trying to get around behind him, catching him at the base of the ear and dropping him flat to the floor. Then he picked up a chair and smashed it over another head, brought it back, and broke the legs against someone else's face. Blood spurted in gushes, while howls of pain mingled with shouts and the noise of falling bodies and breaking furniture.

Baring his teeth in an ugly grimace, Strathman was about to lunge at O'Reilly a second time when the Mountie kicked him again, his foot catching the mine boss full in the chest and lifting him several feet off the ground. Strathman toppled and landed hard on his back, knocked senseless. The savage kick almost broke O'Reilly's foot, but he was so damned fighting mad he barely noticed it.

As the remaining miners pushed toward him, O'Reilly grasped another chair and swung it at the three closest. Two went down under the first smashing blow. By the time he caught the third with his second swing, there was nothing left of the chair but the handle.

The four miners still on their feet stopped where they were, their eyes wide as they stared at the big Mountie standing before them on legs spread wide apart, one foot forward of the other, knees bent slightly, balled fists held menacingly in front of him, left shoulder forward of the right. Slowly they began falling back.

O'Reilly watched them for only a moment before picking up the heavy wooden table on which stood the bottles and glasses the miners had been drinking from, and holding it in front of him, charged them, catching them across their chests with its top and forcing them back against the wall. Laughing like a madman at their howls of protest, O'Reilly pushed with all his might, squashing them into the wall until their faces turned purple. Then he released them for just an instant before smashing the table back against them and pinning them to the wall once more.

Suddenly O'Reilly felt arms grabbing him around the neck from behind. Whirling like a coiled spring, he flung his assailant across the room. Another, picking himself up from the floor, charged but O'Reilly struck him a hammering left-and-right to the face and the miner fell heavily back to the floor.

Fists back up in readiness, O'Reilly stood waiting to pound anyone else who made a hostile move. However, all he saw were bodies lying around the nearly demolished room. Only Lasher's roll-top desk against the far wall seemed to have escaped damage.

Then O'Reilly realized Lasher was gone!

The mining company manager had slipped out while O'Reilly was busy fighting off his cronies. Snatching up his parka from the floor, O'Reilly pulled it on over his head and sprang outside. Looking around quickly, he caught a blur of movement over toward the mine entrance and was just in time to see Lasher disappear inside.

. O'Reilly sprinted across the snow after him, but just as he reached the mine entrance, standing silhouetted against the whiteness, a rifle shot exploded from the blackness inside and a bullet whip-cracked over his head. O'Reilly threw himself sideways, hugging the tunnel wall. He paused for a moment, then crept forward. From the dimness ahead a flash of orange-red stabbed out from the rifle muzzle and another bullet cracked by. O'Reilly could see a large wooden box abutting the wall ahead and he dived for it.

"Don't be a fool, Lasher," O'Reilly shouted into the tunnel once he had positioned himself behind the box. "You're only making it more difficult for yourself by resisting arrest."

"You're crazy, O'Reilly," Lasher yelled back, the sound coming hollowly from within the tunnel. "Your inspector will never let you get away with this. If you take me to Fort Determination, he'll have me released within ten minutes."

"Then, why are you running?" O'Reilly shouted

back.

Lasher's answer was another rifle shot. The bullet bit a long splinter of wood off the box's corner and ricocheted away toward the tunnel mouth.

O'Reilly remained behind the box for two or three minutes, letting his eyes adjust to the darkness. Then he peered cautiously around the box. He was close enough to the tunnel floor that Lasher would not be able to distinguish his head against the lighter background of the mine entrance, because of the tunnel's slight downgrade. He needed to draw Lasher, and he felt around the tunnel floor for something to throw. His hand closed around the hard shape of a rock. Pulling back his arm he tossed the rock down into the tunnel and quickly withdrew his head, expecting another rifle shot to shatter the stillness. But instead he heard the sound of running feet.

Moving from behind the box, O'Reilly crept forward in the blackness. When he reached the spot where he had seen the rifle muzzle-flashes, he felt around the floor of the tunnel until his hand touched a spent brass cartridge case, and then another. Now O'Reilly moved forward at a cautious lope, his caribou-skin mukluks making no noise on the hard rock floor.

Ahead he saw a dim light. As he got closer he saw it was a lantern set into the side of the tunnel, and further down he saw another. Obviously they were there to provide illumination for miners working in the mine. Being Christmas day, no miners were working. O'Reilly and Lasher had the mine to themselves. Still hearing the sound of running boots, the Mountie loped on.

After following the tunnel for what seemed a long time, O'Reilly came to an opening where it joined another tunnel, like a T intersection. There was enough light for him to see two steel rail lines running along the floor. Just as he stepped into it, wondering which way Lasher had gone, a rifle exploded again. Instantly O'Reilly threw himself down. The rifle's noise was deafening. O'Reilly thought his eardrums had been punctured, and his ears rang like the bells of Notre Dame. Only then did he realize he had been hit high in the left shoulder.

At least he now knew which way Lasher had gone. All he had to do was go and get him.

The tunnel ran down a slow grade to O'Reilly's left, where Lasher had fired from. He could see three dim yellow blobs of light from wall lanterns in that direction. There was another light just a yard or two to his right, which had illuminated him enough for Lasher to have hit him with the rifle. About twenty yards further to the right stood a coal car on the shiny steel rails. If he could get to that . . .

Reaching under his parka, O'Reilly pulled out his revolver and took aim at the closest lantern. Cocking the hammer, he held the gun steady and squeezed the trigger. The Enfield bucked in his hand and the lantern shattered into a thousand pieces, coal oil splashing to the tunnel floor and sputtering into flame for a brief moment before extinguishing itself.

The tunnel around him was plunged into total darkness. He was about to rise to his feet when the blackness suddenly erupted into a series of explosions, bullets zooming over him. The noise was devastating and he clapped his hands over his ears, hugging the cold, damp tunnel floor. Despite the noise he was able to count the shots, and he could hear the whining of bullets ricocheting off the rock walls and the iron coal car to his right. After what seemed an eternity, the explosions gave way to reverberating booms that gradually subsided altogether. But he could now hear almost nothing above the ringing in his ears.

Realizing that Lasher must be reloading his rifle, O'Reilly sprang to his feet and dashed to where he knew the coal car to be, in a desperate bid to get to it before Lasher opened fire again.

Reaching the car in safety, O'Reilly ducked around behind it and paused to consider his next move. The car's iron sides would protect him from Lasher's bullets, so he could advance on the mining company manager while using it as cover. First, though, he had to move it. Putting his good shoulder against it, he pushed. It wouldn't budge. His hands groped around until he found the brake. Releasing it, he put his shoulder to the car again. This time it rolled forward. He gave it another push and its momentum increased. Jumping onto the back, he hung low behind the iron body, hanging on by his left arm. His shoulder hurt and he was tempted to change arms and leave his left arm free, but he needed his right to hold his revolver.

O'Reilly couldn't hear the rumble of the coal car's passage for the ringing in his ears, but he could feel the vibration as the wheels rolled along the rails, and he knew the rumble would be loud enough. Then he realized Lasher's ears must be ringing also. Even if he had stuffed something into them, it wouldn't have stopped the noise of the shooting. So Lasher might not hear him coming. But as soon as the coal car neared that first lantern, Lasher would see it.

The first lantern was coming up now, and O'Reilly hung low at the back of the coal car, keeping his head well down, only the knuckles of his left hand protruding over the top. At any second he expected a hail of bullets to spatter against the iron sides, and he tightened his grip on his revolver as he tensed for action.

Then he was past the first lantern and the coal car was rolling on in semidarkness again. Peering around the car's side, he could see the second lantern coming up. Lasher had to be just beyond it—or perhaps just this side of it. But a moment later the second lantern was above him and then it dropped behind. Any second now Lasher would open up. O'Reilly could feel the blood pounding through his temples. Perhaps Lasher might flatten himself against the wall and wait for the coal car to go by, opening fire on it as it passed him. Lasher's bullets would hit him without doubt then, and O'Reilly wondered whether he shouldn't have climbed into the car instead of hanging onto its back.

The car rolled past the third lantern. O'Reilly's eyes probed the shadows behind the tunnel's timber supports as the car rumbled past them, searching for the lurking rifleman. Where the hell was he? Cautiously O'Reilly poked his head over the top of the car's iron sides. He could see more of the dull yellow lights ahead now, marking the tunnel's continued progress. Lasher must have gone further in. But why? O'Reilly asked himself. What did he hope to gain by so doing? How did he hope to escape? Did he plan to ambush O'Reilly somewhere deeper in the tunnel, killing him and throwing his body into some disused shaft, where it mightn't be found for years? And the deeper the coal car carried him into the tunnel, the greater became O'Reilly's discomfiture. He could feel a sense of being hemmed in, of claustrophobia. He would ride a horse anywhere across mountain or prairie, drive a dog team to the North Pole if ordered to, or paddle a canoe all the way to Hudson Bay, but probing the hidden mysteries of a dark, underground tunnel was a frighteningly different matter. He didn't like it, and the deeper the coal car carried him into the tunnel, the less he liked it.

Then he saw it!

It was a large, black, square shadow against the wall coming up on his left. Hooking his elbow over the car's side, he transferred the Enfield to his left hand and braked the car with his right. It ground to a stop opposite the shadow as he stepped off the back.

The shadow was the entrance to another tunnel. It must lead back to the outside of the mountain, O'Reilly reasoned. Had Lasher taken it? It was as black as pitch!

His shoulder hurting like hell, O'Reilly thrust his hand underneath his parka and felt gingerly around to find out what damage Lasher's bullet had done. His fingers came away sticky and wet. From his breeches pocket he pulled out a handkerchief and pressed it against the wound. He didn't have time to do anything else. He had to get Lasher before the wound stiffened up, or before he lost too much blood.

Deciding that Lasher must have gone along this new tunnel, O'Reilly stepped in and followed. Pressing against the wall, he cautiously made his way along the blackness, one foot at a time. Despite the cold, sweat broke out on his brow . . . with his every step he expected the tunnel to suddenly explode and reverberate to the accompaniment of Lasher's rifle. O'Reilly cursed the ringing in his ears. He needed every sense alert, especially his hearing. His only consolation was that Lasher's ears were also ringing. But on the other hand, Lasher knew the tunnel. O'Reilly didn't!

It went through his mind that he could end this now by emptying his Enfield into the blackness ahead, giving Lasher some of his own medicine. But he knew he mustn't do that. It wasn't the Mounted Police way. He had to take Lasher alive. Besides, he didn't want any taint of suspicion that he had hunted down the mining company manager and shot him in cold blood because of a personal vendetta. His dislike for Lasher was well known in Fort Determination and around Coal City. If he killed Lasher, Inspector Kerr could make it look as though he had murdered the man out of vengeance. Even though he was carrying Lasher's bullet in his shoulder, O'Reilly had to take the scheming mining man alive.

His heart beating heavily, blood pounding through his head, sweat on his forehead, his wound aching, O'Reilly probed warily ahead. Blackness completely surrounded him. For all he knew he could even have passed Lasher in the dark. He could go on and on . . . and Lasher might have slipped back out of the tunnel and gone back the way he had come. This tunnel might even lead nowhere. For all O'Reilly knew it could turn around and lead back deeper into the—

Suddenly, over the ringing in his ears, he heard a shout and the crashing of timber. He froze! The noise had come from somewhere ahead. He listened intently but heard nothing more. Then he crept forward again . . . cautiously . . . inch by inch . . . hand against the tunnel wall . . . putting one foot down carefully before stepping out with the other. Then he heard something again. He stopped and once more listened intently, but it was no use. He couldn't make it out over the ringing in his ears. Not until he heard it again—a low moaning.

Something had happened! But what?

He resumed creeping cautiously ahead. Then he heard it a third time. It was definitely a moaning, like someone hurt.

"Lasher!" he called out, his voice echoing back at him.

"Help . . ." he heard thinly. He couldn't tell where the voice came from, but it must have been ahead.

"Where are you, Lasher?"

The voice didn't answer. Was it a trap? O'Reilly had to take the chance, and he moved cautiously forward again.

He had gone another half a dozen feet through the blackness when his outstretched hand touched something in front of him . . . something hard. Feeling along it, he found it to be a wooden railing. Then his slowly moving foot bumped against something . . . a wooden floor or something. Dropping to a crouching position, O'Reilly felt around further. There was a barrier across the tunnel. He felt further along the railing until it gave way. Then he groped along the wooden floor, or whatever it was . . . and suddenly he felt broken boards.

At that precise moment he heard the moaning

again. This time he could place where it was coming from—almost directly below.

"Lasher! Are you down there?"

"Yeah," Lasher's voice came back weakly.

"What happened?"

"Goddamn barrier . . . fell through it. Damn fool Strathman . . . they sunk a shaft looking for a coal seam . . . didn't find any . . . so they put a barrier around it . . . and left the goddamn thing . . . no damn light or anything. Strathman . . . damn idiot . . . didn't tell me about it."

"How badly are you hurt?"

"Feels like . . . my goddamn back's . . . broken."

"How far down are you?" O'Reilly called.

"Don't . . . know," Lasher called back.

"Is there any rope or anything like that around here?"

"Cable in . . . one of those boxes . . . back in the main shaft . . . the one with . . . the rail line."

"All right. Hold on. I'll be back."

Retracing his passage along the black tunnel, O'Reilly soon found himself back in the main shaft. Following the rail line to the closest light, he took it down off its metal bracket and went searching along the tunnel for one of the boxes Lasher had mentioned. Finding one he quickly opened it. Among a collection of picks and drill bits, he found a couple of lengths of cable and a coil of rope. Throwing these around his shoulders, he ran along the tunnel until he reached a second lantern. Taking it down from its bracket, he turned and hurried back along the way he had come toward the tunnel he had followed Lasher into. Holding one of the lanterns out in front of him, he made better time than on the way out and soon found himself back at the barrier. With the illumination from the coal-oil lamp, he could see where Lasher had crashed through the flimsy barricade.

His shoulder was starting to stiffen up now, and O'Reilly felt an urgency about his mission. If Lasher had a broken back, he'd have to return to the mine and organize a full-scale rescue operation. They wouldn't be able to move the mining company manager without a doctor. The mining company employed a so-called doctor at Coal City. He might have been a qualified doctor somewhere years ago, but he'd since degenerated into a drunken sot, and as far as O'Reilly was concerned he was little more than a quack. The big Nova Scotian wouldn't let the man remove the bullet from his shoulder, much less work on a broken back.

Deftly tying the rope to the wire handle of one of the coal-oil lanterns, O'Reilly leaned over the edge of the shaft and lowered the lamp. "Lasher," he called. "Can you see the light?"

"Yeah," Lasher moaned from below.

"All right . . . guide me to your position."

Dangling at the end of the rope, the lantern descended into the darkness. "How am I coming?" O'Reilly called.

"More to . . . the left."

O'Reilly shifted his position and slid the rope along the edge of the shaft. "How's that?"

"A little more . . . yeah, hold it . . . that's it. Keep it coming down."

O'Reilly played out more rope. He had used up most of it when Lasher called out to him. Pushing himself further to the edge of the shaft and leaning out a little more, O'Reilly could look down and see Lasher's sprawled body beside the lantern, about forty feet below.

"Can you move at all?" O'Reilly asked.

He could see Lasher struggling . . . and at last the mining company manager was able to raise himself onto his elbows.

"How do you feel?"

"My back . . . hurts."

"Can you move your legs?"

A pause from below. Again O'Reilly could see the dark figure moving. "Yeah . . . a little . . . my right."

"All right. I'm going to lower a cable. I don't think your back's broken. You probably winded yourself."

O'Reilly lowered one of the cables. When one end dangled in front of Lasher, O'Reilly called out again. "Fasten this end around yourself. Can you do that?"

"What the hell for, O'Reilly?" Lasher shouted back at him. "So you can throw me in jail?"

"Shut up and fasten that cable. Otherwise you'll rot down there."

That was all the inducement Lasher needed, and he fastened the cable around his shoulders and just beneath his arms.

"Now I'll haul you up," O'Reilly called down. "You're a big man, so try to give me some help on the way. Use your feet against the side of the shaft."

Taking up the slack in the cable, O'Reilly moved back along the tunnel, looking for something to brace himself against. The only thing he could find was one of the tunnel's timber supports. In the lantern light, he looked at it critically. "I hope they put these things up properly," he muttered, then leaned into it and braced his left leg against it. There was just enough cable to do the job.

"Can you hear me, Lasher?"

"Yeah."

"Then, here we go."

O'Reilly pulled hard on the cable. "Christ!" he swore, his shoulder sending screaming jabs of pain through him. It was just like pulling dead weight. The cable wasn't moving. "I said, use your feet!" he shouted.

"I . . . can't," Lasher called back. "My left leg's broken."

"Then, use the other."

O'Reilly made a supreme effort. He closed his eyes and gritted his teeth against the pain in his shoulder, at the same time leaning back and pushing hard with his leg. For several seconds nothing happened, then the steel cable moved a few inches. Taking a deep breath, he pulled and strained again. Lasher let out a tortured yell, but the cable stayed taut and O'Reilly moved it a couple of feet this time. Hand over hand . . . two more feet. The pain in his left shoulder became almost unbearable and for a moment he felt as though he was about to pass out, but he pulled the cable up some more . . . hand over hand.

He wanted to rest, and was tempted to call out to Lasher to find a ledge somewhere for a moment, but he resisted the temptation. Perspiration burst out on his forehead and rolled down into his eyes, stinging them with the saltiness. But still the cable came up . . . hand over hand . . . foot by foot.

Finally, after what seemed like an eternity, Lasher's

head appeared at the top of the shaft. O'Reilly made one last, desperate effort before collapsing in sheer exhaustion. But Lasher was over the top. Equally exhausted, he sprawled down on the tunnel floor a few yards from O'Reilly's feet.

Chapter 23

The sled's guide rope in his hand, Sergeant O'Reilly jogged behind his dogs as they rounded the last bend toward Fort Determination. Lying on the sled in front of him, Refflon Lasher stared morosely ahead, an improvised splint around his broken leg and a tightly bound rope holding together three fractured ribs. Both men squinted against the sun's dazzling reflection off the fresh snow covering the valley of the Palliser, the spruce trees and the craggy mountains touching the bright blue sky all about them.

A burst of pleasure surged through O'Reilly, as it always did when he sighted Fort Determination upon returning from a long patrol, but it quickly dissipated at the thought of what awaited him at the post.

Driving right up to the detachment building, O'Reilly shouted the dogs to a stop. There was nothing to be gained by delaying the inevitable, so he had already bent over the sled to pull Lasher up when a red-coated Corporal Rogers appeared at the front door.

"Hugh!" The corporal's face broke into a wide grin at the familiar figure by the foot of the veranda.

"Hello, Dusty. Do me a favor, will you? Ride over to Coal City and arrest Vince Strathman for attempted murder. That'll do for starters. When you get him back here and question him in a few matters, there'll be other charges. Better take a couple of men in case some of those miners attempt to interfere. Try and do this before Inspector Kerr interferes, Dusty."

Dusty Rogers laughed. "Oh, him! Don't worry about him, Hugh. He's . . . Anyway, I'll take Constable Bailey. George has been itching for some action ever since . . . Well, you go on inside. Someone's in there who's been looking forward to seeing you. I'll look after Lasher."

O'Reilly frowned. "Someone looking forward to seeing me? You mean Catherine?"

The laugh remained on Dusty's face. "She's been looking forward to seeing you, too. She was asking about you yesterday, as a matter of fact, but go on in and see for yourself."

Kicking off his snoeshoes, O'Reilly climbed the veranda steps and passed through the front door, where he peeled off his mitts and parka. Then he took the few short paces along the hallway to the office that had once been his. He sensed a presence in there before he reached the doorway, and steeled himself to face Inspector Kerr. But the man sitting behind the desk, although he wore an officer's blue tunic, was not Inspector Kerr. This man wore a superintendent's crown on his shoulder straps and a row of colored ribbons above his left breast pocket. O'Reilly drew himself to attention, but his left arm hung stiffly by his side. His hour of judgment had finally come, and the color drained from his face. He did not appreciate Dusty's sense of humour.

Major John Tarlton Cavannagh, DSO, officer commanding G Division, rose behind the desk and stared unblinkingly at O'Reilly. A distinguished-looking man almost as tall as O'Reilly, with regulation-trimmed silver hair brushed back off a high forehead, he had a strong face weathered to a deep brown by more than thirty years of exposure to sun and wind. The most striking feature about him was his eyes—steel-blue eyes that had unnerved a score or more of dangerous criminals and lawbreakers throughout the North-West Territories, steel-blue eyes that had seen twenty-nine years of the Scarlet Riders' history from Sitting Bull to the Yukon gold rush, steel-blue eyes that belonged to a man who was Mounted Police to the core. It was this man who would have to sit in judgment on O'Reilly, find him guilty of the disciplinary charges, and sentence him to a term of imprisonment in the guardroom and dismissal from the Force.

At last the officer spoke. "You've been gone a long time, O'Reilly."

O'Reilly swallowed. "Yes, sir."

"Hard patrol?"

O'Reilly paused before replying, thinking about his answer. But it was a short, "Yes, sir."

Major Cavannagh's eyes moved to O'Reilly's stiffly hanging arm, taking in the caked blood high on the shoulder of his woolen pullover. "What happened to your shoulder?"

O'Reilly told him.

"Stand at ease, Sergeant. Sit down."

"I'll stay standing, sir."

"As you wish. Is the bullet still in your shoulder?"

"Yes, sir."

"In that event, it's a good thing I brought an Indian Affairs doctor from Edmonton with me. He's been looking into the general health of the Indians in this region. He can attend to that shoulder for you. I think you'd better go and see him and get rested up. After that I'll take your report."

"If it's all the same to you, sir, I'd just as soon get this thing over with right now."

Major Cavannagh studied O'Reilly for a moment, then asked, "Exactly what do you mean by *this thing*, Sergeant?"

For several seconds O'Reilly was at a loss for words. But he felt himself getting a bit ragged around the edges. Everything had suddenly become anticlimactic, and he felt very tired. "Major, I don't think I'm in any mood for Mounted Police formalities. I know the penalty for the charges Inspector Kerr laid against me. I know I'm washed up in the Force, and I'd just as soon save the suspense and get it all over with here and now."

Standing behind the desk, hands clasped behind his back, Major Cavannagh's soldierly face was a study of imperturbability, and it told O'Reilly nothing of what was going through the mind beyond it. Not that O'Reilly cared much anymore.

When the OC spoke again, his voice was quiet and even. If he felt any annoyance at the sergeant's unregimental comments, he didn't reveal it. "You talk as though everything were cut and dried."

"Well, isn't it, sir?" O'Reilly replied almost disinterestedly. "I know the system. In an officer-NCO conflict, the officer is always right. The Force always backs its officers. It doesn't matter whether an officer might just be wrong for a change. All of us in the ranks know officers always stick together. I've served under you on and off for a long time, sir, and you've always been fair, but another officer has brought serious charges against me. It doesn't matter that I might have been pushed into committing the offenses for what I considered to be the best interests of the service. The point is that an officer laid the charges and you have to find me guilty. I'm not blaming you, sir. You have to do it. It's the system. The thing is, I'm too damned tired to go through the farce of an orderly-room trial. I'll plead guilty to the charges right now and take whatever's coming, just to get it over with."

Major Cavannagh unclasped his hands and lowered his erect, military frame back into the chair behind the desk. "Are you sure you won't sit down, O'Reilly? You look all in."

O'Reilly shook his head stubbornly.

Picking up his pipe from a large glass ashtray, Major Cavannagh stuck it in his mouth and lit a match. Holding the flame over the bowl, he looked steadily at the younger man through rolling clouds of smoke. Tired though he was, uncaring or not,

O'Reilly found those steel-blue eyes unsettling.

Major Cavannagh spoke around the stem of his pipe. "I suppose . . . what you say . . . is largely true. But not completely. If an officer is wrong, he must answer for it."

O'Reilly lifted his head a little and thrust forward his jaw. "But how does the Force know when an officer is wrong? With all due respect, sir, how can you, sitting behind your desk down at Fort Saskatchewan—or the commissioner at Regina—tell whether an officer at a distant post knows his job or whether the NCOs and men are carrying him? How can you tell when he's tyrannical, incompetent, unjust?. . . How can you know he's not knocking the hell out of esprit de corps by playing tin-soldier games that not only lower morale but hinder police duties as well? Even when you come up here to carry out the annual inspection, you'd find everything as it should be because your arrival would be expected. You'd ask all the NCOs and men whether they have any complaints. And you know what they'd tell you, sir? They'd tell you, 'None, sir.' Because that's what they're supposed to say, and the officer in command of the post would be present to see they said that and nothing else. And if a sergeant like me were to speak out and tell you exactly what was wrong, there'd be hell to pay because he'd be criticizing the Force's officer corps, and by implication the commissioner himself. Sergeants are supposed to support the system, not condemn it."

O'Reilly's moustache bristled, but the efforts of his diatribe had taken the last vestige of color from his face, giving him a gaunt, haggard look, and he began to sway unsteadily on his feet. But he wasn't quite finished.

"Instead of talking, I did something about it!"

Major Cavannagh took the pipe out of his mouth. "Please sit down, Sergeant!" he ordered. "Before you *fall* down!"

O'Reilly reached out to a chair by the wall and eased himself slowly onto it.

Frowning, Major Cavannagh bit back the cutting edge that hung poised to shape his next words. "Nothing's perfect, O'Reilly! But the system's not that bad, either. I should know—I've been part of it for twenty-nine years. And I haven't always been an officer! I worked my way up through the ranks. It's a good force, the Mounted Police. That's why I've remained in it this long. But to get down to essence— O'Reilly! You'd better get to the doctor!"

O'Reilly had started to slump forward on his chair, but he shook the dizziness from his head. "No, sir! I'm all right. I'd rather get this over with."

Major Cavannagh studied O'Reilly closely, uncertain whether to continue or call the Indian Affairs doctor from his rooms down at the Northern Lights Hotel. Finally he decided to continue.

"Very well. I was on leave in New York when Colonel Perry sent Inspector Kerr up here. On my way back to Fort Saskatchewan, I reported in to headquarters to pay my respects to the commissioner. That was the first I knew of the complaints made against you. Colonel Perry told me he had been under pressure from a certain cabinet minister to send Kerr here to gain some field experience, while at the same time investigating the complaints. He didn't have to add that he did not appreciate a politician telling him how to administer the Mounted Police. However, Inspector Kerr was available and he did need field experience, so Colonel Perry, ever the diplomat, acquiesced.

"I was no sooner back at Fort Saskatchewan than your escort turned up with our old friend, Mike Hannan. At the same time he handed me a confidential envelope containing disciplinary charges Inspector Kerr had brought against you. I was shocked when I read those charges. I know you have a temper, but you're too seasoned for that sort of thing under normal circumstances. So I availed myself of the opportunity to have a chat with Mike. Mike's changed since the old days, but his hearing is just as good. Between overhearing some of your exchanges with Inspector Kerr through the cell bars and yarning with the escort on the riverboat journey down, Mike had a pretty good idea of what was happening, and he filled me in. So you see, O'Reilly, I already knew the other side of the story before I arrived here.

"The first thing I did here was investigate those complaints. As they all originated from the same source, I wasn't surprised to find them mostly groundless. Then I had a man-to-man talk with *Mister* Kerr. He reached the decision that a career in the Mounted Police wasn't what he was really suited for, so he resigned his commission. In fact, he was in such a hurry to get away on the last river steamer before freeze-up that he agreed to drop the disciplinary charges against you just so he wouldn't have to remain to give evidence."

O'Reilly straightened up on his chair. For a moment he didn't say anything. Then he asked, "Does that include the desertion charge, sir?"

Major Cavannagh's steel-blue eyes narrowed. "Did you have any intention of deserting, Sergeant?"

O'Reilly shook his head. "No, sir . . . of course not."

"Well, then, there's no case of desertion. You were on patrol—a successful one, obviously. Now, I suggest you report to the doctor down at the Northern Lights Hotel and let him attend to your shoulder. After that you'd better get cleaned up and take a few days' rest. I want you fit to resume duties as NCO in charge of the post before I return to Fort Saskatchewan."

Grinning, O'Reilly rose slowly to his feet and drew himself to attention, his left arm hanging stiffly by his side. "Very good, sir."

He turned to go through the door out into the hallway, paused and looked back over his shoulder. "When you go back, sir, would you forward to the commissioner an application requesting permission for me to marry?"

"Yes, of course, Sergeant. You must have close to twelve years' service now."

"In May, sir."

Major Cavannagh picked up a pen, dipped it into an inkwell, and held it poised to write. "And might I enquire as to the lady's name?"

"Mrs. Catherine Merrill, sir," O'Reilly replied, quickly adding, "She's a widow, sir . . . the owner of

299

the Northern Lights."

Major Cavannagh smiled. "Well, an excellent choice, Sergeant. I don't think there should be any problem obtaining the commissioner's approval. And I would like to add my congratulations."

"Thank you, sir."

"Right, Sergeant. Carry on."

"Sir."

O'Reilly stepped out through the door.

TALES OF THE OLD WEST

SPIRIT WARRIOR   (1795, $2.50)
by G. Clifton Wisler
The only settler to survive the savage indian attack was a little boy. Although raised as a red man, every man was his enemy when the two worlds clashed — but he vowed no man would be his equal.

IRON HEART   (1736, $2.25)
by Walt Denver
Orphaned by an indian raid, Ben vowed he'd never rest until he'd brought death to the Arapahoes. And it wasn't long before they came to fear the rider of vengeance they called . . . Iron Heart.

WEST OF THE CIMARRON   (1681, $2.50)
by G. Clifton Wisler
Eric didn't have a chance revenging his father's death against the Dunstan gang until a stranger with a fast draw and a dark past arrived from West of the Cimarron.

BIG HORN GUNFIGHTER   (1975, $2.50)
by Robert Kamman
Quinta worked for both sides of the law, and he left a trail of graves from old Mexico to Wyoming to prove it. His partner cut and run, so Quinta took the law into his own hands. Because the only law that mattered to a gunfighter was measured in calibers.

BLOOD TRAIL SOUTH   (1349, $2.25)
by Walt Denver
John Rustin was left for dead, his wife and son butchered by six hard-cases. Five years later, someone with cold eyes and hot lead pursued those six murdering coyotes. Was it a lawman — or John Rustin, himself?

Available wherever paperbacks are sold, or order direct from the Publisher. Send cover price plus 50¢ per copy for mailing and handling to Zebra Books, Dept. 1977, 475 Park Avenue South, New York, N.Y. 10016. Residents of New York, New Jersey and Pennsylvania must include sales tax. DO NOT SEND CASH.